THE CARDS THAT CHANGED MY LIFE

To Chris,

Enjoy!

Love
Joanne xxx.

Joanne was born and raised in Ireland, and has lived in Canada, London and Dublin. From a young age, Joanne has had a vivid imagination fuelled by her love of reading Enid Blyton books. She is an accountant, and in her spare time dreams up stories full of magic and mystery. She now lives in County Louth, Ireland. The Cards That Changed My Life is her debut novel.

JOANNE RYAN CURRAN

One pack of cards.
Infinite possibilities.

The Cards That Changed My Life

First published in 2024 by Cross-eyed Cat Productions

A CIP catalogue record for this book is available from the British Library.

Cover design by Design for Writers

ISBN 978-1-3999-8099-9

To my family, who bring an abundance of magic to my life everyday.

It's not about the cards you're dealt, but how you play the hand.
Randy Pausch.

CHAPTER 1

DECEMBER 2022

JANE

I MAY HAVE JUST RUINED my life. My balance is off and I'm swaying like a drunk. My feet are heavy. Each step is a monstrous feat. A woman loaded down with shopping bags walks right in front of me, forcing me to stop.

'Sorry, excuse me,' she says, annoyed. 'You need to watch where you're going.'

I quickly move out of her way, but then collide into someone else. They give me an angry stare. There are swarms of people all around me. If I don't get out of here soon, I'm going to scream. Ending up on Grafton Street was a big mistake. I need to sit down somewhere to try to calm down and think positive thoughts.

But where?

Gratitude. I read recently that gratitude is the key to happiness. So, what am I grateful for? I am alive. I am healthy. My parents and my sister are alive. They are all healthy. I have clothes to wear. I have shoes on my feet. My shoes are all scuffed, they are too tight and not very comfortable, but nevertheless they are still shoes.

What else?

I have a good job as an investment banker … hmmm … that's debatable. The thought of work makes my heart beat faster. Enough of the gratitude, it's not helping. I'll try counting instead – counting usually calms me.

I count to ten before lots of other numbers float into my mind. 502. That's how many cracks on the pavement I've counted since I left the office today. 375. The number of days I've worked at Becker Bank International so far. 1. The number of times I walked out in the middle of my performance review.

I can't *believe* what I've just done.

As I glance around me, I notice the beautiful chandelier-style Christmas lights are lit, and the street is thronged with people strolling along enjoying the run-up to Christmas. I walk along and hear a busker sing one of my favourite Christmas songs, 'Fairy-tale of New York'. Normally the buskers and street performers never fail to put a smile on my face, but not today. Today is quite possibly the worst day of my life. Terror slowly creeps in. The conversation with Emma races through my mind. I make my way down the street, trying to escape my thoughts and the rising anger I feel inside.

What if Emma fires me? And if I was fired, that would also mean – I may not see Ben again. Ben. Handsome, smooth-talking Ben. When Ben walks into a room he lights it up and everything works out well for him. Most of the girls in the office have a serious crush on Ben. Even though I know it's pointless being in love with him, I can't help it. From the first moment I spoke to him I knew he got me. He saw me for who I really was, and he couldn't care less about my sister's fame. Ben makes an effort to get my attention and I feel alive when he's around.

When I'm not in the office I try so hard to stop thinking about Ben, but despite this he still comes into my dreams most nights. I have many recurring dreams that start off with Ben calling at my door to give me something. What that something is I can never quite make out. It's blurry in my dream. We end up drinking way too much mulled wine and watch my favourite Christmas movie, *The Holiday*. He rests his head on my shoulder and tells me that he wants to book a flight to go away with me and that he loves me or something along those lines. And then the dream ends and when I wake up, I tell myself the dreams are ridiculous and that would never happen in real life. I really need to move on with my life and stop obsessing about Ben because he's not mine to love. Going after a guy who's already committed to someone else is just wrong. Aside from that it's pointless; while I'm sitting at home alone daydreaming about him, he's living his best life with his girlfriend. He probably doesn't give me a second thought.

Today didn't start like any other day. For starters I didn't have the usual dream about Ben; I can't remember what I dreamt about, but I woke up later than usual and time got the better of me. Everything I did took longer than usual. The recent late nights at the office had worn me out, and my body refused to move at the speed I needed it to. I wasn't too late leaving the house – only by about ten minutes, but still that put me off. My bus was also late, and the elderly man I helped cross the road shuffled as if he was a baby turtle. I didn't get a chance to sit and organise my thoughts, compile my to-do list or read over my notes for my appraisal, like I had originally planned.

The elevator took forever. It stalled at the fifth floor, the light glowing red. Now that I think about it, it was like an omen. What were they doing on the fifth floor? Loading cattle? By the time it did crawl back to the ground floor, beads of sweat had gathered under my arms, and I was hot and bothered.

Reaching the fourth floor, I rushed along the glass corridor past rows of bankers, who sat at their desks engrossed in their work. Towards the end of the corridor the interior changed. This is where some of the management team sat in sought-after corner offices. The floor to ceiling glass walls were glossier. The light was brighter and sparkled on the beautiful white marble floor. Soon one of these offices would be mine, I thought. Well, that was the aim anyway. I was ready for my promotion today. Ready and quite late. I took a deep breath as I crossed my fingers. *Please universe, make this happen,* I whispered.

'Hey Emma, is now a good time?' I said as I rapped on my manager's door and opened it gently.

'Jane, how are things?' Emma raised an eyebrow, leaned back on the chair at her huge mahogany desk and eyeballed me from head to toe. She let out a tiny sigh. 'Take a seat and we'll get started once I finish this. I expected you earlier than this.' She cocked her head to one side and fiddled around with her mouse.

'Sorry,' I said. 'I got delayed.'

I walked into her office and took my seat, feeling the chair behind my back. Even the chairs were fancy.

I stared at the clock above her head in silence, counted to one hundred while I listened to the tick tock, tick tock, and tried to still my thoughts. The office was sparse, with not one personal possession. Lever arch files lined the shelves along the walls, sorted in alphabetical order. The strong smell of Emma's perfume lingered in the air and caught in my throat. Emma looked at me, and then back to the screen. She always looked glamorous for work, owning a wardrobe of tight skirts and expensive looking silk blouses. Today she was wearing a pair of Louboutin shoes. They weren't even scuffed. I gazed down at my white shirt and grey skirt suit that I had carefully picked to impress Emma and fidgeted on my chair. I looked like a little mouse compared to her. A scruffy, sweaty one at that.

Finally, Emma lifted her head and spoke to me. 'Let's start with how you think the last year went for you. I know you submitted your appraisal form already, but I want to hear it from you directly.'

'Sure, where do I start? I think things have gone great ...' I said, trying to remember my key achievements over the year.

'We don't have all day,' she said, smiling. 'I want to get out of here at a reasonable time tonight.'

'I know that ...'

'Hmmm ... let's just crack on, shall we?'

I nodded my head in agreement. I loved my job at Becker Bank International – a merchant bank in the Irish Financial Services Centre – mainly because I loved dealing with my clients. My portfolio was small, but it performed well. Not only was I making more money for my clients, but I genuinely believed by breaking down all the finance jargon, they were making better business decisions.

My job was full of procedures and policies. Everything had a place or a system – transactions went in and out, for every debit there was a credit and I found the order and logic soothing. I loved that I understood the complex reporting. It was something I was good at and I'm not good at much. Well, compared to my sister, Gillian, I'm not. At home everything my sister did she excelled at. She was a star performer from a young age. The bank was the only place I felt like I was smart and fitted in.

Emma flicked the stack of papers. 'Mmm ... you gave yourself some very high ratings. I see here ... what was your most considerable achievement ... interesting ... hmm ... so you consider the work you do for Mr. Feltz to be that significant. I'll need to check a few of these details.'

Mr. Feltz was my favourite client. That was a good account to talk about. I was ready for this. I attempted to talk, but Emma looked back and forth from the form to me, and that made me hesitate. 'Eh ...' I said. My mind went completely blank because Emma's not normally like this.

What's rattled her cage?

My stomach gurgled. In the rush this morning I didn't have breakfast. I thought of the box of pastries I'd seen outside the elevator. I'd love to have one now with a huge cup of coffee.

She cleared her throat. The tone of her voice became sombre. 'I'm not sure about some of these ten out of tens you gave yourself. Perhaps they are more an eight or a seven, even.' She flicked back her long jet-black hair and gave a tight smile. 'Hmmm ... technical ability, determination ... I agree with you there. I'll let you keep those tens. I'd like to see more leadership though before I can justify giving you a ten for that section.'

I winced. It was all right for Emma, she was born confident. She had no problem leading a meeting or a team. When Emma spoke people listened. She didn't go to pieces when asked to talk out loud.

We met on the first day of our induction week. A group of ten of us were being groomed to become some of the country's brightest financial minds. We were told you either sink or swim and most people weren't cut out for the fast-paced environment. Ben, Emma and I were the only ones to finish by the end of the week. I'm not sure what happened to the others – we were never told. My guess is they left when they realised how much work was involved and how our lives would soon revolve around the bank. At the end of the induction, we called ourselves the three musketeers, and it stuck. Emma was lucky and got promoted first, hence why she was now our boss.

'More leadership,' I said. My voice crackled in shock. My throat was raspy. I took a sip of water. 'Can you give me an example?'

'The rate of return on Mr. Feltz's account could be higher.'

'Well, I didn't think that fitted the client's needs. He's a cautious investor. I've achieved the business goals set by the client – to find more cost-saving opportunities and hence obtain a higher profit margin.'

'I understand Ben spoke to you about this account. He felt differently. The operating model he prepared for me was more aggressive.'

Ben? What had Ben been saying to Emma? Why was Ben producing operating models for my clients?

'Well, we … yes, we talked about it and didn't agree on the direction of the portfolio,' I said.

'So, Ben was right?'

'Well, in financial terms, yes … the client would have made more money, but I felt he was in safer hands with my strategy—'

'But ultimately, the client wants to make more money.'

'Yes.'

'As we do.'

'I understand that, but the client trusts me.'

'That's the leadership I mean. You need to take more risks, you're far too conservative to the detriment of your portfolio.'

I went quiet. I know my approach is right – at the end of the day it's about keeping the clients happy – but she's not listening to what I have to say. I hated the thought of Emma and Ben discussing my accounts. I felt like I'd been betrayed. I thought Ben cared about me. I imagined the two of them huddled together whispering. Like in the early days – they spent a lot of time in meetings alone together.

Emma's phone rang. She answered it curtly and I heard the receptionist tell her the pastries she ordered for our 11am team meeting were waiting to be collected at the bottom of the elevator.

'Oh, they look nice,' I said after she hung up.

'What does?' she said, taken aback.

'The pastries.'

'You saw them?'

'Yes. Beside the elevator on my way up.'

'And why didn't you bring them up?'

'I didn't know who they were for.'

'And you didn't think to ask?'

'It didn't occur to me.' I shrugged my shoulders.

Emma shook her head. 'Another example of where more leadership is required.' She sighed.

I shifted awkwardly in my chair. I felt like this wasn't going well. Still, I had to ask. It was now or never. I took a deep breath. 'I was wondering if now would be a good time to talk about my promotion?'

She frowned. 'Sorry, Jane, but no … it's not the right time.'

'I'm good at my job, Emma, and I work late most evenings,' I said quietly.

As Emma well knew; we had spent many a late evening together in the office, sometimes blasting music through our laptop speakers before heading off for a drink.

'I'm not saying you're bad at your job. Your work is up to standard, but you need to do a little bit extra.' She pinched her forefinger and thumb together. 'It's not about the longer hours. I need more from you.'

'How can I give more?'

'I'm sorry, Jane. This is so awkward. I can't do this anymore.' She put her hands over her face, lowered her voice to a whisper as if she was sharing the biggest secret in the world. 'Between me, you and these four walls, I'm told by Tim I can only give one promotion this year and they want it to go to Ben – he's bringing in new clients. Executing deals. It's already been decided. I'm sorry.'

Those whispered words made my throat burn and I wanted to throw up.

'Ben … Ben? Ben doesn't want this. He told me I deserve this.'

'It's not up to Ben to promote you. He was probably just being nice. Look, I know it's difficult to stand out. It's a competitive environment.' She waved her hands around the room. 'I can promote you next year providing you take on board my suggestions.'

'Suggestions?' I raised my eyebrows.

'Yes, definitely. I can see you being promotion material in a year's time.' She grinned to ease the tension. 'Move away from your desk and network more – join some activities like … the Golf Society. Make yourself visible!'

'I'm not really interested in golf.'

The tick tock, tick tock, sound of the clock got louder and louder by the second. It ticked to a gentle rhythm. Don't do it ... don't do it ... walk away ... walk away, it sang to me as I counted the ticks.

'You know I deserve this, based on my portfolio performance. It outperforms others in the bank. I retain my clients and bring in a lot of money.'

Ben's father was good friends with our CEO, and he did the bare minimum to get by. I had outperformed his portfolio by three, if not four times. I hated that I was being compared to him.

'This isn't easy for me, you know. You avoid going to most of the corporate events. That's the perfect opportunity to network.'

'I thought you were my friend,' I said. I stood up and the bendy chair shot out behind me.

'Jane, where are you going?'

'One of my best friends. You told me you were going to share my work with them. You can't expect me to just accept this. I'll ...'

'You'll what?'

The clock changed its tune. Walk away, walk away, walk away, it sang repeatedly like a woodpecker pounding through my head.

'I've had enough ...,' I said trembling, convinced I was about to have a panic attack. It was as if the room was closing in on me and if I didn't get out of there it would squeeze the life out of me. 'I have to get out of here.'

I turned, opened the door and ran out of the corner office. I ran past Ben who was standing at the coffee machine in his Santa hat, by the receptionist gazing up at him, and straight past the elevator that would surely take forever. I grabbed my coat and bag as I passed my desk and thundered down the stairs and onto the street, my feet a whirr, until I ended up at Grafton Street.

And now here I stand, looking at the Christmas lights, at the shoppers, at the cracks in the pavement, trying to count, to calm down. *Please don't scream*, I tell myself. Even though I may have ruined everything I worked so hard for. *Gratitude. Be grateful*, I think as I close my eyes. *Be grateful for everything you have.*

But, a panicky voice in my head says, *what if you can't fix this? What the hell are you going to do then?*

CHAPTER 2

MY HEART POUNDS FASTER as I turn down a side street, anxiously looking for a quiet place to sit. A sign stands out from the wall beside me. Alley I Bhfolach. Hidden Alley. I walk down the curve of the alley, as it winds and turns. I pass by a vintage clothing shop, a quaint toy shop, a craft shop and there at the very end stands a huge second-hand bookshop.

Seeing the shop again feels like being engulfed in a warm hug from an old friend, protecting me from the harshness of reality, and all the anger that's eating me up inside. It's exactly what I need right now: to count the books, compose myself, read a book and embrace the characters inside. Characters with complex and complicated lives who will help me forget about my own.

I stretch my arms out and put my back against the wall. The giant purple brick walls, four storeys high, stand strong, tall and proud as they lean in towards me. The coolness of the walls helps me breathe gulps of fresh air. Large Georgian windows and an arched brick doorway with an old-fashioned bell above the door give me a welcoming nod.

I breathe in for ten, hold, and breathe out for ten.

I do this several times until my vision becomes less blurry. I read the sign over the door. It has the engraved fancy lettering of the shop name, Hidden Secrets.

I think I'm going to be okay. *I'll be safe here.*

I walk into a kingdom. A mesmerising kingdom. Makeshift book-shelves pile all the way to the ceiling. I turn my head from side to side not knowing where to go next. Stepping on the cracked concrete floors I smell that savoury, musky book smell I've loved ever since I was a child.

I used to come here at the weekends with my dad while my sister, Gillian, was at one of her acting classes. I got to know the owner, Tara, well.

I make my way over to a red armchair, in the snug by the window, right beside the crackling fire. It hasn't changed much since I was last here. Lamps still sit on tables at the little snugs dotted around the room. Huge piles of books lean against the walls waiting to find their place on the shelves, and into the hands of a new owner. Memories come flooding back to me.

As I close my eyes and lean back in the armchair, I sense someone watching me. A short guy in his late twenties approaches me from across the room.

'Are you all right?' he asks.

'Just popped in out of the rain and I'm trying to dry off ...' I mutter, hoping I sound normal.

'You looked unsteady when you walked in the door.' His face looks concerned or puzzled by me. I can't work out which one.

'I'll be fine now that I've found somewhere to sit down,' I say.

'Is there anything I can help you with? I work here. You look familiar. I'm sure I know you from somewhere—'

'I don't think we've met before, but I used to come here when I was younger. Does Tara still work here?'

'Yeah. Tara's still the owner. She's sorting out some books now, but I'll go get her. I'm Gus by the way.'

'That would be fantastic. Thank you, Gus.'

He walks off, but then turns and just stares at me with his mouth open. 'I definitely know you from somewhere.'

A black cat rubs up against me purring loudly and curls its tail around my legs. It can probably sense I need some comfort. It jumps up on my knee and I stroke it gently.

'Get back here, Sooty. Leave the poor girl alone. Could you take over sorting that pile of books for me, Gus? I've something else I need to do,' I hear a faint voice say, and with that, Gus and Sooty walk off.

I know who he's on about. My sister Gillian. I get mistaken for her sometimes. People are usually disappointed when they realise I'm not her, so I didn't want to bring her name up.

I make my way over to the self-help section and scan the books. I love self-help books. I've every one of them under the sun – read in hope that I uncover some secrets or rules I'm missing out on to make my life better. I'm searching for answers, which is ridiculous, I know. It's going to take more than a book to solve my problems. It's like an Aladdin's cave here. You never know what you might find. Vintage comics and magazines still sit on the shelf next to me, *Dandy, Beano, Twinkle* and *Jackie* to name a few. Underneath these are the board games Tara played with me whenever there was quiet time in the shop.

It seems only fitting that I end up here as my life is falling apart. The first time I came to the bookshop and met Tara, I was also having a bad day. I remember it was winter, and it was lashing rain. When I woke up that morning my mam wasn't there. The night before, she promised me she would finish my Christmas costume for the school play. The play was in a few days, and I was worried I would have nothing to wear, and of course I was worried about my mam. She never told me she was going away anywhere.

Whenever I asked my dad about her whereabouts, he didn't seem to have any answers. He was a calm man and nothing really seemed to faze him. He would just sigh and say things like, 'Life will go on, Jane. With or without your mother. Whatever happens, I'll make sure you girls are taken care of.'

That made me think that she was gone forever and I was anxious.

That same day, my dad and I had dropped Gillian to her acting class; I couldn't wait for Gillian to finish her class so I could find out if she knew any more than me about Mam. Dad was looking for somewhere he could get some paperwork done, and I had crayons and a notebook to keep me occupied. I spotted the bookshop first, because the Hidden Secrets sign caught my eye, and I imagined it as a place full of secrets and hidden treasures. Through the window I saw twinkly lights, and a dainty, old woman with a pretty face sitting in a red armchair beside a roaring fire. I thought she looked happy and reminded me of a fairy from a book I read. She seemed very rich, as she was wearing a beautiful green dress with jewels that shone in the light and had matching shoes. I wanted to feel happy like that, and I wanted a dress just like hers. I thought I could persuade my dad to get me one if we went inside.

I remember how quiet the customers were. They were all engrossed in the books, like they were reading the most interesting thing in the world. I didn't have a book to read. I wanted to ask my dad to get me one – full of adventures and escape. But I could tell his mind was elsewhere, so I just wandered around gazing at the shelves. I'd never seen so many books in one place piled up high to the ceiling. I heard whispers, and I was so intrigued by them I went looking to find out where they could be coming from. Each time I was convinced if I turned the corner, I would figure out the source of the whispers, but I ended up just walking around in circles. I stopped and sat down in a dark part of the shop full of shadows, listening to the rain pounding down on the pavement. The whispering got louder when Tara appeared. The jewels on her dress were even bigger up close. I looked up at her in awe, and she asked me if I was okay, and if I was lost. Her voice had a sweet musical lilt that instantly put me at ease.

'I'm here with my dad,' I said. 'He's in the shop somewhere, I'm sure I could find him if I wanted to.'

'Why the sad face?' she said.

'My mam has gone somewhere and I want her home. I miss her,' I blurted out.

She tilted her head to the side. 'How about I bring you back to your father? He could be worried about you.'

We found my dad quick enough, and they chatted for a while before she brought me to the café area and gave me a hot chocolate and a brownie with ice-cream and sprinkles. I still remember the taste of it. It was the nicest brownie I had ever tasted.

'Your father agrees with me you could do with some cheering-up, and he tells me you need an angel costume for your Christmas play rehearsal tomorrow,' she said. 'How old are you?'

'I'm eight.'

'What a coincidence, I may have just the thing,' she replied, but she never elaborated any more than that. She went off somewhere and a few minutes later came back with the most fabulous costume I had ever seen. The dress was like a big fluffy cloud with pieces of silver sewn all around it and a shiny halo. I remember thinking that my mam could never make something as good, and that my friends in school were going to be so jealous of my costume. She also handed me a book, and said I could keep it.

'It will cheer you up until your mam gets back,' she said.

I smiled up at her. 'I love books. And unicorns.'

'Well, how about that. This book is all about unicorns who are searching to find out what their talents are.'

'And do they find out?' I replied.

'You'll need to read the book to figure it out.' Her eyes gleamed as she laughed.

'Is this place full of treasure? You've given me lots of lovely things today.'

'Well, I think it is, and I just love finding treasure ... especially in the shadows.' She looked at me seriously. 'I want you to remember something, Jane, when you're feeling down.'

'What is it?'

'Every storm cloud has a silver lining.'

No one had made me feel instantly better like she had. It wasn't my birthday or Christmas, but she had given me the most wonderful presents.

I wondered where had she got them?

My mam came home a few days later, without any explanation. I soon realised that her disappearing act would be a common occurrence, but being with Tara in her bookshop was where I felt special and protected from the drama at home. Most of all I trusted her completely.

I see Tara now, beside the Mind, Body and Soul section, placing books on the shelves. Despite the passing of time, she hasn't aged much. She must be in her seventies or eighties. She's well-dressed in a black and white Chanel suit. Expensive looking pearls hang around her neck. Her grey sharp eyes look bright, and her golden wavy hair sits around her shoulders. Life has been good to Tara.

I walk over to her and pat her gently on the arm. 'Tara, it's so nice to see you. How have you been?'

'Jane McAlister. Is it you? What a nice surprise – after all this time you're back. I wondered when we would meet again.' Tara smiles. 'My, you have grown. After all these years I still think of you from time to time.'

'Tara, I haven't seen you since ...' I say.

'Since you became a teenager and had more important things to care about than me and my old books,' she says. 'How are you? How's your family keeping? Good, I hope.'

I'm twenty-three now. How do you summarise the last ten years of your life?

I don't know where to begin. Lately my life has shrunk down to the size of a pea. A pea so soft and vulnerable that it would be squished if anyone were to step on it. The only exciting thing about my life is work and being around Ben. But not anymore.

The truth is that it wasn't my decision to stop going to the shop. After five years of coming here most weekends, I was devastated when my dad told me that he couldn't bring me anymore. He was working hard to get a promotion at the time, and had to work in the office at weekends. Gillian had moved then to a more prestigious acting class, on the other side of town, so I had to spend time with my mam and hang around until Gillian finished classes. I hated not seeing Tara anymore.

'My parents split up, but they're grand. They're better off apart.'

'Why, whatever is the matter?' she says gently.

Tara's kindness sets off tears that stream down my face. Once the floodgates open, I can't stop.

'I'm sorry. I'm having a bad day. It's a mess really. I'm a mess.'

'Ah, now you're not a mess. What happened?'

'I got turned down for a promotion. Emma said I'm not ready because I need to take more risks, network more and something about carrying up a box of pastries.' As I say the words, I'm aware of how ridiculous it sounds. The whole thing makes no sense even to me.

'Who's Emma?'

'My friend who recently became my boss. I should go back and apologise for storming off, but then I'm stuck. It's all very complicated.' I bite my lip as I wipe more tears from my face. 'What do you think I should do, Tara?'

'I think you should have a nice cup of tea and relax. If she really is your friend, she'll understand.' She leans forward. 'Is this promotion really what you want, Jane?'

I shrug my shoulders and sigh. An unexpected lump rises in my throat. More tears fall from the tip of my nose and onto my grey suit jacket. 'I want more than anything to be promoted ...'

My voice drifts off into silence as an emptiness slowly soaks through me. As I think about the mess I'm in, I'm dizzy from the enormity of what has happened.

When I glance up, Tara meets my gaze directly as if she can see right through me. Right into my heart and soul. It has been so long since anyone looked at me like that.

The bell above the door rings and a group of customers come in for a book club evening.

'You stay here. I'll be back after I get this group set up with teas and coffees,' she says as she walks off.

I check my iPhone, hoping for a message from Emma asking me to come back to work. There is a text, but it's not what I was expecting.

> **Jane. I understand why you were upset. I suggest you take a few days off to calm down.**

I'm so shocked, I don't know how to respond. I don't think time away from the office is what I need though. I want the old Emma back. The one from before she got promoted and became my boss. Back then she loved to bitch about our colleagues to me and we drank in the pub across the road from the bank most Thursdays after work because she fancied the barman.

I go through my social media. There's no messages or comments on any of my latest postings. A notification pops up about some activity on Gillian's Twitter account. My sister has now 1,798,058 followers. I move on to her Instagram account and swipe through her perfectly presented pictures. She's living the ultimate dream – her life is a frenzy of snapshots where she's drinking champagne on private jets with celebrity friends or surrounded by groups of adoring fans taking selfies.

My dad always said I was the clever one in the family, so how come I've ended up like this, while Gillian is living her best life?

As I browse through the shelves, I hear whispering that I can't quite make out. Similar to whispers I heard in the shop as a child. I settle in to count the books, and try to make sense of the whispers, but a velvet blue drawstring bag on the very top shelf catches my eye. I can't reach it so instead, I pick up one of my old favourites, *Wuthering Heights.* I get a cup of tea and one of Tara's homemade fruit scones from the café section. Tara is surrounded by customers. She seems well respected and liked.

I get engrossed in the world of Catherine and Heathcliff, oblivious to everyone else around me, when Tara approaches me.

'I still remember the first time I met you. Your father brought his big old briefcase and was focused on his paperwork. He didn't even notice you had gone. He worked too hard, that man.'

'I was glad you found me. All the books you introduced me to … there were nuggets of wisdom in each one. I could really do with some of your wisdom now, Tara.'

As I look up at her I notice the drawstring bag again.

'Well, I'm all yours now,' says Tara. 'What are you looking at?'

'The blue drawstring bag up there. I like the look of it. What's inside?' I ask.

'Why, you are the first customer to notice that bag. It's been up there untouched for many years.'

'The colour caught my eye.'

'Inside is a pack of cards. A very special pack of cards. I've been meaning to pass them on, I just haven't found the right person. It seems, however, the cards have caught your attention. How interesting.'

'Cards. Is it a card game? I love card games.'

'Not exactly a game.'

Tara climbs up sixteen steps (I count them all) until she reaches the bag and holds it out in the palm of her hand.

I can't take my eyes off it. Something is glowing inside. Whatever it is I want to find out. My fingers tingle as a shiver runs through me. 'I'll buy the bag. How much does it cost?'

'It's not for sale, Jane,' she says quietly, 'and it never will be. The cards will only be given to someone who I – as their owner – trust with their powers.'

'What powers?' I ask, frowning.

'It's only right someone else gets a chance to use them and they seem to have taken a liking to you. Perhaps it's a sign they have chosen you.'

I can't concentrate on what she's saying. All I can think about is seeing what's inside the bag.

She hands the bag over to me. 'This is for you, Jane. A gift from me.'

I breathe a sigh of relief. 'Oh, thank you,' I say.

The bag is worn around the edges. It feels so soft to touch. I tug open the drawstring and the contents gleam like a bar of solid gold, blinding my eyes. I take out the cards and the atmosphere in the room changes like a cloud lifting. A note falls out. It drifts slowly to the floor. A white feather follows and then floats out the open door. The handwriting is both elaborate and elegant. The gold gilded edges on the notepaper glisten in the light as I pick it up and read it aloud.

As the rightful owner of these cards, you now possess immense power. You are truly blessed. It's your time! The Universe is listening, and it wants to support you. Use these cards whenever you feel necessary with your intent clearly in mind. Depending on your wishes and circumstances, the cards will provide you with the answers needed to fulfil your dreams. You must take the cards' advice. As their owner you will gain more energy, motivation and lessons will be learnt. Choices should not

be made lightly as there will be consequences, and once
you pick a card there's no turning back. Good Luck!

'I read this same note many years ago,' says Tara. Her bright eyes twinkle. 'It seems so long ago now, so much has happened since. So many magical things.'

'Magic? I don't get it, Tara. How can a pack of cards solve all my problems?'

'They can and they will. See for yourself how magical they are.'

They're like nothing I've ever seen before. Each one is slightly bigger than the size of a standard playing card. There are colourful pictures and advice written on them. I count them. All eighty-three of them. The cards shimmer again as patches of light slip slowly into the room. Everything in the shop seems brighter and sharper. The colours and light are even different.

I pick a card at random and read the advice on the back. I feel a strange, tingly sensation. Blood rushes to my head and I begin to get lightheaded.

'That's not how it works,' says Tara.

'But I just wanted to understand what's written on the cards, and the pictures.'

'You must ask the universe for what you want first and then select a card and do whatever it says. Otherwise it will be meaningless.'

'And then what? The universe waves its magic wand and hey presto, my life is suddenly wonderful? I'm sorry Tara, but I don't get it,' I say.

'I know you don't believe me but try them and you will experience their power.' Her grey eyes turn misty. 'What this power is I do not know, all I know is it exists.' She appears to be deadly serious. None of this is logical. I'm not a child anymore, I know there's no such thing as magic. 'The cards will push you to go for your dreams and take action. They will change your life.'

Tara's words fall around me and hit a nerve. I feel a longing so strong and sharp it catches my breath.

'How do the cards work exactly?'

'First you tell the cards what you want. Shuffle them and then pick a card. On one side there will be advice you must take to make your wish come true. On the other side there will be an image of what is to come if you take the advice … once you pick a card there's no turning back … what have you got to lose, Jane?'

'Nothing … I guess … it can't hurt if I give them a go, but I'm not sure they'll work,' I say. I turn to Tara wondering how she'll respond. What else can she possibly say to make me believe they are magic?

'Try them,' she says as she walks off to take some donated books from a customer.

Can a pack of cards really sort out my life? I doubt it.

CHAPTER 3

I STOP OFF AT THE corner shop on my way home to my apartment. As soon as I walk in, I notice my elderly neighbour, Mary, has a pile of groceries lined up at the till. She's upset so I rush over to help her. I love old people, and I'm very fond of Mary. She's wearing a cute pink headscarf and some of her grey curls peep out.

'Hello, my dear,' she says. 'I forgot my purse. I'll need to go back home and get it. How silly of me. I'd forget my head if it wasn't screwed on these days. I wonder where I left it.'

'There's no need for that. I'll get this for you, Mary,' I say as I scan my bank card.

I carry her groceries and we walk home together. The bag is heavy. I don't know how she would have managed this herself. I offer to do her shopping in future, but she tells me she prefers to do it herself.

'It gets me out of the house, Jane. Now tell me about Gillian. I watched her on *The Late Late Show* the other night. She was only marvellous. Can you get me her autograph?'

I watched Gillian on the show too. She had the host eating out of her hand, and she charmed the pants off the audience. It was some performance. But that's her job. She's an actress.

'Of course I will. I've merchandise from some of her movies too – mugs and posters. Would you like some?'

'How kind. God bless you, my love.'

'Take care, Mary. If you need anything else, just give me a shout,' I say, as I pop a fifty-euro note discreetly into her shopping bag when we get to her door. Just in case she's short of a few bob.

One of the downsides to living alone is that when I make a mess there's no one else to clean up, regardless of how upset I feel. I hate cleaning. I've been meaning to get a cleaner for a while, but I've got quite lazy about the whole thing. When I enter my living room, last night's Chinese takeaway cartons are lying around. The smell of curry makes me gag. I decide the cleaning can wait. Wine, however, can't. A few glasses of wine might make the mess disappear, and make everything feel better for a while. I think about changing into my pyjamas but then decide against it. I'm afraid I may never want to get out of them again.

I throw my handbag on the coffee table as I enter my galley kitchen. The cards fall out of my bag. I glance down at them waiting for something to happen. I'm not sure what exactly. Perhaps a pulse or a glow. Something to show me that Tara was right about their powers.

My stomach grumbles.

My fridge is empty apart from cheese, a tub of Kerrygold butter and a bottle of Chardonnay. I never got a chance to buy any groceries for myself as I was too focused on helping Mary. I grab the wine and pour myself a generous glass. It goes down nicely in about thirty seconds. My fingers twitch as I pour myself another. This one is even bigger. The cold liquid swirls around my head playfully and wets my throat.

I grab some Jacob's crackers from the almost-bare cupboard to go with the Red Leicester cheese. I wait for the crunch as I take a bite, but there's none. It tastes disgusting. The mould on the cheese becomes obvious as I spit it out on the magazine beside me. A face on the cover stares back.

It's Gillian on *Vogue*.

I can't imagine her ever eating mouldy cheese.

I read the label on the bottle of Chardonnay. A rich aged oak with flavours of coconut, vanilla and spices. A strange feeling arises in the pit of my stomach. Reality hits. I'm not getting the promotion. What on earth am I going to do next? I pour myself another glass and gulp it back and then I have one more.

I'm so attached to the bank. To work anywhere else just seems so wrong. I'm going to have to brush up on my CV and search for a new job. I'm obviously not valued there. If I leave, who else will finish all my work projects? Probably Ben. I should be pissed off with Ben, but I can't. I can't imagine ever being pissed off with Ben. Just as I'm about to pick up the cards my iPhone rings.

'Hello, my darling,' my mam's voice slurs when I answer.

She's been hitting the drink from the sounds of it. Something must have happened. I hate when she's drunk. Either she's high on life or morbid about how her life never turned out the way she wanted it to. And then it occurs to me, hitting the drink is exactly what I'm doing now. I've really hit rock bottom if I'm behaving like my mother.

'Hi Mam. How's things?'

'Michael proposed. She's getting married.'

'Who's getting married?'

'Gillian is.'

'She's engaged again? This is her third engagement. Which one is Michael? I can't keep up.'

'You must know Michael Boudet, they starred together in that movie where he played an action hero. I couldn't have picked a nicer son-in-law. He's such a nice chap and so handsome too.'

My sister's boyfriends are all nice, handsome chaps. She falls in love with whoever she is filming with, usually the male lead. The problem is her relationships don't last very long. Gillian is a hopeless romantic.

'She flew straight home … she couldn't wait to tell us in person.'

'That's nice. Do you think he's the one?'

'He is. They're clearly besotted with each other. You'll see for yourself when you get here.'

'I can't wait to meet him. I have some news too. I had my appraisal today and well … it didn't exactly go the way I wanted it to. I lost out on a promotion. It went to my friend, Ben. You know, Ben. The guy I sit beside.'

'You're not still fantasising about him, are you? You need to get a real boyfriend. And I don't know what the big deal is about this promotion. It's just an office job. You should want to move on to something bigger – onwards and upwards as they say. The sooner you move on the better.'

'My work may not be as glamorous as Gillian's, but it means a lot to me …' I say faintly, still taken aback by my mother's throwaway comment about my job and Ben. Can't I just be miserable? And then pick myself back up.

'Moving away from the bank could change your life, Jane. I always wanted you to be a model. You're pretty enough … you just needed to get used to the camera, but your father would have none of it. He steered you towards numbers and books instead. What a waste of time that was. You could come and work for your sister. Be one of her assistants … she'll set you up with a nice man … she's here, she wants to speak to you. Hold on and please don't upset her with your problems.'

I couldn't think of anything worse than being Gillian's assistant. My mam really doesn't get me.

'Hey sis,' says Gillian squealing. 'So … aren't you going to congratulate me?'

'Of course, congrats.'

'Are you coming over to Mam's place to have some champers to celebrate with us? It's just a quick visit. We came on Michael's jet, and I fly back to London soon, so I don't have much time,' she says.

My sister speaks very fast. I think it's because she has so much to say and she's always in a hurry. She's like a whirlwind, a few minutes in her company and I'm exhausted.

'I'll just get changed out of my work clothes and I'll be straight there.'

'Come as soon as you can and dress smart. I can't just wait around for you.'

'You're busy. I get it. So, tell me about Michael?'

'There's not much to say really. We met and fell madly in love. We want to get married within the next few months. Before I turn twenty-five … I always said I wanted to be married before I'm twenty-five.'

Tiredness swamps me. I can't help but yawn. My head hurts. It's always stressful dealing with Gillian. The online images of her pop into my head. It's been so long since I last saw her in person. I think the last time was at Aunt Áine's wedding that she dropped into for a few hours. I never even got to talk to her that day. She was surrounded by guests wanting her attention.

'What's that yawn for? You can show a bit more enthusiasm than that, Jane.'

'So have you decided on bridesmaids yet?' I ask, trying to ease the tension. I hope I'll be one.

'Hmm ... no ... not yet. I have a few options. I want at least five. If I were to ask you, promise me you won't spoil the photos. There'll likely be a magazine deal, so I want no poses with your eyes closed or that lopsided thing you do with your mouth when you smile. Everything needs to be perfect. Let's be honest ... you're not very photogenic. Are you, Jane?'

My face turns bright red. I can find no words to answer back. I count to ten and then twenty before I end the call.

I get changed quickly and make my way over in a taxi to Abington, Malahide. My mam's place. Gillian bought her a mansion there on Millionaire's Row after she became famous. The traffic is heavy and it's lashing rain. When I arrive, the house is in darkness. There's no one there. Gillian sends me a text a few minutes later.

Jane. You took too long! We've gone to meet some of Mam's friends on the way to the airport. Slán abhaile. X

I'm wet from head to toe. I want to call them and ask them why they made me come all the way over here for nothing, but I don't. I don't want to make a scene with Michael being there, and it would probably be turned on its head and made out to be all my fault. I can't win no matter what I do.

When I get home, I get changed into my pyjamas, I plonk myself on the couch, stare into space. I plan on never moving from this spot again. Everything feels surreal, like I'm living someone else's life or just watching it unfold from the sidelines. This can't be my life.

I remember the strange conversation with Tara. I pick up the cards and shuffle them as they gleam and shine. The brightness I experienced in the bookshop happens again. Everything in my apartment looks vibrant. Is it all in my head or is it the wine? I promised Tara I would give this a chance, so here goes nothing.

'Hello cards, can you get me my promotion, please?' I say loudly to the walls. My voice seems to echo back to me as I pick a card.

The word *Success* is engraved on the front of it; below this is an image of what is to come: a smiling blonde-haired woman with her hands in the air. The colours are so striking they appear to jump out from the paper. I read the advice on the card.

You will come out from wherever you are hiding and take centre stage, for whatever you have put effort into is about to blossom into something wonderful. Make others aware of just how valuable you are, and success will come.

I wait in silence for something to happen. Anything. A flicker of light, a spark or a bang even.

Isn't that what happens in movies?

I count to two hundred and still nothing. There – I've done it. I can go back to Tara tomorrow and return the cards and tell her I tried, but nothing happened.

I turn on Netflix, but I can't focus on anything. Instead, I scroll through my phone. There are no pictures of Gillian's ring yet, but her engagement has been officially announced through her social media accounts. There are 160,451 comments so far on her latest Facebook post. Some suggest her engagement is all for publicity. A few are downright mean. Comments like 'what a bitch she is and it's no wonder the other engagements were called off.' Some others say she's clearly desperate to get married. Another one claims she can't act, and she has insider information that Gillian slept her way to the top and she's a coke head. The last one I read says, 'she's too above her station that one. I heard she grew up in a two-up two-down terraced house you couldn't swing a cat in.'

The comments give me no satisfaction, only a duller ache in my head. I know how hard my sister works and I feel strangely over-protective of her when I read anything negative.

There are many reasons why I dislike my sister, but they're for none of the reasons that get mentioned on social media or in the tabloids. I hate her for the fact that she left when I was a teenager to live in Hollywood and at the time, I missed her so much my heart hurt. When she did come back, with her Oscar in tow, our relationship was different. She changed. Something happened to her that made her closed off and secretive. My sweet, caring older sister became an enigma to me and she never divulged to me what happened in Hollywood. Our communication broke down, we were no longer best friends. Instead, I watched her live her life out through the press and on social media. I began to see her as an entitled spoilt brat.

I also hate that once she became famous, I was no longer just Jane McAlister to others. Instead, I was mostly addressed as Gillian O'Hara's sister. It became obvious most people were only interested in me because of my sister and I never knew who to trust anymore. No one ever seems to think what it's like for the siblings of famous people, and from my perspective, no matter what I did with my life it would pale in comparison to my sister's achievements.

But there are times when I'm so proud of her that my heart screams with happiness. Like when she won her Oscar, I couldn't sleep for days with excitement. The same when she's nominated for any awards. I love that she's achieved so much in her life at such a young age, and she really is an outstanding actress. In the early days I kept scrapbooks of all the newspaper articles about her success. She deserves every bit of goodness in her life, it's just a pity I don't get to share it with her anymore.

While I get ready for bed, the photograph on the wall catches my eye. The one of myself, Ben, and Emma taken after we finished our induction period with the bank. The three of us were slouched on a couch in Café en Seine with a table full of cocktails. Ben has his arms around both of us while Emma is glancing over at him. You can tell from the photo, I was happy. Happy because I thought I had finally met my soulmate. I've never had the courage to tell Ben how I really feel about him. I'm too afraid in case he turns me down and I make a fool of myself.

I think back to the conversation I had with Ben in the office yesterday. His tanned face was turned towards me. He had a box of Christmas decorations beside him. He's on the social committee, who were tasked with decorating the entire fourth floor for Christmas.

'Does the Santa hat suit me, Jane?' he said.

I just stared at him with my mouth open. Despite the goofy hat, he looked good. Really good. His striking blue eyes looked tired. I couldn't help but notice the dark circles under his eyes. Perhaps he'd had a few too many drinks the night before. Probably out with his girlfriend, Sarah. He was clean-shaven as usual. His dark hair was styled carefully and he wore a made-to-measure suit from one of the most expensive tailors in Dublin. It fitted his tall, well-built frame like a glove.

'Here's an elf hat for you to try on. You'd make a great elf.' He placed some tinsel over my long blonde hair as he passed me the hat. 'Put on the hat ... let's take a selfie.'

He took out his Polaroid instant camera from the drawer, placed the hat on my head, and put his arm around me.

'Stop messing.' I giggled. I tend to giggle a lot when I'm nervous.

'There we go. Perfect. Smile,' he said as the flash from the camera made me blink.

It wasn't the most flattering picture of me, but Ben didn't seem to notice. He placed it on his desk beside the rest of the photos. I had this weird lop-sided look on my face and my eyes were slightly closed while Ben looked perfect.

'Ah, I like this one,' he said. 'You look cute as an elf.'

'No more photos. I'm nervous about my appraisal tomorrow. I really hope I get promoted.'

He stopped what he was doing and looked at me intently.

'Why do you want it so much?'

'I want to learn management skills and become better at my job. Isn't that what everyone wants?'

'No. Not everyone. Most of the people here just want to make money, Jane. They don't care about learning management skills or becoming more productive.'

'But I want to move on with my life. To be somebody.'

I cringed at how desperate I sounded.

'You are somebody.'

'No, I'm not.'

'Yes, you are.'

'You're teasing me again,' I said. 'I just want to do something with my life, Ben. What's wrong with that?'

'Nothing.' He shrugged his shoulders. 'But you have years ahead of you to decide what you want to do. You're only twenty-three. There's more to life than being a slave to this place.'

'You don't get it.' I frowned.

Ben grew up on Vico Road in Dalkey. His neighbours were the likes of Bono and The Edge from U2. Work is just something he fits in around playing rugby or travelling to exotic locations with Sarah. It's a well-known fact that Ben got this job because of family connections. Ben doesn't need to worry about making a splash in the ocean. He was born into it – a bit like the royal family. No matter what Ben does he will always come up smelling of roses.

He walked towards me and leaned against my desk. His leg was practically touching mine. Being so close to him made me jittery. I could smell his aftershave. He wore my favourite one.

'If I was putting as much effort as you do into your job, I'd prefer to do it for a cause that means something,' he said.

'Like what?'

'I don't know. I haven't figured that out yet. That's why I'm still here.'

'That's not helping me right now … I just—'

'Ah, I've upset you. Don't be. I think you're great at what you do. You just have to believe it. You deserve to be promoted more than anyone else here.' He waved his hands around the room. 'If it was up to me … I'd promote you in a heartbeat,' he said as he gazed at me with his hand on his chest.

He says the nicest things to me sometimes. My heart melted and I wanted to reach out and hug him, but I didn't. Instead, I thought about what it would be like if I put my arms around his neck and kissed him. I blushed and shook my head to bring myself back to earth.

'You know, sometimes I feel like just quitting life and going travelling,' he said, interrupting my thoughts.

'With Sarah?'

'No. Just by myself. I'd have freedom. Total freedom. No pressure from my old man asking me when I'm ready to take over the family business and no commitments. Sarah's great and all, but lately she's been getting too clingy. Way too clingy. I think she wants to get engaged soon ...' He winced.

'Well, she is a lot older than you. The clock is ticking—'

'Yeah, but there's no way I'm ready for that. I don't know if I ever will be.'

I shook my head. Even though Ben talks about going travelling, I doubt anything is going to break them up.

CHAPTER 4

THE NEXT MORNING, I wake up with an anxious feeling in the pit of my stomach. My mouth is dry. My head is pounding. I check my phone for any messages from Emma, but there's none. Last night before I went to sleep, I called her three times and sent her a text apologising for walking out of our meeting. I told her I'll be back in the office today and asked if we could meet to clear the air. I really hope I haven't jeopardised my job.

As I walk to work, trying to shake off the hangover, I go over and over in my mind about what I should say to Emma. I feel awful as I count the cracks in the payment along the way.

It's as if my life is on the brink of change, and nothing feels normal anymore.

When I get to the fourth floor of the bank, it's pretty much empty. It always is at this time of the morning. I love to be one of the first into the office, it's quiet and calm then before the rest of the bankers arrive and I can knuckle down and get straight to work.

'Anyone know where I can get a strong cup of black coffee around here?' says a man walking towards me with a strong German accent.

I direct him to the coffee dock beside my desk and show him how everything works.

'If you don't like the coffee,' I say smiling, 'I can pop out and get you one, I know where they sell the best coffee in the IFSC. I was just about to go out and get one myself. Ah, there you go. You've figured out how to work it now.'

'I'm sure this will be fine, but thank you for the offer,' he says.

I hear my phone ring, so I rush off to answer it in case it's important. It's my client, Mr. Feltz. He requests heaps of information to do with his investments. I have a photographic memory so I go through his entire financial portfolios. Numbers roll off my tongue; I quote all his revenue, and investments for the last five years at his request. I know his account like the back of my hand.

'If you have any further questions, or need anything else please don't hesitate to contact me. Your business is very important to us,' I say once I know he's satisfied. The thing with Mr. Feltz is he wants to feel important, so I make sure I do that. Having a sister like mine makes me well-equipped to deal with difficult people.

It's only after I hang up the phone, I realise I'm being watched by the man who I sorted out with coffee. He's sitting down on a chair at the coffee dock sipping his drink. My cheeks flame red at the thought of someone watching me so intently while I'm working. He's a tall man, in his mid- to late-fifties. He's silent for a moment, as he stares at me, and then a smile spreads across his face.

'Are you new? I've never seen you here before,' I say.

'I'm here for an interview. It's just a short visit.'

'Oh, what's the job for? Is it for a finance position?'

'A bit of everything really,' he says vaguely. 'Who are you?'

'Me ... well ... I'm ... I'm ...' I say, shocked.

'What's your name?'

'I'm Jane,' I say. 'Jane McAlister.'

'Nice to meet you, Jane. I'm Walter.' He shakes my hand. He looks around the floor of the open plan office. 'You're in early.'

'Oh, always the first one in and the last to leave, that's me. Nothing better to do with my time or so my family tell me. I really need to get a life ...'

I laugh at my own joke, waiting for him to laugh back, but he doesn't. He just continues staring at me.

'I may have an opportunity for you, Jane. My secretary will be in touch to set up a meeting,' he says before he walks away.

Who is this man? And what opportunity could he have for me?

Walter's secretary arranged for us to meet later that evening. It turns out that Walter is actually the CEO of Becker Bank International, which makes me question even more what he wants to talk to me about.

And why over dinner?

Walter is rarely in the Dublin office and if he is it's usually only to meet big investors. None of my colleagues on the fourth floor have ever met him before, apart from Ben. He's met him a few times with his dad. Ben said Walter comes across to him as a ruthless man who's just out to make money and who enjoys firing people. Because of this, my first thought when I found out Walter was the CEO was that I was in trouble. Big trouble. I went over in my mind the phone conversation I'd had with Mr. Feltz earlier, searching for any inkling of something I'd said that could have come across the wrong way. Walter was watching me so intently and sitting very close to my desk, I'm sure he heard my every word.

Surely he's not bringing me to dinner to fire me? I wish I didn't need to go to the meeting. I thought about backing out, but I'm not stupid. No one turns down a meeting with the CEO.

What if he thinks I'm engaging in fraud or wants to question me about Mr. Feltz's financial affairs?

My stomach is sick with the thought of it. At least I know all my paperwork is in order. I'm a stickler for detail and always follow procedures.

Our meeting is at a hotel situated on Grand Canal Square, which is one of the coolest parts of Dublin city – known as Google-land. Surrounding the hotel there's wide open spaces, vegan restaurants, an organic market and a vibrant theatre. Ben's river-facing apartment is close by.

When I get to the hotel for the meeting I'm right on time. Inside it's all sharp edges with a modern design. I get a sense I've entered a spaceship filled with friendly faces. Everything is Instagrammable and futuristic. There's a smell of Christmas. I tell the receptionist that I'm here for a dinner meeting with Mr. Becker.

'Are you Jane McAlister?' she asks.

I nod my head and she gives me a wide smile.

'We hope you enjoy your evening. Please let me escort you to the rooftop terrace for dinner.'

I glance at myself in the mirror on my way to the elevator. My brown eyes twinkle back at me despite the fact I'm on edge. I'm wearing a black knee-length Prada dress suit and high heels, both of which are Gillian's hand-me-downs. My sister is quite generous giving me things she no longer wants. She follows fashion trends and sends me boxes of clothes on a regular basis, usually the previous season's stuff.

I look more like her whenever I wear her clothes. We have similar shaped oval faces and are around the same dress size. It's just our hair that sets us apart and how we carry ourselves. Gillian swaggers and sways. *Look at me*, her body screams, and when she enters a room, everyone knows she's arrived. I, on the other hand, like to fade gracefully into the background. Becoming quite an expert at it by now.

My cards are in my handbag. I wonder if they had anything to do with this meeting, but then I realise how ridiculous that is. How could a pack of cards set this up?

I count to twenty as I get out of the elevator and step onto the rooftop terrace. The most stunning, unparalleled three-sixty views across Dublin open up. I can make out the Dublin Mountains, the Irish Sea, and the Dublin Docklands. My first thought is, I can't wait to tell Emma how beautiful this is. We were due to come here for a girls' weekend in a few weeks, but there's no way I can tell her now. Instead I imagine myself here with Ben. In my mind he has his arms wrapped around me while we look out across at the view, and he's kissing my neck.

Someone coughs, bringing me back down to earth.

There in the middle of the terrace I spot Walter sitting at a table, observing me carefully. He's wearing a pale blue shirt unbuttoned at the neck with black chinos. His arm is loosely draped across a rattan couch. Two waiters fawn over him as he sits at the only table on the terrace, lit by outdoor heaters and fairy lights. The lights twinkle and shine as if they're cheering me on. White sparkly Christmas decorations are placed on the table while a huge Christmas tree is close by.

'Jane, please take a seat,' he says with a strong German accent as he pulls out my chair. 'I hope you don't mind, but I reserved the whole terrace for us for tonight.'

'Thank you, Mr. Becker,' I say and I shake his hand.

What the hell is going on?

'Please call me Walter.' His eyes don't leave me as he assesses me. 'Let me explain why I asked you here tonight.'

I sit down and shift in my seat to get a good look at everything. The candlelit table is laid elegantly with white linen and the cutlery and glasses gleam. Everything screams money and wealth.

'I'm sorry I didn't know who you were earlier.'

'That's my fault. I should have introduced myself to you. There's a position that I've been trying to fill for some time in Dublin. The candidates I met so far weren't the right fit ... and then I met you. I did some investigations to find out about you but it's best you tell me yourself.'

I falter. The thought of someone investigating me fills me with dread, but at least I'm not about to be fired. 'Well, I greatly admire hardworking and successful people like yourself.' I gesture with my shaky hands. 'I love working at the bank ...' My voice is shaking.

His face is expressionless. 'Your clients had a lot to say about you.'

It's as if he's studying me like I'm some exotic animal at the zoo. I can't help but blush. I'm too hot. I take off my jacket and place it on the back of my chair. He pauses and looks down at his notebook. At this point everything I'm wearing feels wrong, my dress is uncomfortable and I can't think of anything to say. I feel self-conscious. I shouldn't be here. Tonight is going to be a disaster.

What does he want from me?

Walter seems oblivious to my discomfort. 'Can I get you a drink? Champagne?' he asks.

'Champagne would be nice. Thank you.'

Walter selects a very expensive bottle from the menu.

'What exactly do you want to do with your life, Jane?'

I'm tongue-tied, hot and bothered, but then I hear Tara's voice speak to me in my head. *You have endless potential. What have you got to lose, Jane?*

I feel more confident, I sit up straighter. I glance down at my clothes and they don't seem so bad after all. I look Walter straight in the eye. 'I want to be as successful as you, Walter.'

He laughs. 'I like your way of thinking. We have lots to talk about tonight, Jane, but first we eat.'

He clicks his fingers. Waiters surround us as they bring out food. Delicious smells waft around me. First come the seafood dishes, crab, mussels, lobster, salmon and tiger prawns. Hot steam rushes out from the plates. Then mozzarella with ripened tomatoes on sourdough bread, Parma ham, huge garlic mushrooms, chicken wings and various salads appear before me.

'I ordered all the starters from the menu. This is the best way to decide.'

I've never seen so much food in my life. My glass is filled with more champagne. I gulp it down and once it's empty it's topped up again. My eyes bulge in wonder, but I only take small portions of food. I don't want to come across as a greedy guts. I've gone from eating mouldy cheese yesterday to this. An envelope is placed beside my wine glass. Inside is a complimentary ticket to a sound bath session for tomorrow morning at the hotel. I've always wanted to try one. This must be the sort of service Gillian experiences on a daily basis. I could get used to this.

'Where do you get your drive from, Jane? What pushes you to want more?'

'From my sister,' I whisper.

'Your sister. What does she do? Does she also work in finance?'

I was hoping he wouldn't ask that. Now's not the time to give Walter the run down on how many Oscars Gillian has.

'She's an actress. You may not have heard of her, but to answer your question her success drives me to be just as good as her.'

He smiles. 'That's very different to banking, but it's impressive all the same. As far as I'm concerned, you're an asset to this company. I need you on my team. Who is your manager?' he asks, frowning.

'Emma.'

'Emma who?'

'O'Brien. She's been my manager for about a month.'

He takes out his phone and I can see he's looking me up on the staff directory. 'Her boss is Tim O'Halloran.' He passes his phone to me with a picture of Emma on it and her reporting line.

'From now on you will report directly to me. No more reporting to Emma O'Brien.' He waves his hand as if he is swatting a fly. 'Whatever your current salary is it's now tripled. You now oversee some of the bank's high-profile clients. If you give them the same service as Mr. Feltz you can't go wrong. Does that sound good to you?'

'It sounds perfect. Thank you.' I gulp back more champagne.

'I'll get the paperwork drawn up. Please excuse me while I deal with this.' He takes out his phone and has a short conversation in German with someone. He hands me his business card. 'I'll make arrangements for your new office.'

I nod in agreement. Finally, all my hard work has paid off! We say our goodbyes. When I leave the hotel, I'm on cloud nine.

In the taxi on the way home I keep refreshing my email on my iPhone for the contract. I'm so excited yet full of disbelief, it's almost too good to be true. The drive home is taking forever. I can't keep this to myself. I have to tell someone. Ben. I need to tell Ben what happened. I ring him, but all I get after the ring tone is, 'Hey it's Ben, I'm unavailable to take your call right now. Please leave a message and I'll get back to you. Cheers.'

Unavailable.

It's moments like this that hurt the most. The ones when I'm bursting with excitement to tell him something, but he's unavailable. That sums him up in one word.

I put my iPhone back in my handbag and I notice the drawstring bag is open.

How did that happen? I was sure I had tied it tightly.

The cards gleam like they did before in the bookshop – or maybe I just imagined it. Could they really be magic?

I hear a ping, and refresh my email again. The contract has arrived. The position even comes with my own penthouse office apartment situated within the bank. I've never heard of an apartment situated within the bank before, but I'm not complaining. This is a dream come true.

I'm used to sleepless nights. I often wake up in the middle of the night and listen to every creak and sound of my apartment, and find it impossible to go back asleep. Tonight is different, though. I wake up confused. A layer of sweat covers my skin as my damp nightdress clings to me. Scraps of my dream flash through my mind; a dream so vivid it feels more real than reality. Moths chase me while I try to find my way home. Each time I reach my front door it moves. Then there are fireworks. They scatter bursts of light like shooting stars in space.

I hear the creeping of footsteps getting louder and the creaking of the floorboards. The digital clock says it's 3:47 am. It sounds like an intruder is in my apartment and they're about to barge into my bedroom at any second. I try to wiggle my toes, arms and legs, but I can't. I'm paralysed with fear, waiting for the handle of the bedroom door to move. I need a weapon. Anything sharp or heavy should do. A glass of water sits on my bedside locker. I try to move my arms to pick it up, but it's useless. They still won't budge. Another noise. A slam this time. Something has fallen to the ground. I try to make out shapes in the dark, but everything looks more sinister. Shadows look foreign. The curtains rustle as if they're trying to tell me something.

My mind continues to wander, questioning what the noises could be. I get my movement back but lie awake for hours counting until the morning light slowly slips into my bedroom and the noises cease. I then drag myself out of bed and check around my apartment. Nothing is out of place. It's like there was no one there.

If it wasn't a burglar, what the hell was it?

CHAPTER 5

BEN

I COULDN'T CONCENTRATE WHEN JANE had her appraisal. The whole time she was in Emma's office I was worried about how things would pan out. I was hoping Emma would do the right thing, but I had a sneaky suspicion she wouldn't. When I saw Jane run past me it was clear she was upset. I shouted after her to come back, but I don't think she heard me.

What had Emma told her? I wondered how much she knew.

I wanted to run after her and make it better, but I was worried she didn't want anything to do with me and that I'd only make it worse.

Did she hate me now?

The whole thing was fucked up and I'd no idea how to fix it. Especially as it was mainly my fault. I have many regrets with how things panned out between myself, Jane and Emma. If I could go back in time to those first few months that we started working together and change everything I would.

I'll never forget the first day I met Jane. It was about a year ago, at the beginning of our induction week on the graduate programme with Becker Bank International. The first thing I noticed was her intensity. She wrote so many notes and always walked around with a pen and notebook. Poised and ready for action. Her blonde hair and brown eyes made a stunning combination, and I couldn't take my eyes off her. She had fantastic legs too. Jane was like the opposite of me. While I was more interested in finding out about the free booze on offer, she was at her laptop reading up on the bank's policies and procedures. I thought out of the three of us she'd be the first one to be promoted as she wanted to succeed so badly. It was like her life depended on it.

On the second day I went out to get a coffee. I needed fresh air and some headspace from all the information we were being bombarded with.

'I came to visit my sister. She works nearby, but she turned me down,' said a voice in front of me as I stood in the queue.

She sounded eloquent and spoke fast, very fast. Her voice annoyed me, but it didn't seem to bother the guy serving her the coffee she asked for. I saw him throw some extra croissants into a bag and pass it to her.

'You're a gorgeous looking woman,' he said with a wink. 'How could anyone turn you down? I know I never would.'

She replied with a laugh. A dirty loud laugh.

Intrigued by what the barista said, I had to check her out for myself. Was she as gorgeous as he was making out? She was standing with her back to me. Her bright fire engine red hair trailed down her back. She had toned thighs and wore tight black shorts. They appeared stuck to her legs. Her black tank top showed off her slim waist. I eavesdropped on their conversation to find out more about her. I only caught fragmented parts. She said something about how she wanted to settle down and have a quiet life. That her life was a whirlwind and she was exhausted.

What did she do for a living? Was she a model or an actress? She was too dramatic to just work in an office. That outfit wouldn't be appropriate anyway. Who was this exotic creature? Was it her face or her body that made her so gorgeous?

I inched forward to get a glimpse of her face. She directed her gaze towards me, aware she was being stared at. I turned away as I was caught out, but she didn't flinch. She carried on the conversation as if this is what happens to her on a regular basis. Like being watched was the most natural thing in the world. When I saw her face, I realised who she was. The billboard pictures with Gillian O'Hara's face splattered all over them were everywhere.

When I got back to the bank, I told the rest of the group who I just saw, and the room filled with chat all about Gillian. Everyone had something to say about her. Everyone apart from Jane, she just listened to all the conversations with an odd look on her face and walked off by herself.

'Are you all right?' I said.

'It's not something I talk about much, but Gillian O'Hara is my sister. O'Hara is her stage name,' she mumbled to me. 'All the comments about her get to me sometimes.'

'No way! She said you were too busy to meet her.'

'Gillian just showed up and asked me to go off shopping with her. She forgets sometimes other people have things to do. I wanted to go with her, but I didn't want to miss the induction. This job is important to me. I really want to do well.' Her eyes filled up with sadness. 'My relationship with my sister is ... well, it's complicated. She lives in a different world to the rest of us.'

That was it. End of conversation. I had so many questions, but I knew after that not to push it any further. She looked so fragile when she spoke about Gillian, I wanted to protect her.

She's prettier than Gillian. She's more of a natural beauty by far, and her eyes are a deeper shade of brown. Gillian is styled and groomed to perfection. A bit fake-looking, though. Every photo of her in the magazines or newspapers looks staged.

I made sure I got to sit beside Jane in work. I cracked jokes constantly, to make her laugh. I loved the way her face lit up when she smiled, and I could tell she was into me.

She worked for hours fixing things to make everything perfect for her clients. She turned down nights out if she had projects to finish instead. Nights when everyone left the office early. Everyone apart from Jane and Emma.

The clients loved Jane. She went over and above to please them. No matter who was watching she acted the same and I admired that about her. There were so many chancers in the bank, and she was like a breath of fresh air. She never bragged or boasted like the rest of us. She didn't care about the bonuses or making money, she just wanted to do the right thing.

'Stop it, Ben,' she'd say whenever I told her she was better-looking than Gillian. 'You're such a tease. You love to wind me up.'

I tried a few times to ask Jane out, but it never went to plan. She never took me seriously. I even resorted to flipping a coin. *Tails she loves me, heads she doesn't*, I'd say to myself. It landed on heads way too much for my liking.

Instead, I asked Emma to go for a drink with me. Purely just to pick her brains to get a female perspective on things. The three of us were becoming so close I thought Emma might tell me what the craic was, and I'd finally know where I stood.

'What do you think my chances are with Jane?' I said. 'Do you think she'd want to go out on a date with me?'

She laughed right in my face and said something so significant it stopped me in my tracks. I wish I never listened. I should have just walked away because what she told me stopped me from pursuing Jane.

CHAPTER 6

JANE

MY MIND BUZZES AS the hot water scalds my skin. It drums to a rhythm against my neck and shoulders. The intense heat soothes my sore muscles. Was there really an intruder in my apartment last night? At the time the noises were so real, terrifying me. As I think about them, I feel like I'm drowning; it's as if the water is filling my lungs.

What if they come back?

I jump out of the shower quickly and wrap a towel tightly around me. The water drips down my body. A reflection stares back at me in the mirror – eyes uncertain, afraid, with dark shadows underneath. My complexion is grey and gaunt. I'll need a full face of make-up today.

Cracks in the ceiling run all the way across the room. I never noticed them before. Maybe they were always there. I was on top of the world last night, I floated to bed, but now I'm shaken. Afraid of my own shadow. The room is black, the colour of fear that seeps into my blood and bones. I need to get out of the apartment. Get away and be anywhere but here. The sound bath starts in an hour so that will give me somewhere to go and then I'll call Walter to accept his offer.

I get dressed and walk around taking everything in. For the first time I'm aware of how empty it is apart from a few photos and pictures – mainly of myself and Ben. There's no fruit in bowls or flowers in vases. My cupboards are practically bare, I rarely shop for food as I eat most of my meals in work or get takeaways. I've lived here for a year, but I've never really made it into a home. I had great plans to decorate but I've never had the time because of work.

I bought this place with money for a deposit that Gillian gave me. It was enough to get me a one-bed apartment on Clanbrassil Street, which is within walking distance of Dublin city centre. She phoned me one day to tell me Mam was sick of me still living at home, but she was too polite to tell me herself.

'Get something basic with the money I send you,' she said, 'nothing too fancy. It's just to get your foot on the property ladder and out of Mam's hair.'

I've lived on my own ever since I moved in.

Am I destined to live alone forever?

I will be if I can't shake my feelings for Ben. I need to get over him once and for all.

A pang of loneliness washes over me, reminding me how much I want to have a boyfriend. Someone to share my life with and eventually have kids. It's so hard for me to meet anyone.

Normally I would call my old school friend, Sorcha, when I'm feeling off, but I can't right now as she's working night shifts in the hospital this week. Sorcha moved to Sydney, Australia a year ago and works there as a nurse. She's like the nicest person in the world and gets me like no one else. When Gillian's career blossomed, she got a huge part as an actress – in a Disney movie. She needed to be in Hollywood to film and she didn't want to be on her own, so I stayed at Sorcha's house, while my mam accompanied Gillian for the period she was filming. Sorcha's parents were strict, and I loved the sense of order in her house during my time spent there. We became as close as sisters.

It's times like this I wish she didn't live so far away. I could call Ben, but his kindness would probably only make my crush worse. I can't talk to my mam as the conversation would only turn to Gillian. Anyway, this would never happen to Gillian. She lives in a top security, gated apartment complex in Knightsbridge in London. She probably has her new fiancé sleeping by her side every night.

The cards are beside me. As I hold them the room becomes sharper and brighter. I get a sense of clarity and focus. Tara said they're magic, but they can't be. Magic, real magic, doesn't exist, but what's happening now feels magical. The way the colour and light change in the room is almost enchanting. The note said they're from the universe and something about it being my time.

It can't hurt to give them another try and see what happens.

I shuffle the cards and say, 'Hello cards, I want to meet a new guy, someone who can help me get over Ben.'

I pick a card.

The words **Sudden Movement** are engraved at the front of it, and there's a picture of a dark-haired man with blue eyes. I read the message.

> *When this card appears, it is a caution that a new adventure is approaching. Someone unexpected is coming and you must be ready. He will swoop into your life and take you by storm. He can be hard to tie down, so you'll need to move fast. Act with confidence and courage.*

Is this a coincidence? It probably is.

The sound bath on the rooftop terrace is just beginning when I arrive. I lie down on the only available spot on a yoga mat. The air feels cold, but a cosy fleece blanket keeps me warm. The therapist's voice is soothing.

'Sound therapy is deeply rooted in science and based on the principles of quantum physics and sacred geometry. You will experience the healing power of Tibetan singing bowls, gongs, ocean drums and chimes. The healing frequencies and vibrations will take away all your stress and cares. Lie down and allow the beautiful sounds and vibrations to wash over you, healing your mind, body and spirit,' she says.

The music sweeps around me. It's as if every musical note evaporates leaving a multi-coloured mist like a faint rainbow. Sounds fill me, evoking tender emotions as I feel myself starting to nod off. I dream I'm lying on the grass in a park. It's sunny and my arms are wrapped around a man. Not just any man. In my dream he's my boyfriend. I reach over for a kiss. My hands caress his thick dark hair, I stare into his deep dark blue eyes while my lips find his. I can't stop kissing him, and why should I? He is my boyfriend, after all. This is one of the best dreams I've had in a long time. The kisses are nice. I wouldn't call them passionate, more slow and sensual, but very nice all the same. As I melt into his strong, broad chest I wonder who exactly is this guy and how I met him, and then everything feels like it's in slow motion. He's holding onto me; his arms are wrapped tightly around me. Right under my rib cage. It's the perfect fit, but why has he stopped kissing me?

I glance around slightly confused. It's cold. Where's the sun, grass and the park gone?

This is bad. Very bad.

I'm still at the sound bath. I've rolled off my mat, right over to the guy next to me. I'm lying on top of him and my arms and legs are wrapped tightly around him.

I gasp and untangle myself. My body is on fire. I was expecting things to get hotter and then just like that it stopped.

'Hey there,' the stranger's voice says softly. His lips are parted and he has a flicker of something in his eyes. Something that makes me think he liked it just as much as me.

'Oh my God. I'm so sorry. I didn't mean to throw myself at you like that,' I say.

'I don't usually get that kind of attention at a sound bath. No harm done though,' he says as he kneels beside me smirking.

He's a cocky sort of guy, I can tell as soon as he opens his mouth. He puts his fingers through his hair and fixes his clothes. A lock of wavy glossy dark hair falls across his forehead. His blue eyes are playful and full of life. He's wearing all black – tracksuit bottoms, a t-shirt that's slightly ruffled at the collar, and scuffed black runners, and there's an energy that radiates from him.

He's very attractive, in a rugged, unshaven way. I can't stop staring at him. I imagine he's a life-and-soul-of-the-party kind of person. I doubt he wastes his time obsessing over one of his best friends or falling asleep and kissing random strangers.

I wonder whether being that good-looking opens lots of doors and makes his world easier. Like Ben's life, because he comes from such a wealthy family, he has connections everywhere. Why is it I'm still thinking about Ben?

'I'm Jane, I'm so sorry … wrapping myself around a perfect stranger like that, well that's a new one for me—'

'Perfect. Huh. How did you come up with that?' He looks at me like I'm crazy. Like I'm a stalker or something.

'I don't mean you're perfect. I don't even know you. It's just I was dreaming and I thought you were my boyfriend. Look I'm so sorry, can we just forget all about this?'

He laughs, amused by my predicament and then stares at me for ages before he says, 'Sure. No harm done.'

He's a good bit taller than me with a muscular build, and at least five or six years older. He shakes his head. 'You look so familiar. Are you sure we haven't met before? I'm Jay.' He's puzzled now trying to figure out where he knows me from. I'm just waiting for him to bring up my sister, but he doesn't. 'Here, let me help you up.'

When our hands touch a sudden shock runs through me. Like a bolt of electricity running down my spine. I'm rooted to the spot. He's smiling, a slow, sexy kind of smile as he holds onto my hand longer than necessary. He studies me up and down.

'So, Jane, what makes a beautiful girl like you fall asleep at a drop of a hat? Did you have a late night partying?' he says.

This is another one of those rare moments, where all the stars are aligned and something extraordinary has happened. The enormity of what just happened hits me. Maybe it's the fact that I didn't get much sleep last night and the stress I've been under leading up to my appraisal that's making me act like this. Or maybe all the excitement of getting the new job is making me go a bit loopy. Or perhaps … just perhaps there is something to the cards after all. The more I think about it, it's possible that it could be down to the cards. I can't remember the last time I've had this much excitement and it's all to do with what I asked the cards for.

Feck.

Imagine that. I own a pack of magical cards. Real magical cards. Cards that can change my life. The universe must be listening after all. Holy crap. What should I do next?

I turn to Jay, he's waiting for me to answer him. I wish I had my cards now, but I left them at home. I need to say something smart, funny and unforgettable.

'No partying. I just found it hard to sleep,' I blurt out. Okay so that wasn't the best chat up line ever, but I'm just warming up.

'Oh, right. I best be off. You should go home now and try to get some sleep. Everyone else has left.' He turns away from me and walks off.

I notice for the first time that the rooftop terrace is empty. The sound bath is over. I open and close my mouth. My mind goes blank and I just stand there like an idiot for ages watching him walk away.

He wasn't meant to leave, the cards brought him to me and I've just let him walk away. I may never see him again. They told me what I had to do: I must be confident, courageous and act fast. I need to say something that will spark further conversation. It's now or never. I sprint after Jay and as I get closer to him I shout out his name. He stops and smiles when he sees me.

'What's wrong, Jane? Is everything okay?' he says looking me directly in the eye.

'Yeah. Everything is great. What I meant to say earlier is that, I've had a busy week, because I've been working hard for a promotion,' I say, out of breath.

'Ah, and did you get it?' His voice is soft and low.

'Hell, yeah. Of course I did.'

'Beauty and confidence, I like it. What do you do?'

'I work for an investment bank. I'm a banker.'

'So, I hope it's not all work and no play,' he says as the corner of his mouth twitches upwards.

'There's never a dull moment with me, Jay.'

I cringe as soon as I say those words. I hope I don't sound too cheesy. I'm totally out of my comfort zone right now.

'I can see that. You've made an impression on me already and we've only just met.' He winks and we both laugh.

We stand close together grinning at each other. Our hands touch again and I feel a pulse of energy rush through me again. This must only be happening because of the magic from the cards.

'Did you feel that or is just me?' he says. 'It's like an electric shock.'

'I feel it too. It's a spark of something.'

I notice for the first time how intense his blue eyes are. There's definitely something about him that feels right. I really want to see him again.

'I came after you because I want to see you again, Jay. Let's exchange numbers.'

'Sure, why not,' he says as he takes out his phone and smirks. 'This could be fun.'

I leave on a high and I punch the air. I'm on fire.

My phone rings.

'Jane, are you all right? I saw how upset you were and I was worried about you. I saw your missed call. Sorry, I only got a chance to call you now, I've been busy with Sarah ...'

'I got a new job ...' I say.

'But I'm not going to take the promotion. The whole thing is a load of bollox. I told her it should be yours. You should come back to work. Don't leave. The place wouldn't be the same without you. Anyway, you know the plan is for me to eventually work in my old man's business.'

That's Ben all over. He's as cool as a cucumber – ready to turn down the promotion just like that without breaking a sweat.

'I got a new job working directly for Walter Becker. He asked me out for dinner and offered it to me. I'm not leaving the bank, just moving up. I even get my own office.' My face erupts into a huge smile.

'Well done. I'm delighted for you. A new office, huh. You're going up in the world now.'

I wonder what my new office will be like. Will I understand how to do my new work? My new clients are high-profile – which is like nothing I've dealt with before.

'Seriously though, Ben. What do you think of it all?'

'You know my feelings about Walter, but he may not be like that with you.' He pauses. 'I think I'm going to miss you sitting beside me.'

'Stop teasing me. Be serious. I mean about the work—'

'I am being serious. My day will definitely be duller without you around. Listen, don't worry about it. You'll be grand. Better than grand. This is what you wanted for so long. It's great you got this job. I'm proud of you. Walter Becker better watch out, you'll be taking over his job in no time. Hold on a second. Sarah is beside me. We're having breakfast together, and she wants me off the phone. I have to go.'

I can picture him rolling his eyes, he hates it when Sarah tells him what to do. He usually gets annoyed and she promises to stop nagging him and then they kiss and make up.

'Okay. No worries, Ben. I'll catch up with you when I'm back in work.'

'Grand. I'll look forward to it.'

I really want to see Tara to find out more about the cards. As I approach Hidden Secrets she's sitting beside the crackling fire with a blanket wrapped around her legs. She looks sick. Her eyes are sullen and misty like a dense fog. When I enter the bookshop, I realise there are no customers. It's such a change from the other day, it's as if a piece of its joy and sparkle are missing, like it has some of Tara's illness.

'Jane, I was just thinking about you,' she says in a hoarse voice. 'I was hoping we would meet today. You look like a different girl to the one who was upset. What a difference a few days can make. So how are you?'

'Are you okay, Tara?' I say, concerned.

Seeing Tara sick like this gives me a strange feeling in the pit of my stomach. I've never seen her sick before.

'A bit under the weather, but some ginger and lemon will soon fix that. Please tell me what's been happening with you.'

'I'm good. Great in fact … I got a promotion in the end after all, but a different one. A much better one. I also met a new guy. It's so weird. The cards you gave me … I think they work. It's like they predicted these things would happen or do they make it happen? Where did they come from?'

'I'm afraid I can't tell you where they came from. All I can say is that they appeared one day in the bookshop. I found them right in this very armchair I'm sitting on. They have worked for me and

I'm sure they will do the same for you.' She coughs uncontrollably and gulps back a glass of water. The coughing continues for some time. Her face becomes pale and drawn.

'Tara, those coughing fits aren't right. Please let me help you. Let me bring you to the doctor ...'

'Not at all. I hate doctors. I'll be fine. If the ginger and lemon doesn't fix me, I've some flower remedies that will do the trick.'

I remember back to a time when Tara took care of me when I was sick. I had been off school for a few days with a cough and sore throat. At the weekend, I pretended to my dad that I was better so he would let me see Tara in the bookshop. When I got there she knew I wasn't well. She told me to rest in the huge red armchair, and gave me a honey and lemon remedy that took all the pain away.

Perhaps all she needs now is one of those home-made remedies.

'Please sit down, Jane. There is something important I need to tell you. It's about the cards.'

CHAPTER 7

I SIT DOWN ON THE armchair beside Tara in front of the warm fire. She strokes Sooty, her cat.

'Jane, you must think about what will really make you happy before you select your next card,' she says.

'I am happy. What I've asked for so far has worked out much better than I expected. I got a new job and met a new guy. I don't know what the problem is,' I say as I shrug my shoulders. The sharpness in her voice has thrown me slightly.

'The cards are very powerful, and you must listen to your heart and select your wishes wisely. I don't want you to go through what I did.'

'What happened to you?' I ask.

'I had no one to guide me, I had to figure out how the cards worked. If you use them properly wonderful things can happen.' Her voice becomes faint to almost a whisper. 'All I ever wanted to do was to help others.'

'And you have. The cards have changed my life already.'

'You must take the cards seriously, Jane. There are consequences that you must take seriously. I want to guide you, but I feel sleepy.'

How did she get sick? She was fine before she gave me the cards, but she's not making much sense now.

'That cough seems nasty. You should rest.'

Tara's eyes close. She's fallen asleep on the armchair. Her blanket falls to the floor, so I place it back on her gently. As I touch against her skin it feels paper thin. Her hands are freezing cold. I put the closed sign on the door and turn the lock to allow Tara to sleep longer.

Poor Tara.

Now I know my cards work, I want to use them to find out more about Tara. There's so much I don't know about her.

'Hello cards, please show me something so I can understand Tara better,' I ask as I shuffle them.

The words **Hidden Truth** are engraved on the card I select; there's an image of a room filled with clothes and a rocking chair.

The message reads,

> *The veil has been lifted and you must search for the hidden truth. Something big is coming and although you don't know what yet, all will be revealed soon. Prepare to receive messages and experience synchronicity.*

What could be coming?

I browse around in wonder at the books that fill the shop from floor to ceiling. Some out-of-print, rare and first editions sit proudly on the shelves. This place really is a treasure trove. I remember my dad told me how this place was just an empty shell before Tara bought it. She's turned it into something special. I could easily spend the entire day here.

What is it about the comfort of books?

How long would it take to count them all? I run my fingers across some of the book spines and fixate on the jumble of colours and letters. As I count them my brain awakens. It's as if neurons are firing up making new connections. My fingertips tingle.

As I think about how happy I am being in the bookshop, my mind goes back to Gillian's first time here. It was a very different experience to mine.

It was a short while after I had just met Tara, and talked for days on end to Gillian about how amazing Tara and her shop full of treasure was. She was excited to see it for herself. I had convinced myself that Tara was magic and she made my Christmas costume from thin air. I wanted Gillian to feel exactly like I did when I visited.

She arrived after her stage performance class, and her face was flushed with joy, because she had just found out she would be playing the lead role in an upcoming show. She was an understudy and the person who was supposed to play the lead had injured their leg and couldn't perform.

I was eating one of Tara's brownies with ice-cream when I introduced her to Tara. Gillian just stared at her with her mouth open for ages.

'You have lovely clothes,' she said, eventually. 'I've heard a lot about you from my sister. She can't stop talking about you.'

Tara smiled, and I noticed her smile matched her eyes, which looked all twinkly and playful. 'How wonderful,' she said, 'I'm delighted to finally meet you, Gillian. Jane has talked a lot about you too.'

'I'm going to be the lead in a new show, and soon everyone is going to know my name because I'm going to be a star. My mam tells me I will be, if I work hard enough, and do what she tells me to, and believe in myself.'

Tara looked at us both mysteriously, like she knew something we didn't.

'Would you like a brownie and ice-cream? I'm sure you would after all the running around on stage. It must be a lot of hard work.'

'No treats for me. My mam doesn't like me eating too much sugar. It makes me hyper, and I'm going to be a famous superstar so I need to watch what I eat,' said Gillian.

'Really?' said Tara. 'How extraordinary. I've never met a child before who refused one of my brownies. Never mind, I've also picked out a book for you to bring home.' She handed Gillian a book with a picture of a movie star on the front of it.

'I love it! This is the most perfect book ever,' she shouted.

She was so enthralled by the book, she read the whole thing in the shop without stopping.

'I'm so sorry, but I can't bring this home with me,' she said, after she finished. 'As much as I'd like to, my mam is not a fan of books. She says Dad and Jane are wasting their time here, filling their heads with nonsense. Reading won't make me a star.'

I elbowed my sister. I wish she didn't listen to everything my mam said. All she wanted to do was make Mam happy. I knew I would never would be a movie star like Mam wanted. I was too clumsy and shy, so I stopped going to stage performing classes after the first week of starting. I loved reading, despite what my mam said.

Tara didn't seem put out by Gillian's comments. It was like she was expecting it.

While I sat and read books, Tara asked Gillian about her acting and stage performing classes, and she listened to her every word.

'My mam says if I practise every day and believe in myself, I will achieve whatever I want. She never got the chance to be a star and now she regrets it, but I will. What do you think, Tara?'

'There's no doubt about it. I believe if you work hard enough and believe in yourself you can create whatever you want. Knowing what you really want is the hard part though,' Tara sighed before she walked off and came back with another present for Gillian.

I was so annoyed listening to Gillian going on about being famous. Why couldn't she see how kind Tara was?

When I told her this she stuck her nose up in the air.

'We better go now. The shelves are very old looking. I hope they don't come apart, and fall on my head, and it smells musty. I don't want my dance costume to get dirty. Mam won't be pleased,' she said.

'Don't be ridiculous, Gillian,' I said. 'The shelves won't fall down, and if they did Tara will fix them. She makes everything better. You'll soon love her just as much as I do.'

'I like her, Jane, she is kind, but she goes on a bit in riddles. Anyway, Mam wouldn't like me staying here for too long,' she whispered to me. 'I need to go home and practise performing for the show.'

I was so disappointed. I had imagined us both hanging out here until Dad made us leave. Gillian obviously had other ideas. She never sat still after that, she kept running up and down to Dad asking him when could we go home.

Gillian never came back to the bookshop again, but it still didn't put me off coming. After a few months of visiting every week, I realised that it wasn't just me Tara was kind to, she made a fuss out of all the children who visited. There was one boy in particular who had a vision impairment, and Tara took time out of her busy day to pick out braille books that she thought he would like. He also loved it when she sat and read to him. His mother told us it was the highlight of his week. There was another boy I remember, who never spoke, but he loved to come to the bookshop and sit with myself and Tara, and create the most amazing pictures of peacocks. The colours and details were outstanding.

Tara loved children, she was so natural with them. When she found out how much I liked counting, she let me count and stack books on the shelves. Over time, I even worked in the shop serving the customers, and counting out the change. I was the only child who she let do that, so it felt like I was her favourite.

In the middle of counting the books now, I hear footsteps behind me. When I turn around there's no one there. Someone coughs. Has Tara woken up? No, she's still fast asleep. The door opens, and then slams.

How did that happen?

I was sure I locked it. Perhaps I didn't. A young child stands inside the doorway. She's no older than eight or nine years old. Too young to be on her own. She's wearing a smart long red coat, with a black collar and a pair of black Mary Jane shoes. Her blonde hair is in neat pigtails with red ribbons either side. Her face is pale.

'Can I help you?' I say.

'I'm lost,' she says as her brown eyes watch me intensely.

'Oh, you poor thing. Come in and sit down. Let me help you.'

She stares at me blankly.

Tara coughs in her sleep and with that the girl turns, walks out the door and then runs off.

I chase after her. She's too fast to catch and as she turns the corner of the alleyway, I lose her. The street is empty, apart from Sooty meowing at me loudly. There's nothing there only dark shadows. Maybe she found her parents. When I go back to Hidden Secrets, Tara is awake. I head home and pray whoever was in my apartment earlier doesn't return.

When I arrive at my apartment, I check for signs of an intruder, but there's none. Everything is just as I left it. I'm beginning to think

I imagined the whole thing last night. Perhaps it wasn't as bad as I thought. Every creak or noise always seems worse at night.

Sorcha calls me while I'm having a glass of wine in the bath.

'Well, hello there, stranger,' she says.

'Sorcha, I was thinking of you earlier. How are things down under?'

'Tiring. I just finished a thirteen-hour shift at the hospital. It was manic. I was rushed off my feet, but I'm dying to hear your news. Did you get the promotion?'

'I did, but not the one I was expecting. It's a long story … I got a different one. It's much better than what I was hoping Emma would give me. It all worked out well in the end.'

'That's amazing. Congrats. How's the lovely Ben? Is he still with Sarah?'

'Yeah. He sure is.'

'When are you both going to get your act together and get it on? You're made for each other. You just need to get your head out of the sand and tell him how you feel.'

'You know I can't do that.'

'I read both our star signs today and yours is referring to Ben. You need to just tell him how you feel. I'll read it out to you … hold on a second. Okay, so it says under Virgo, December is a pivotal month for your relationships. Now is the ideal time to tell your crush how you really feel. Your love will be requited. Your popularity is on the rise, and you must take a leap of faith to see what comes your way.'

As much as I want to believe it, I need to be realistic. Ben's not interested in me romantically.

'Anyway, I met a new guy called Jay. He's gorgeous and I'm mad about him already,' I say.

'More gorgeous than Ben?'

'Yeah … well. He's definitely in the same league as Ben.'

'Wow, that's a first for you. How did you meet him?'

'You'll never believe this, or maybe you will. This is right up your street. I was given a pack of cards that make the universe give me whatever I ask for, if I take the cards' advice.'

'What? What type of cards? Are they Tarot cards? Angel cards? Oracle cards?'

'No. These are different. Tara, the owner of Hidden Secrets book-shop gave them to me, she said they're magic. I asked them to help me meet someone new to get over Ben and then Jay appeared shortly afterwards. They helped me get my new job too … Sorcha … Sorcha. Are you still there?'

There's silence.

'What sort of advice? They're not asking you to do anything crazy, are they?'

'No. Nothing like that. So far, it's been fine. I'm not sure how exactly they can do it, but I really think they work. I thought you would get this. You're into cards, crystals and all that spiritual stuff.'

'Sorry Jane, I'm thinking. You always said there was something otherworldly about Tara. So, who knows what the cards can do? Just be careful. I don't want you getting in over your head. Remember what happened to Jen and Liam when we were in sixth year in sec-ondary school. They messed around with an Ouija board and were never the same again. Liam disappeared off the face of the earth. No one knows where he is now. Jen is a nervous wreck. She still lives at home with her parents, and I heard she barely leaves the house.'

'The cards are nothing like that. I'll be grand. Tara wouldn't have given them to me if they were bad. My life is finally going the way I want it to.'

'Hmmm … well that's good, keep me posted. Oh, I saw on Instagram Gillian got engaged. She's some woman isn't she? Where does she find all the men? Actually don't answer that. It's probably off some glamourous movie set.'

'Yeah, there's no shortage of men in her life, that's for sure.'

'I can't keep up. I noticed she's been in the papers a lot lately. I'm glad I'm your friend and not Gillian's; that girl sure knows how to party.'

'Yeah, I know. Different world huh!'

'Seriously, though. How does she do it, and hold a job at the same time?'

'Who knows.'

'Where does she get her energy from? The mind boggles. I have to go. I need sleep.'

'Wait, you never told me what your horoscope said …'

'Oh, it was something along the lines of December being the month I get romanced by someone I least expected. If only ... huh. I'd need a pack of cards like yours to make that happen. My bed is calling me now. Chat soon, Jane.'

'Bye, Sorcha. Take care.'

'You too, Jane.'

As soon as I hang up the phone, I feel sad that our conversation is over. I wish she didn't live in Australia so we could see each other more often. I know we'd have so much fun together and my life would be easier with her by my side. I think about using the cards to make her move back to Ireland; I'm not sure if I should, but it's something to consider.

The next morning, I collect the key for my new office at the bank's reception desk. I got here early, about six am. I couldn't sleep. I was tossing and turning all night thinking about the girl I saw at the bookshop yesterday. I wish I knew what happened to her. I hope she found her parents and isn't still lost. The poor thing. Noises interrupted my sleep too. Lots of strange, weird sounds, but when I checked my apartment there was no one there. This time I checked everywhere. In the cupboards, wardrobe, and even under the bed.

I push these worries out of my head and focus on the receptionist who tells me my new office is on the thirteenth floor. There must be a mistake. No one ever goes to the thirteenth floor. No one is allowed there. It's completely empty of staff as far as I know.

'This floor used to be kept for the Board when they were visiting from Head Office, but Mr. Becker asked for your office to be here.'

We take the private elevator to the top floor and when I step out, it's into a small glass atrium. She walks briskly ahead of me. Her high heels click on the marble floors. A shiny brown door is in front of me. There's no one else around. It's as if I'm Alice, except I'm wearing a business suit. I'm half expecting a white rabbit to run by any second.

She passes me the keys. 'I'll let you open the door,' she says.

I turn the key and walk into my penthouse office. There's a smell of disinfectant combined with vanilla. She closes the door behind her.

The lights come on automatically. It's very tastefully decorated in creams and mahogany with a polished cream marble floor. Fresh flowers and expensive paintings are dotted around the room. Huge cream leather couches sit around a multimedia conferencing system. A large flat screen TV is placed next to a treadmill. On the other side there's a library with shelves filled with financial books. A beautiful mahogany desk sits on the other side of the room with a round table and chairs beside it.

Floor to ceiling windows wrap around either side of the room and through them is the most magnificent view of the river Liffey. I walk out onto the large balcony to take in the spectacular views. There's the neon lit Convention Centre and in front of me the Samuel Beckett Bridge spans the river. Its beautiful white winter lights reflect against the water. The iconic rustic red and white striped Poolbeg stacks stand tall in the distant Dublin skyline.

I watch the lights turn on in the neighbouring buildings as they wake up for another day of business.

'Through that door is an apartment for you to use as you see fit. Mr. Becker wants you to be as comfortable as possible. Please think of it as your home,' she says. She points to a door past the office area.

I swallow, trying to take it all in.

'The office will be cleaned daily by our office cleaners and the kitchen will remain fully stocked at all times. If you need anything at all please let me know.'

I wonder how many employees have stayed here before. I walk past the office area and through the door that leads into the apartment. With each door I open I become more impressed by what's inside. The apartment contains a massive dining room. A luxurious sitting room. A huge bedroom with a four-poster bed, a fully stocked kitchen and a bathroom with a large sauna. My office and apartment span the entire thirteenth floor of the bank. This place is amazing.

I go back out to the office area after I've had a good look around. There are piles of folders placed on my work desk.

'Oh, those folders tell you everything you need to know about your job. I'd advise you to read them as soon as possible.'

'There's quite a lot of folders,' I swallow again.

'Is there a problem Miss McAlister? Do you have any questions?'

'No questions. I'm sure I'll be fine.'

'Right, I've covered everything. If you need anything please let me know. Goodbye, Jane and good luck.' She walks out the door.

Hours later the phone on my desk rings.

'Hello Jane, I know it's still early, but I wanted to check in with you. How is everything going so far?' says Walter.

'Morning, Walter. It's amazing. You didn't need to do all this for me,' I say.

'You're an important member of my team now.'

'I'm going to arrange meetings with my new clients and I'm looking forward to meeting them all.'

'If you treat these clients with the same level of service as Mr. Feltz they'll never want to leave us. Do you understand?'

'Of course. I won't let you down.'

I rub my temples. I can't stop yawning. I spent the morning going through the folders. Apart from some high-net-worth individuals, my new clients are mainly American multi-nationals, tech and international construction companies who have set up base in Ireland due to the country's low corporation tax rates. They have serious money with the bank and it's above and beyond anything I've ever dealt with before.

I pace up and down, but then a sense of calm comes over me. I know I can do this. The cards just gave me the break I needed to get this, but I have the talent to see it through. A sense of control washes over me.

My new role was officially announced and there's a stack of emails coming through from my colleagues. Emails like, 'Jane, congrats. It couldn't have happened to a nicer person. You deserve this.' Some say, 'Jane, you smashed through the glass ceiling.' Another one says, 'You'll be next in line for the CEO job soon.' The last one I read says, 'You're an inspiration to the finance team.'

A photographer, a stylist, make-up artist and hairdresser arrive and tell me they need to take a picture for the company's website and some of my social media accounts will now be managed by the bank.

Once I'm camera-ready, pictures are taken of my best poses standing against my office desk looking out across the IFSC. I come across as being professional and confident and I feel it too. It must be because of the cards. I check my social media after the pictures are uploaded and there's thousands of new followers, connections and likes.

When I go to the fourth floor later that day the whole floor claps when I arrive. I'm presented with a huge bouquet of flowers. The good wishes touch my heart.

I can't see Emma anywhere, but I catch Ben's eye and he shouts, 'atta girl,' and blows me a kiss.

I go up to my office afterwards with a swagger.

Later that morning I remember my cards. What was it Tara said? To think about what would make my happy before I chose a card. Well, meeting Jay made me feel incredibly happy.

'Hello cards,' I say as I shuffle them and tell them my wish – to experience a great romance. I want Jay to ask me out on a date. I choose a card from the middle of the pack. *Romance* is engraved this time with an image of a woman with blonde hair holding a dark-haired man's hand. She looks just like me. The text on the card reads,

You are about to meet or have already met someone and will experience a great romance. You must step out of your comfort zone yet stay focused on your values and beliefs.

CHAPTER 8

I WORK FURIOUSLY FOR THE rest of the morning, completing more work than I ever thought possible and only stop to take a break when I hear a knock on my office door.

'It's me. God, you were hard to find. I brought lunch – a mozzarella, tomato, and pesto panini. Your favourite.'

'Is it lunch time already? Come in, Ben.'

He walks around my office with his mouth wide open in shock. 'Woohoo, Jane! Becker certainly means business with you. What's this? A fully stocked kitchen? I know where I'll be coming for lunch in future. This beats the cafeteria any day.'

'Ha-ha Ben. You're gas. How about we sit out on the balcony to eat? The views from here are fab. I'll turn on the outdoor heaters. There we go. So how are things with you?'

'Holy fuck, Jane. You've gone up in the world. Why has Becker put you up here? Why not in one of the company apartments in the IFSC?'

'I've no idea but look at the place – it's fabulous.' I grab Ben's hands and jump up and down with excitement.

'You'll end up living in the bank …'

'No … I won't. I don't need to move in. It comes with the job, so who am I to complain?'

'You'll never want to leave this place …'

'Of course I will.'

He narrows his eyes. 'Hmmm … well make sure you do. Don't kill yourself with work.'

'Don't worry about me, Ben. I'll be grand, I have everything under control. Did you decide if you'll accept the promotion yet?'

'Not yet. I haven't even had a chance to speak to Emma today. She's been in meetings all morning with senior management. She's stomping around the place and slamming doors. I'd say she's holding on to her job by a thread. You know what she's like though, she'll try to talk herself out of it just like she always does.'

'She has a way with words that's for sure.'

'I know, but I think Becker wants her gone now because of the way she treated you. You're his star performer and guys like Becker don't suffer fools gladly. She messed up with you and now she's paying for it.'

As we talk about Emma, I realise I want our friendship back to the way it was before all this work stuff got in the way.

'Listen, I get that it was awkward for her when she became my boss, but not promoting me has actually been a blessing in disguise because I got all this.' I wave my hands around. 'Why is she ignoring me? She still hasn't responded to my apology text. It's like she dumped me and I've no idea what I did wrong.'

'Don't be upset. Seriously put her out of your mind. If she doesn't want to be your friend it's her loss.'

When I first joined the bank Sorcha had recently moved to Australia. Meeting Emma and Ben helped fill the void of Sorcha's departure. Not only did I fall headfirst for Ben, I also felt immediately like I'd known Emma for years. When she spoke everyone in the room listened. I was so drawn to her.

'What's happened to us, Ben?'

'Us. You mean me and you.'

'No. I mean the three musketeers. We're drifting apart. Once Emma got promoted it went to her head.'

He shrugs his shoulders. 'That's what happens sometimes, but enjoy all of this. You worked so hard for it,' he says as he moves closer to me. 'Just don't let this change you. You're too nice for that.'

His words spark something off inside of me. I want to reach over and hug him, just as friends, but I don't. He walks towards me and just as I think he's coming for a hug he walks slightly past me and turns off the heater. His closeness and the pleasant smell of his aftershave catch me off guard. I wonder what scent he's wearing. It's like a citrus aroma, but it's musky at the same time.

I need to stop smelling him. I jump up from my chair abruptly. I blush and turn away so he can't see my flushed face. This is way too awkward for my liking.

'It's weird being down there without you, Jane.'

'Haha … but it hasn't been that long since I left.'

'I know, but the place feels empty.'

I avoid looking at him. 'I'm not gone forever. You can come and visit me anytime.'

'Thank God for that,' he whispers in my ear.

'I have a meeting with a client to prepare for. Thanks for the chat and the lunch. It was nice,' I say, blushing.

'Sure. No worries. I best be getting back to work myself. Mind yourself Jane. I'll let you know what happens with Emma.' He strolls out of my office smiling.

I check my emails, which are way more intense than what I'm used to, and I want to get through them all.

My iPhone rings. Jay's name pops up.

My heart leaps.

'Hello there, I was wondering when I'd hear from you again,' I say.

'I know it was only yesterday that we met, but I can't get you out of my head,' he says. 'I don't know what's going on, but you're all I can think about.'

'Me too.'

'I need to see you, Jane. Where are you? I'll come and pick you up.'

'I'm in work …'

'What time do you finish at?'

'I'm not sure …'

'How about I make that decision for you? I'll be outside your work at five o'clock.'

'I don't normally leave work that early. Could we meet a bit later? About eight? I usually work til then.'

'Eight pm. No way. That's too long to wait. Surely they can do without you for a few hours?'

'Hmmm … I guess I can leave a bit earlier today. Okay. I'll see you then. I'll text you the address.'

God, he's keen and intense. Very intense. I can't remember the last time I left work that early, but I can come in early tomorrow.

I should hang up now but I don't. I just stand there and listen to his breathing.

'Bye, Jane,' he says. 'If I had my way I'd be over to see you now. It's going to kill me waiting.'

I laugh while I hear my heart beating. Thank God he's not in front of me. I'm blushing like crazy.

What on earth have the cards done to me?

'Bye, Jay.'

'I'm counting down the minutes till I can see you again.'

'Me too,' I say with longing. I wonder what tonight will bring. I can feel his warmth coming through the phone.

I stand outside the bank waiting for Jay. I check my watch every few minutes, wondering if I've been stood up. He's ten to fifteen minutes late at this stage. I hope he hasn't had a change of heart and it's just the traffic that's making him late.

Just in case, I decide to take matters into my own hands. I take out the cards and ask them to make sure Jay doesn't stand me up.

The card I pick has the words **The Date** engraved on it. I read the card.

> *The wait is over. The time has come for you to be swept off your feet. The one you ask for will soon arrive. Prepare to be spellbound and trust in the process of the cards.*

I hear a whistle and then I see him, he's leaning against a blue Vespa scooter holding a helmet. He's dressed the same as the last time I saw him except he has a black leather jacket slung over his shoulders. I remember how attractive he is.

'Hey Jane, I'm over here, come over,' he shouts and then makes another whistle sound. 'The traffic was mental.'

I swagger across the road towards him with a huge smile. I'm getting used to this swagger thing. My stomach churns with the excitement. As I reach him, I notice men and women glance at him as they pass. People stare from their cars. It's as if he's going to stop traffic. He's not the usual type of guy I'd go for. I'm attracted to smartly dressed men in suits, like Ben, but despite this I find myself very drawn to him.

'Stand back,' he says. 'I want to get a good look at you. Hmmm ... so, no yoga pants today. A business suit instead. It's a nice look on you but then again, I'm sure you would look good in anything,' he says.

He takes my hand and plants a kiss on it. I wonder if he is this flirty with all the women he just met. I'm amazed by his confidence.

'You're even more beautiful than I remember. Your chariot awaits my lady,' he says as he points at his scooter.

'Is this your Vespa? I've always wanted one,' I say standing back, thinking how to match his forward comments.

'Yeah, it's mine. God, it's so good to see you.'

'You too.' I smile.

'So, I packed a picnic. You just say the word and I'll bring you wherever you want.'

'How about you choose?' I say.

'Perfect. Come closer so I can put this on you.'

He touches my long blonde hair to smooth it down, pushes it back from my face and then kisses my forehead. I blush nervously. I want to play it cool, but inside I'm shaking as the helmet goes on.

'It suits you. Hop on and don't be afraid to hold on tightly,' he says.

'Where are we going?' I ask.

'We're going to my place.'

I imagine his place is like Ben's. All shiny and new. One of the city's fancy apartment complexes. There I go again. Ben.

He drives so fast, it's like we're going to lose balance and topple over at any second. I grab on tighter as my stomach flutters.

Why on earth did I agree to this?

As we speed around another corner, I realise Jay must know what he's doing because we didn't topple over. I slowly move my head from his back where it was hiding. I focus on things I've never noticed that much before. The changes of lights. Traffic zooming by. I notice pedestrians' clothes and get glimpses of their faces. The sights, sounds, smells and even the leaves falling from the trees are different. It's like experiencing the city from a whole new perspective. It's freeing and exhilarating, but slightly dangerous at the same time.

'Stay where you are, and I'll help you off. We're going over to the island,' he says as he parks the Vespa.

He grabs a picnic backet from the back of the scooter and he helps me get off. There's a sign to the right of me. *Droichead an Oileáin. Bridge of the Island.* We make our way to a wooden bridge. There's a locked gate blocking access. Jay runs towards it and presses a few buttons on the keypad. It swings open. As we walk across the bridge, he has his hand on the small of my back. I can feel the heat of his skin burning through the fabric of my clothes.

It's dark, but a faint assortment of orange and red hues float all around us. The contrast between the sea and the sky makes the horizon look like an encounter of two worlds. The sky reflects on the water. I wasn't even aware this place existed. It's the most romantic place I've ever seen in my life. We reach the island and apart from the seals and the birds, it's deserted. He lays out a blanket on the sand.

'Where are we?' I ask.

'Gull Island. This is my home for the next while.'

Jay lives on an island! Is he homeless? Ehh … why? None of this adds up. I've so many questions for him, but I'm trying to act cool.

'You live on the beach …'

'God, no.' He laughs. 'I started working as a park-ranger on the island a few days ago. I'm staying in a cottage further up the beach that comes with the job, I'm only here for a month or two to cover for a friend who's away.'

'What will you do after that?' I ask.

'Well, that all depends,' he says, and he gives me a look as if to say I'm an important factor in this decision.

I'm in awe over how quickly this has happened. We've gone from total strangers at a sound bath to him including me in his plans. My cards are amazing.

'I'm a bit strapped for cash at the moment so this picnic is the best I could do,' he says as he unpacks the basket. There are some deli sandwiches, fruit and cans of beer. 'I hope you like it. You're shivering; here, let me give you my jacket. I can't have you catching a cold.'

What? Strapped for cash. Why? I'm taken aback at first, but then I think feck it. I'm not interested in him for his money, and I don't care about the food. My appetite has gone due to nerves. My only real care right now is to not simultaneously combust with excitement when he puts his jacket around me.

'So, tell me. What is it you do in that huge bank anyway? I'm curious.'

'I know it sounds boring, but I'm one of the few who report directly into the CEO, which is kind of cool.'

'Clever girl, and no it's not boring to me. Fair play to you, you seem to have it all sussed. So, what is that like? Is it all meetings and emails?'

'Ha-ha! Kind of and lots of spreadsheets. I'm just settling in really. We don't deal with the public, only large corporations or the super-rich. It's commercial loans, financial advice and investments.'

'It sounds impressive, but I've never been a big fan of banks myself. I don't trust them, they just seem out for themselves.'

'But everyone has bank accounts these days—'

'I don't really use mine anymore, but enough about that. None of that matters though. I want to know more about you.'

The concept of not using a bank account seems alien to me.

We chat about our favourite TV programmes, favourite food and then the conversation turns to family. He asks me if I have any siblings and I tell him I have one sister. I don't want this to be about Gillian yet though. Not just yet. I want him to like me for me, so I quickly change the focus back to him.

'Do you have any brothers or sisters?' I say.

He puts his arm around me. 'We don't need to share everything straight away. We've plenty of time to get to know each other. My life has been complicated, Jane.' He leans towards me and kisses my forehead, next my cheekbones and then stops. 'I didn't have the best start in life. I've come from a dark place.'

We look out onto the shore. 'Complicated … huh,' I say as alarm bells ring in my head.

'Yeah, but that's all about to change. Now I've met you.'

Something tells me I shouldn't get involved with Jay. That I'm out of my depth. I should walk away and get off this island, but I don't. I can't. For some reason I'm fascinated with this guy. Enthralled by him. I want more, much more. It's almost like I'm under his spell.

'I can tell you're an incredibly special person, Jane,' he whispers to me.

'I think you're incredibly special too, Jay,' I whisper back.

He wraps a blanket around us, while we watch the waves crashing along the shore. I take in his every feature, to memorise for when we are apart.

'Let's go for a walk,' he says.

As we walk along the beach together holding hands, lights shine in the distance, and I hear carousel music.

'That's a Christmas market, but it's on the mainland,' he says as he follows my gaze. 'My place is just around the corner.'

We soon approach a small, traditional Irish thatched cottage. *Teachín Oileán Gull — Cottage of Gull Island* is written on the plaque above the door. It has whitewashed walls. A sunshine-yellow half door, with high door frames, and three small windows. I smell a musky, fresh smell just before drops of rain fall.

He opens the door and gestures for me to walk inside.

'That was good timing. Let me show you around.'

The cottage is warm and cheery. Downstairs there are curtains on all the windows. There's a living room with a small fireplace and a tiny kitchen just off it. Two bedrooms and a bathroom. It's tidy and organised for someone who just moved in. All the furniture is wooden. It reminds me of Goldilocks and the three bears. There's a dreamy fairy tale quality to the whole place.

'What's up there?' I ask and point to a staircase to the left of the living room.

'Ah,' he says, 'that's the attic. The most important place of all.'

'Really, can I take a look?'

He hesitates and just when I think he's going to refuse, he nods and tells me to go ahead. I walk up the dark staircase and come to a locked door.

'I need to keep this stuff safe … it's very valuable,' he says as he takes the padlock off and we enter the room.

The first thing that hits me is the noise; it's like a whirling sound, going around and around, hurting my ears.

'What's all this?' I ask as I take everything in.

To the right of me there's loads of computer stuff. Hard drives, wires and motherboards. Some of it is broken. At the back of the room, there's even more computer equipment. The monitors have numbers and some sort of data flashing up constantly like something is being processed. The room is hot, and the energy is electric. Something odd, very odd, is going on.

'I'm into computers. I take them apart, rebuild them, add stuff like integrated circuit chips and graphic cards to make them stronger with more processing speed and memory.' His voice is loud. He's almost shouting to be heard over the noise.

'The speed is astonishing. Your electricity bill must be through the roof.'

'Yeah, I have programs set-up to work on algorithms and they need to be left on all the time.'

I walk closer to the monitors and scrutinise all the information. I start to identify slight patterns in the data. I'm not an expert in computer programming by any means, but I've done a few coding courses through the bank. I want to fiddle around a bit to figure out what's going on.

'I think we've spent enough time here. How about we go downstairs and get more comfortable.'

We move into Jay's bedroom and lie down on the bed. He asks me to stay the night. I'll stay for another twenty minutes I tell him, but I really don't want this night to end. He's pissed off, I can tell. I hate first dates; I never know how I come across. I tend to finish them as quick as I can.

'Can I kiss you?' he says as his mouth twitches upwards, 'a proper kiss this time. One when you're not asleep.'

'Haha … okay,' I say, feeling shy.

He gazes deep into my eyes and kisses me as he runs his hands over the curves of my body. 'It's getting hot in here,' he says and he takes off his top.

I can't tear my eyes away from him. I can't get over his confidence or his body. It's honed to perfection, and he's lying down on the bed all easy breezy with not a care in the world. Yet I'm so nervous.

What do I do now?

'Come closer. Don't be shy. I don't bite. Well, not unless you want me to. I love your lips.' He traces his fingers around them. 'God, you look so familiar. It's like I met you before. Seriously … I feel like I've known you my whole life,' he says softly.

We kiss again. I grab the blanket and place it over me, feeling self-conscious. He takes it off me and tosses it to the floor.

'You're beautiful,' he says. 'What is it with women and their bodies? Why are they so hung up over them? Just relax and trust me, we don't have to do anything you don't want to.'

His touch is gentle yet strong, he stares at me the whole time. All thoughts I have of anything other than Jay just go out the window. So much for only staying for twenty minutes. It's like nothing I've ever experienced with a guy before. He's so confident and self-assured and he makes me feel special. Like I'm just as attractive as him.

My heart beats as if it's going to explode.

I shift positions to lean on my elbow and just stare at him as he's lying on his back beside me again.

'You're amazing.' I stroke his face and run my fingers all over his body.

'I'm not the only one. Where have you been all my life, Jane? I could get used to this.'

'Ha! We moved in different circles, I guess.'

'Not anymore. I want to keep you here forever.' He reaches over and holds me in his arms and we kiss again.

Eventually he gets up and lights a cigarette, takes a big drag and blows smoke circles.

'I didn't realise you smoked,' I say.

'I've been trying to give up, but it's too hard. I've no willpower.'

'So do you do this often,' I ask, 'like bring a practical stranger back home?'

He reaches over towards me, and kisses my head. 'Now, I found you. I never want to let you go.'

'Me too. I feel the same.'

At some point I must have dozed off. I wake in the middle of the night on top of Jay's bed. His arms and legs are wrapped around me. I hear a strange noise like a loud whirring sound. I get up, and try not to wake him as I walk around the rooms in the cottage. The noise must be coming from the computers in the attic. I walk up the dark stairway and try to open the door, but it's padlocked.

There are shadows all around me as I walk back down the stairs and lie back in bed. I hear footsteps. The same footsteps I heard in my apartment before. Someone is coming and they're very close from the sounds of the creaking of the floorboards. I'm being followed. It must the same person who was in my apartment before. Why are they following me? Terror floods me and I scream.

'What's all the fucking screaming for? Calm down. Jesus, Jane, what's wrong?' he says, softening as he sees my terrified face.

'I hear noises. There's someone here. Have you locked the door?' I scream.

'I don't know … we fell asleep. There's no noises. I can't hear anything. I'll check. I'll be back in a minute,' he says as he kisses my forehead.

He takes a bat that's stored under the bed and leaves me on my own to search the cottage. The noises are getting louder and louder. Thoughts race through my mind as to who could be following me. Is it a stalker after Gillian, but trying to get to her through me? This is Ireland, though. It's the one place in the world Gillian says she doesn't get bothered by the public. The noises only started when I got the cards, so someone might be following me around to get them.

I'm shaking when Jay comes back to the bedroom ten minutes later. He puts his arms around me, and we lie back down on the bed.

'There's no one else here. I looked everywhere. I even went outside. I can't hear a thing. Just relax. You're safe with me.'

He kisses me and I get the impression he's enjoying being my protector.

But why can't he hear the noises?

'I should go,' I say. 'I need to get to the office early, I've loads of work to do.' I just want to get off the island and be around people. I'd feel safer then.

'It's too early for the office,' he says. 'I'll drop you into work in an hour or so.'

He wraps his arms around me and the way our skin connects it's as if his body melts into mine. He falls asleep quickly, but I still can't. I take out my cards and stare at them. The room is vibrant again. I wonder if they can stop the noises. I shuffle them and ask them to make the noises go away. The card I pick has the words **Darkness of the mind** engraved on it. I read the message at the back.

> *The noises will not cease until you face your fears, for they represent the troubles in the darkest part of your mind. Speak to the one who understands the power of the cards and you will gain more clarity and understanding.*

Tara. I need to go back and talk to Tara. She's the only one who understands how the cards work. My mind continues to wander, questioning what the hell is going on. I count over and over again until I eventually fall asleep out of pure exhaustion.

CHAPTER 9

BEN

THIS EVENING, I'M AS grumpy as hell and I find myself snapping at Sarah. She asks me questions that I have no interest in answering. Questions about our relationship and nailing down a time for our next date night. To get her off my back, I tell her we can go out for breakfast soon and chat properly then. My mind is elsewhere. I can't stop thinking about Jane. I hope she's okay, and I wonder what she's doing now.

The truth is I never should have asked Emma to go for a drink with me, back then, to find out where I stood with Jane. I think back with regret to what happened that night. I made a right mess of it.

We were in a pub on Suffolk Street and the place was packed with tourists. There was an Irish Trad session that was in full swing when we arrived, and we found a nice spot in the snug behind the main bar. I was expecting Emma to tell me Jane was into me and to go ahead and ask her out. I had even planned our first date. I was going to bring her to Paris for dinner. The owners of the restaurant were friends with my old man, and I knew they'd treat us like royalty, but Emma didn't think that was a good idea.

'You're mad even to think about making a move on Jane,' she said.

'Why?' I said. My confidence took a serious blow.

'Jane's in love with someone else. Her ex, Colm. She's still mad about him. You haven't a hope in hell. And don't tell her I told you any of this. She'd hate it if she knew I was discussing her love life with anyone.'

I still couldn't get Jane out of my head, and I couldn't stop talking about her to Emma. I kept asking her what was going on with Jane and Colm. Any glimmer of a chance I had with Jane, I was going to go for it. Emma's reply was always to forget about her.

One night, after way too many drinks with Emma, things got a bit out of hand. She moved closer to me and whispered in my ear. 'I don't want to hear anything else about Jane. You're wasting your time. I know what I want and it's you.'

She kissed me and came back to my apartment which led to us spending the night in bed together. It was a very bad, drunk mistake.

'No one in the bank needs to know about this, it might affect our careers. Don't even tell Jane,' she said as she wrapped her legs around me the next morning.

I never told anyone. No one had a clue. Not even Jane.

In front of others at work, Emma acted professionally, like nothing was going on between us, and nothing was, because I made it clear to her I wasn't interested in taking things further.

She then called around to my apartment at random times. She'd buy me clothes and try to dress me. It was really pissing me off. I didn't mean to hurt her, but I told her to back the hell off. Eventually she got the message.

A few weeks later, myself and a few guys from the bank ended up in a nightclub after work. I met Sarah there. She was a small, pretty little thing with long black curly hair who laughed a lot. I took her number and brought her out for dinner a few nights later. I dropped about four or five hundred euro between the wine and the food.

She was impressed by my job and loved hanging out with me. We quickly became an item. It was an easy, uncomplicated relationship which is exactly what I needed. I splashed the cash and spoilt her, and she was happy, and I was happy.

At the back of my mind, though, I always wondered what I could have had with Jane.

CHAPTER 10

JANE

WHEN I AWAKE IN Jay's bed it's to the crashing sound of the waves and the sun beaming in through the curtains. It's like paradise. His skin feels warm against mine. As I watch him sleep all I can think of is my cards. I wonder whether Tara fell strangely in love like me, and what about those weird noises? Did she experience them too? I won't know until I talk to her later.

Am I the only one in possession of cards like these?

There's no doubt how powerful they are. What about really successful people like the Irish Taoiseach, the President of America or Nobel Prize winners? Do they have a pack of these cards? Is that why they are so successful? What if Gillian has cards like these? It would explain why *she's* so successful. I wonder if she would tell me if she had.

I'm getting everything I want super quick. My thoughts really are shaping my reality. Since Tara gave me the cards my life has been a whirlwind between Jay and my new job. Most of all Jay. I've fallen for him, hook, line and sinker. I imagine our relationship will be like the type of love I've read about in old classics like *Wuthering Heights*. The closest thing I've ever come to love before Jay (that wasn't about Ben) was my relationship with Colm. It ended on the night of my twenty-first birthday party. I knew Colm from secondary school. Everyone fancied him back then, but our paths never really crossed. He was the most popular guy in school. I couldn't believe it when he asked me out years later after bumping into him in the pub. I was holding two pints of Guinness at the time. It sloshed all over my white top as he brushed past me abruptly. He stopped and turned towards me. He was wearing blue jeans and a white shirt and his boyish handsome face looked at me confused.

'Don't I know you from somewhere?' he said. 'Oh, you're Gillian O'Hara's sister.'

'I'm Jane McAlister. We were in the same year at school,' I blurted out.

'Really,' he says. 'I can't place you in any of my classes. Actually, are you the one who got the highest results in the Leaving Cert in our year? Yeah, I remember you now. Here let me buy you more drinks. What are you having?' As he took the glasses off me, I could feel him checking me out.

'That's me, thanks. Two more Guinness would be nice. I'll be over there.' I pointed over to where Sorcha was sitting.

'He likes you,' Sorcha squealed at me when I sat down beside her. 'I saw the way he was looking at you.'

'There's no way he'd be interested in me,' I said. 'He's out of my league.'

'Stop putting yourself down, Jane. You're just as good as him.' That was Sorcha all over. She was always trying to boost my confidence.

Colm brought the drinks over with his friend and sat with us for the rest of the night. He was full of chat and was so attentive towards me all night. He took my number at the end of the night and called me the next day. We were inseparable after that. Our relationship was a funny one. It wasn't equal. I never fully relaxed around him. I tried too hard to be the perfect girlfriend.

We were together almost nine months before my party. It was held at my mam's house in Abington. Mam hired a professional party planner and the place looked amazing. A load of Colm's friends were there, and he was on a high. He loved to brag to his friends about who my sister was and jumped at any opportunity to meet her.

Word got around that Gillian was due to make an appearance and in the weeks leading up to my party I was in demand with anyone who knew me really. They all came out of the woodwork. People I haven't seen in years wanted to catch up with me. Of course, they all mentioned Gillian.

The day of my party, I waited and waited for Gillian to arrive. A parcel arrived from her in the post. It was a pair of silver Gucci shoes and a matching bag that would go perfectly with my pink dress I had planned to wear. I was so excited. She called me just before the party was due to start to say that she couldn't come, but she'd make it up to me.

I was devastated, but my mam told me to basically just get a grip and get on with it.

'This is your sister's life now. You've no right to be upset,' she said. 'You shouldn't have put that pressure on Gillian to come to your party. I hope you haven't upset her.'

So I tried to pretend like Gillian being there wasn't a big deal. I put on a fake smile, but I could tell everyone was disappointed when I told them she wasn't coming. The room was filled with whispers and rumours as to why Gillian wasn't there. Colm was off with me all night. At the end of the night when we were on our own, I broke down in tears over what happened.

'My party was a flop, but at least I still have you,' I said, and I brought up the 'L' word that had never been mentioned before. We were happy and content. He didn't lie or cheat. I could imagine us getting engaged pretty soon. I believed he was the one.

I asked him if he loved me.

'I can't see this being a long-term thing,' he said. 'It's not what I thought it was going to be. I thought we'd get to hang out more with Gillian, but sure she didn't even turn up tonight.'

'But … I'm not like Gillian …' I said.

'You're way too serious for me. I'm done,' he said as he walked out the door.

He obviously thought going out with me would give him access to some of Gillian's life. To the parties and premieres she frequently attends. I knew he was being an asshole, but his words cut through me. I've been afraid ever since to get excited about falling in love again.

I think that's why I had such a crush on Ben. His confidence reminded me of Colm in a way, but Ben is nicer. He's unavailable which suited me, as being off-limits means he could never hurt me the way Colm did.

Jay tells me I'm special and likes me for who I am, not who my sister is. He doesn't even *know* who my sister is and I want to keep it that way. He's opened up my heart.

He gets up out of bed to make us breakfast and I google like mad to find out more about the cards. I type in 'cards from the universe' and a load of other card decks pop up, but none of them are like mine. I even type 'cards from the universe makes the owner hear weird noises' and I land on some website about Einstein's theory of space time which states the universe is not silent but is alive with vibrating energy. It still doesn't explain the strange sounds I've been hearing though.

After all my googling I'm no nearer to finding out about the cards. But what I do know is they work, and I'm excited to see what else they can do.

Jay arrives back to the room with poached eggs, toast, and orange juice.

'I hope you like eggs,' he says. 'Take your time.'

'I have a meeting at eight with my boss. I can't be late for it.'

'Eat your breakfast and then we'll leave. It doesn't take long on the scooter from here. I might even get you there a bit early.'

When I get into work, I settle into my meeting with Walter. He's really impressed with my work so far and he asks me if I would take his place and do an interview for *Forbes* magazine. They're doing a feature about the world's best places to do business and he wants me to represent the bank.

The morning is a flurry of excitement. My office is overtaken by staff from the magazine. The interview goes well. I tell them the factors that make Ireland one of the best places in the world to do business. We discuss the country's friendliness, innovation, taxes, monetary freedom, and investor protection and I'm on a roll. They also ask me about my rise to the top and the secret of my success. If only they knew it was down to my magical cards.

'Rather than seeing work as a way to just pay the bills, I see it as a huge part of my life. I don't believe in a work-life balance because I love my work so much. It's about making new choices, stepping out of your comfort zone and deciding what's good for you in your life,' I say.

I imagine myself as a motivational speaker, inspiring others to reach for the pinnacle of their careers.

My iPhone pings constantly with congratulation messages. Gillian even texts me. I didn't tell her about my new job so she must have found out through my social media accounts.

Well done sis. Just focus on the business aspects of your job and don't tell the press anything about our home life. X

I think back to what it was like at home when we were growing up. It was full of drama.

When my parents were still together, I'd feel the shift in the atmosphere before the shouting and screaming started. I never understood what had happened to kick it off, but I instinctively knew to stay out of their way and not ask for anything until things had calmed down. Which could take weeks.

I heard bits of their arguments – it was the same stuff re-hashed. My mam would say my dad was a workaholic and never had any time for her. Although my dad was always calm with me, he didn't have the same patience with my mam. He would tell her to stop trying to live her unspent youth through Gillian, and Mam's partying drove him mad. She'd go through phases where she wouldn't drink for months, but when she started again, she'd throw parties and have her friends over. They'd take over our kitchen, drinking and smoking while Gillian and I would be called in to perform a song or do a dance. I never joined in, I hated being put on the spot. It felt as if they were in some sort of exclusive club that I wasn't qualified to be a member of. Instead, I'd sit with my dad in the living room. We'd read books quietly while the noise from the kitchen would seep in through the walls. At bedtime, especially on those nights, I was terrified someone would burst into my room uninvited. It happened from time to time. Counting was the only thing that could make me fall asleep. I was about six years old when that obsession started, and my fear of loud noises began.

If my mam wasn't having parties during her binges, she'd disappear off for days on end, and left us to muddle along and, my dad had to take care of everything.

Living with an alcoholic is full of highs and lows. When Mam was off the drink she was full of love and hugs for myself and Gillian. She would rave on about how she would make Gillian a star, and that she would never leave us again. We were all she needed to make her happy, she said. The sad thing was she really believed it at the time.

I was about ten years old when I realised Mam was an alcoholic. One morning, I was playing with Gillian in her bedroom, when Mam stumbled in covered in muck after being away for three days. She had a bottle of whiskey in her hand. She leaned on the TV, which came crashing down and glass smashed to the floor. My dad came and screamed at her. She slurred something incomprehensible back, and then sobbed loudly.

'Geraldine, just go to bed and sleep this off,' he replied, 'I'll deal with clearing up this mess. You've really outdone yourself this time.'

He told us to wait for him in the car. We sat in the car in silence until Dad came back, both of us afraid to verbalise what we saw.

'I want you to stop Mam drinking alcohol,' Gillian said eventually with tears in her eyes, 'it turns her into a monster. And she's not. She is nothing like a monster.'

Up to that point, I had imagined Mam was a secret spy on a mission to save the planet or a superhero, and that's why she left us so much. Never to turn herself into a monster.

That same day, Dad wanted us to stay with his sister, Áine, for a few nights, but I persuaded him to just bring Gillian there and take me to see Tara instead.

When I confided in Tara over what I saw my mam do, she hugged me and told me to look up at the sky that night and count all the stars twinkling above. I was to gather my thoughts, focus on the brightest star and ask the universe for my most cherished wish to come true.

She went off somewhere and came back with a soft wool-haired doll with bright blue eyes. I held that doll tightly in my aunt's house that night, and when I looked up at the stars I made a wish – for my mam to stop drinking. My mam didn't come home for about a month after that, and when she did, she stopped drinking, but she became more obsessed than ever about making Gillian famous.

When my parents eventually announced their split, I was devastated. I pleaded with my dad not to leave. But nothing I said or did could change his mind.

Gillian, on the other hand, didn't seem bothered.

'I don't care if you go your separate ways as long as I get to live with Mam. She told me she'd do whatever it takes to make me a star,' she said.

'I'm living with Dad,' I said.

I wasn't stupid; I knew the break-up was coming. I had practised phrases, while looking in the mirror. 'I left this at my mam's house' or 'I'll be spending Christmas with my dad.'

My dad wanted me to come and live with him. He had been transferred to work for a bank in Toronto. The plan was he'd go there alone and get set up, and in a few weeks, I was to come over and start a new life with him.

My mam refused to let me go. It was too far, she said, and it wasn't fair to take me away from my friends. She presumed he'd be working all the time and didn't want him to neglect me the way she was. So apparently, I was better off with her.

Once he left, the darkness started. I spent most of my time in my room. I barely spoke to anyone. I was so angry with my dad for moving to Canada. Without him around, I felt like my life was ruined. Everything felt unsafe. It was as if my whole being was vacuumed up and all that was left was fear and panic. Leaving the house was a difficult task.

In fairness to Gillian, she did try to help me, but at that point she was so full of life and confidence I couldn't relate to her. She was deadly serious about becoming famous and the break-up didn't hit her as hard as me.

I had some close friends, but they didn't know how to help me, apart from Sorcha, who was recovering from an eating disorder. She reached out to me, and we became close. Soon Sorcha was the only one I wanted to be around.

Eventually things settled down a bit. Mam still wasn't drinking. I put everything into my schoolwork and became the biggest nerd. Most of my time at home was spent studying in my room. My grades were amazing. I aced every single exam and was a teacher's perfect student.

Everyone in school was in awe of me over Gillian's success, but I didn't see her much when I was in school. I had already lost my dad, and then I felt like I lost my sister too when she went to live in Hollywood. She was seen at every movie premiere and every Hollywood party going and was drinking pretty hard, often with my mam by her side. I guess the temptation in Hollywood was too much for both of them.

My iPhone rings. This time it's my dad. Over time, I learnt that although Gillian and I look similar, people think she is way more interesting than me. When I told Dad this he said I was like a hidden gem. Once someone realised how precious I was, they'd never want to let me go.

Although I was so angry with my dad for leaving, I got close to him again about five years ago. He insisted I come to his wedding in Toronto. He married a sweet Canadian called Kate who works as a human rights lawyer. He's much better suited to her than my mam.

'I always knew you had it in you, Jane. It was only a matter of time,' he says. 'My hidden gem has finally been discovered.'

'Thanks, Dad,' I say as I'm beaming from head to toe.

'You know, never in my whole career did I ever get to the level that you're at now. What an amazing achievement.'

'I know, it's all amazing! I've just been interviewed by *Forbes* magazine,' I say.

There's silence for a few minutes.

'Wow! I probably never told you this enough when you were

younger, but I'm so proud of you. I hope you realise now just how special you are.'

Today is possibly the best day of my life.

Throughout the day, Tara and the cards keep popping into my head. I need to find out about the noises. As soon as I finish work, I go straight to see her. It's cold and foggy. The misty air clings to my hair and clothing. I pull my long black wool coat tighter around me and put up my collar to provide protection from the cold, dewy sensation against my skin. My visibility is restricted. The sounds of the buskers singing Christmas carols fill the air, but they appear as faint shapes hidden through the dense fog. As I turn down a side street off Grafton Street, I realise I'm right outside Hidden Secrets.

What hits me when I enter the shop is the strong smell of mulled wine. The aroma of the spicy herbs, nutmeg and sugar evokes memories of happy festive times of Christmas at home with my parents.

What could be better than a warm glass of mulled wine after a walk in the cold? I wonder whether Jay likes mulled wine just as much as me.

The bookshop is decorated with gold twinkling fairy lights across the shelves. The staff are wearing Santa hats with bells on the top, working away happily. I breathe in the musty smell of books combined with the mulled wine. There are satisfied smiles on the people visiting, some just browsing while others are sitting in snugs reading peacefully. I grin, feeling happy to be there.

This place is like a little Santa's workshop. So joyful.

'Jane, what brings you here on this foggy evening? Can I interest you in some mulled wine? It's my special recipe,' she says in a croaky voice. I can tell she's not well, but she's trying to put on a brave face.

She's wearing a Santa hat, just like the rest of her staff, with a long, red and white Dior dress. The usual sparkle has vanished from her eyes. She's even sicker than the last time I saw her. Her homemade remedy hasn't worked.

'You read my mind. I'd love some. Only a little glass, though.'

'Take a seat, Jane. Let's chat.'

CHAPTER 11

S HE HANDS ME A generous glass of mulled wine. I relax and sit back in a huge armchair.

'I must get your recipe. This is delicious, Tara, and it's busy today.'

'Business is picking up again. There was a lull for a while, but that seems to have settled now.'

'I feel like I have so much to tell you,' I say.

'Take your time, Jane. I'm all ears,' she says.

'I can't thank you enough for giving me the cards. My life is unrecognisable. I could never achieve what I have now without them.'

'So, are you happy?' she whispers.

'Yeah. Unbelievably happy, but there's been strange noises. I thought I was being followed, but no one else hears them. It's some-thing to do with my fears. The cards told me to come and talk to you to get answers.'

She turns and stares at me for what feels like forever.

'The cards bring the good and the bad. Your fears and anxieties may seem larger than life,' she says.

'But I don't want to have to deal with my fears,' I say, shaken.

I look at Tara in a new light. I'm annoyed with her. Really annoyed. Why would she do such a thing – give me a pack of cards that have the potential to scare the living daylights out of me? I know she said the cards appeared to me for a reason, but she didn't have to give them to me. She could have left them up on the shelf.

'You read the note, it said there would be consequences—'

'Yeah … but there was nothing mentioned about facing my fears. I wasn't expecting this to happen.'

'There's no need to be afraid of your fears, Jane; just because something scares you doesn't mean you should avoid it. Your fears are there to show you what matters most. They will show you what you truly want and what is good for you. When you face them you will come out stronger and afraid of nothing and no one. You are more capable than you realise.'

As she says this, I think about my many fears. I have loads of them and dread to think what would happen if they came true. I make a mental list of some of the first ones that float into my head: I'm afraid of the dark, people I care about leaving me, flying, I've a strange fear of going mad – like totally insane and losing my mind. I'm also afraid of loud noises, being followed, death, being rejected, discovering I'm talentless, being alone and not being good enough for anyone to really love me. That's part of the reason why I could never tell Ben how I felt about him. Even if he wasn't with Sarah, I know I could never have the confidence to tell him.

Being followed has been a huge fear of mine ever since I was followed by a man when I was walking home from college one night. No matter how fast I walked he was right behind me. I hid inside a pub, and I lost him, thank God, but ever since then being followed still plays on my mind. I remember that feeling of terror that ran through me.

'Can this be changed? Can we stop this?'

'No. We can't … you must let the cards do what they need to.'

'But how do I stop the noises, Tara? I hate them,' I say, as I wonder what other fears the cards will throw at me.

'Only when you learn what you need to will you come out stronger and your fears will disappear. Follow your inner compass that guides you to the light and you will always be safe. When you close the door on your fears, you will have the courage to open up to new possibilities. The cards are not out to get you.'

'Did this happen to you? The noises I mean …'

'Yes. It did,' she whispers. 'I heard every creak of the floorboards at night and imagined all sorts of dreadful things were happening to me. I had other fears too. For now, I suggest you figure out where you feel most at home and the rest will fall into place.'

'If only it was that easy … I've been wondering who else has cards like these. Am I the only one?'

'Does it matter?' she says, staring at me intently.

The silence and the atmosphere are uncomfortable. Why is she looking at me like that?

'I do wonder if Gillian has cards like this … she could have found them in the shop the day she came here all those years ago … it would explain how she became so famous—'

'When I first met Gillian, I could tell she was going to become a star. I could tell it without a doubt.'

'How?'

'Because she believed it more than anything else in the world, and nothing was going to get in her way.'

'True, but it's just something I wondered because I can achieve things now, that I couldn't before. If I follow the advice of the cards, I can't go wrong, and I think that's what Gillian's life must be like. She'd never tell me anyway. She never tells me what's going on in her life anymore. But … are the cards some sort of secret that other people are aware of? I mean … their power is so strong I could do anything. This is mind blowing, Tara. I could even ask them to make me president if I wanted to, I don't but I'm just saying.'

'The most important thing I believe, is that you use the cards to make some sort of a difference,' she says.

'Like what?'

'I mean that you change something.'

'Like, change the world? Oh, I never thought about using them for that. I wouldn't know where to begin, but now I realise how selfish I've been. I've used them for all the things that I want.'

I move my gaze, and look to the ground. I think of all the things I could have wished for. Like world peace or to stop world poverty. There are so many things I can think of. I could wish for a cure for any incurable disease or solve global warming. I imagine myself as a type of UN Ambassador or Mother Teresa. My mind is flooded with all the problems of the world I could solve. I get panicky. I'm afraid of making all the wrong choices.

'Oh no. I've so many people to help,' I say. 'How am I going to help them all?'

Tara laughs. 'I don't mean to change the entire world. That's a big ask. Just focus on your world. The bit around you. Change isn't easy, but it is important.'

'My world has changed so much already,' I say.

'Maybe you could have a think about what you need rather than what you want all the time. Where are the cards now?'

'My cards are in my handbag. Now, where are you, cards? Oh, they don't seem to be here,' I say frantically.

I empty out my bag. Out comes my make-up bag, keys, wallet, chewing gum, hair ties and all the bits and bobs that live in my handbag, but there's no sign of the cards. Anxiously I search around. Finally, I find them on the floor under the armchair next to me.

How did they get there? They must have fallen out somehow, but my handbag was zipped closed. Did Tara know they were there the whole time?

I feel slightly foolish that I lost them. I take a bigger gulp of mulled wine.

'You look tired, Jane. By the look of those dark circles under your eyes, I take it you haven't been sleeping much lately.'

'Life is just too exciting to sleep. I think I'll just go get myself another glass of mulled wine,' I say, to avoid further interrogation from Tara.

'Don't let the cards out of your sight. I dread to think what could happen if they were in the wrong hands,' she whispers into my ear. She walks away to serve a customer, coughing loudly.

I get myself another glass of mulled wine, and think about Tara's cough. It really doesn't sound right. I wonder why she looks so ill.

I hold the cards in my hand. *Hello, cards, can you make Tara better?* I ask before I shuffle them and read the top card.

The picture shows an old lady with golden hair by the beach. **Recovery** is engraved on this card.

*This card relates to a person who has problems accept-
ing professional advice, and who feels younger than they
actually are. If there are any conditions, recovery will
now be fast, however it is of great importance that one
does not overdo it, otherwise exhaustion will set in. The
balance between mind, body and soul is vital. Complete
recovery can only exist when one realises it's time to let
go and move on.*

The next few days go by in a blur. My new job is still amazing.
I'm getting on wonderfully with my clients and compliments from
them are flying in. Everything I do is greeted with praise. Every
meeting I have goes better than I expected. When they first met
me, I got comments about how young I am to be in such a high
position in the bank, but I quickly assured them I am the best
person for the job. I'm getting used to being this new, confident
version of myself.

I've fallen into a little routine where I go to see Tara straight after
work and then I meet up with Jay. I am full of energy, whereas I
see Tara getting sicker each day. I'm more energetic than I've ever
been in my life. Everything feels easier and effortless. My mind is
sharper, and my clients' investments are performing at an unbe-
lievable level, under my guidance.

I feel guilty how Tara's life has taken a turn since she gave me
the cards. Her illness is on my mind a lot, I keep checking if she's
getting any better. It's hard to tell though. She seems so up and
down, and she's ageing before my eyes.

Most of my time with Jay is spent in bed. Making love feels so
natural. The chemical connection between us is amazing. He's like
a drug to me, but anytime I ask him something about himself, he
changes the subject. The only thing he's opened up to me about
is about his computer stuff in the attic. He's told me he's mining
cryptocurrency and and he is convinced it's going to turn him into

a millionaire. He's so into making money and becoming rich, which I find annoying, but I admire his ambition.

One evening he brought me back up to the attic and I got a chance to really dive in and examine his computer coding.

'You've done a great job, but a few small changes are needed and you need to limit the number of coins in circulation. Twenty-one million euro is way too much. It's way too ambitious.' I burst into giggles at the absurdity of it all, but that just got his back up.

'Leave it alone,' he said. 'I don't want anything to go wrong. I'm on the cusp of a breakthrough here.'

I didn't want to push it further in case I hurt his feelings. I've learnt he's a very sensitive guy who hates to be wrong and a tad delusional when it comes to his cryptocurrency project.

I'm in work the next day when I get an email from Sorcha.

> Hello there lovely,
>
> What's been going on with you? I want to know everything you've been up to. Your social media accounts are looking sensational. Well done girl. I'm so proud of you. You must have worked so hard! So, have the cards made all your dreams come true yet? My horoscope was wishful thinking. I've been waiting for my secret admirer to appear but there's been nothing. Did you see Jay again? How's Ben? Please tell me you've taken my advice and told him how you feel ... you would make the perfect couple. I hope one of us is getting some action.
>
> Miss you so much.
> Sorcha xxx

I'm so happy to get her email, I reply back straight away.

> Hey, my lovely Sorcha,
>   It's great to hear from you.

My job couldn't be more perfect. Life is amazing, and it's all thanks to the cards. They work Sorcha! They really work and I can pretty much get anything my heart desires. You won't believe this, but I've fallen in love with Jay. I'd love you to meet him. I think you'd like him. Any idea when you'll be home again?

Lots of love
Jane xxxx

She must be online, as her next email comes through within minutes.

Jane!!!
From the sounds of it you're rocking it. I want a pack of those cards! Jay must be pretty special for you to have fallen for him and to forget about Ben so quickly. I'm not convinced he could take the place of Ben. I'll have to meet him in person to find out. I have some news. I'm finally going to be home soon. I was planning to surprise you, but I can't keep it in. I'm hoping to make it back in the New Year. Although I love it here, I want to settle down and I'm considering coming back for good! There are loads of jobs for nurses back home.

Will let you know my travel dates as soon as I know, and we can make plans.

Sorcha xxxx.
PS Can you send some of that heart desire stuff my way?

How amazing that would be if Sorcha was back home? I take the cards out of my handbag and shuffle them as I think of Sorcha. I ask them to give Sorcha whatever her heart truly desires and then pick a card.

There's a picture of a man holding a bouquet of flowers. The message says *Sudden Shake-up.*

Luck will now come the way of a sweet and dependable person, if you so wish, but they are not fond of change; moving home may not be in their best interests. This sudden shake-up will turn out to be positive if you give them as much encouragement as possible to stay where they are. They will attract attention through work, which will be perfect to achieve their heart's desire and find love.

I wonder whether if I do nothing, if Sorcha will still come home. Surely, it's up to her to make that decision herself. She wants to come home, and I want her home. Perhaps she may be happy here. She could meet the man of her dreams in Dublin. I don't want to disobey the cards, but this is something I feel strongly about. I put the cards out of sight and try to forget about what they asked me to do.

I can't forget about them, though. They are the only thing I can think of, like they have some sort of power over me. It's almost like I must obey them. I guess this is what the note meant when it said I must follow the cards' advice, and there's no turning back.

I reply to Sorcha, and I tell her I asked the cards to grant her heart's desires and she should consider staying in Australia, and to keep an open mind about meeting a guy through work. I'm gutted that she's not coming home now, but I really want what's best for her. At least the cards aren't consuming my thoughts anymore and my mind is clear.

After work Jay collects me outside Hidden Secrets and we go to a Christmas market. There are loads of huts selling Christmas gifts. The lights are twinkly and there's a Christmassy feel in the air. We get something to eat from one of the food trucks.

'I don't know why, but I find food from a food truck always tastes better,' he says. 'Anyway, everything tastes better when I'm with you.'

I smile, we kiss and everything feels right in the world. As we walk around, we can't keep our hands off each other, we're turning into one of those annoying couples I usually hate the sight of, but any sense of logic I have goes out the window when I'm with him. I feel more alive than I ever have. Invincible, but at the same time addicted to him.

'Look at the beautiful Christmas decorations. They can be personalised. How cute,' I say as I turn to Jay, but he's not even listening to me.

'It's almost time for the market to close,' he says, annoyed. 'I don't get why you wanted to go to the bookshop first. It's just a big dusty old place. I wanted to get here earlier.'

'But we still have time to have a look around. Anyway, if you bothered to come inside instead of hanging around waiting for me you would understand its beauty,' I say as I give him my most angry stare. He walks off and I lose him in the crowd. I get this dreadful feeling that he's going to replace me with someone else. When we're out together I notice he constantly looks at other women. My moods have been erratic over the past while because I'm scared Jay is going to dump me for a new, improved version. Most of the time I'm so happy, in control, full of energy and excited about what else the cards will bring, but there have been moments where I feel like I'm walking on a tightrope. It's so hard being this in love with someone.

'I just bought this for us,' he says as he reappears behind me. 'I'm sorry for being an asshole. If it means so much to you. I'll go into the dusty bookshop sometime.' He hands me a large red shiny decoration. It has the words "Jane and Jay's first Christmas together" on it. 'What do you think, Jane, will you spend Christmas with me?'

A strange warm sensation sweeps over me, and I feel like I'm under his spell again. It's as if I'm in a Christmas movie, because I'm standing here with the most beautiful man in the world, and he wants to spend Christmas with me. No more having to go back to my mam's house and feeling like the odd one out again with her pitiful looks, wondering why I'm still single while Gillian has men falling at her feet.

I'm sure she won't mind if I decline this year. Even if Gillian isn't there, Mam will have her boyfriend Seamus with her.

My mam met Seamus on a night out with Gillian a few years ago. Seamus is the cousin of Gillian's bodyguard and when they met it was love at first sight apparently. He's also a trained bodyguard who's about twenty years younger than Mam, but she doesn't care. He's her drinking partner, and it gives her a sense of importance that she has her own personal bodyguard.

'Yes. I would love to spend Christmas with you,' I say. I lean over to kiss him again and then delicate snowflakes fall and land all around us.

'Let's get out of here, before the snow gets heavier.'

When we get to Jay's cottage, it's dark and our clothes are soaking wet from the snow. We take off our coats and I shiver. Jay lights the fire.

'You need to get out of those clothes,' he says. 'I'll just go sort out something to warm you up.'

I sit on the couch and warm up in front of the crackling fire. I hear a bath running, but Jay never told me he was going to have a bath.

I go to the bathroom. The room is hot and steamy. He's sitting on the side of the large free-standing bath placing rose petals over the bubbles.

'I've left fresh towels out, so relax and enjoy. Is the water all right? There's something I forgot,' he says. 'I'll be back in a minute.'

I undress and stretch out in the bath. I put my head back as my body relaxes with the heat. He comes back into the bathroom with a large bucket of champagne on ice and champagne glasses with juicy strawberries on the side.

'I thought you might be thirsty,' he says grinning. 'Only the best for you.'

He stands in front of me and takes his jumper off slowly and flexes his muscles.

'I used to be a body builder,' he says as he pulls off his pants. 'I won professional competitions.'

'Ah, a body builder ... huh,' I say. 'So, what was that like?' I try to hold in my laughter discreetly as Jay poses.

'I enjoyed it, but my ex-girlfriends got jealous of how much attention I got.'

That's my chance to ask him about past girlfriends. When I broach the subject, he gets defensive and tells me now's not the time and kisses me instead.

There's so much I want to know about him. Why will he not tell me?

He gets into the bath, places my legs either side of him and massages them, sending shivers up my spine.

'I told you before, my life is complicated.'

'I remember, but that doesn't stop me from wanting to know more.'

'Fine then,' he says as he looks pissed off. 'What do you want to know?'

'Okay. Let's start with your family. Do you have any siblings?'

He frowns. 'I don't want to go there.'

'Why? What's wrong?' I reach over and rub his arm.

His face hardens. 'I'm an orphan. My parents died when I was a baby and I was brought up by different relatives living in England. I moved to Ireland when I was thirteen to live with my aunt.'

'What was that like? Was she nice?'

'Yeah, she was nice. A bit wacko though, she was into cards, fortune-telling, casting spells and crystals – mad shit like that. She believed she was psychic too, and did tours around the country, so was never at home. We were stony broke. She never made enough money. Growing up, having no one at home made me self-sufficient. I learnt to rely on no one but myself. I'm a loner, Jane, through and through. Most of the time all I need is my computer and I'm happy.'

'You don't need to be alone anymore. You have me now.' I squeeze his hand and he smiles. I vow to never tell Jay about my cards in case he thinks I'm crazy like his aunt.

'My cryptocurrency project is going to make us so rich and we'll never want for anything ever again.' His eyes darken with intensity.

'It's not all about money, Jay.' I lower my voice.

'Money is power and when you grow up poor like me, you long for that. Having no money is shit, Jane. I never want to go back to that life. There was times growing up when I had no lunch for school and I went without meals. I had no choice, but to steal to get food and to survive. I ended up doing time in prison for a few years …

for a robbery. I got in with the wrong crowd ... we robbed a bank. I was stupid, but when I was inside, I got big into doing weights and fitness. I had to learn to protect myself.'

I don't know how to reply to that. I feel sad for him and ashamed of myself for even contemplating I had problems before, because my life has been a lot easier than his. Okay so I've had issues to do with my parents' break up, my mam's problems and my sister's fame, but none of that compares to what he's been through. I've never ended up in jail. I've been lucky in life and even luckier now I have my cards.

'You deserve so much good in your life,' I say as my eyes glisten.

'And I will ... all the good will come when I get my crypto business up and running. Money makes things easier and protects you from the bad stuff ...'

He gets out of the bath and hands me a towel. He takes my hand and leads me into his bedroom. The bed is covered with rose petals. There's jazz music playing softly, as we lie on his bed facing each other.

'It takes a special kind of person for me to trust like this ... so now you know why I had a hard life but hopefully that's all about to change. You're a good person, Jane. Probably too good for the likes of me.'

'Don't say that ... you're so lovely.'

'Before I came to Ireland ... my early years ... I blocked them out. I was passed around from aunts to uncles, but I never stayed. There was always hassle. I've had cigarettes put out on my back ... I was homeless for a while—'

'That's so awful ... no one deserves that.'

'No, they don't, but I don't want to think about that anymore. I just want to focus on the future and you. I feel like we were meant to be together.'

'Yeah, I know what you mean. Like we attracted each other.'

His face becomes dark and intense. 'No, I don't believe in that shit. There's things we can't control. A lot of things. I didn't ask to have no parents—'

'Of course not, but what about the universe? I think it brings people and things we need most into our lives. Do you ever think about how we met? It happened so fast – almost like it was *meant to be.*'

'I'm sorry, Jane, but I don't buy in to any of this shit. You're preaching to the wrong person. But what I do know is I'm madly … in love with you,' he says.

'Me too,' I say as a rush of excitement runs through me. 'I love you too, Jay.'

We spend the night making love many times over until the early hours of the morning, and eventually drift off to sleep in each other's arms.

CHAPTER 12

THE NEXT DAY I go to Hidden Secrets again. The *Irish Daily Mail* sits on the chair in the snug beside me. On the front page there's a photo of Gillian.

What ridiculous story is it this time?

Gillian only has to leave the house to get milk or bread and the paparazzi make a meal out of it.

I flick through the newspaper looking for the article. There it is. A double page spread with the headline 'Celebrities and their sisters'. I wasn't expecting this. There's Kate Middleton and Pippa, Beyoncé with Solange. There's also two photographs side by side of myself and Gillian. The photo of me is the one taken by *Forbes* Magazine.

I read the caption under it.

Oscar-winning actress Gillian O'Hara with her business tycoon sister, Jane McAlister.

I look like a success just like Gillian. The article shows just how far I've come because of the cards.

I see Tara across the room. She yawns in between coughs. The shutters are down and it's partially lit inside. The Christmas tree lights are on, it's quiet and peaceful. The last customer left a few minutes ago. I tell her to sit down, rest and I'll finish closing the shop.

'It would be nice to rest my tired bones. I'm so tired all the time,' says Tara, confused. 'I just don't get it. Why is this tiredness not going away?' She sits down on the nearest chair and sighs.

Why have the cards not made her better by now? Perhaps she just needs more rest.

'You need to take it easy. I can help you. Just tell me what needs to be done.' I smile at her and pat her hands. They're older and more wrinkled. More bones and less skin than before. She's thinner too. It's like she's wasting away. I wonder if she's eating properly.

'There's a whole pile of books in the corner over there that need to be organised and there's invoices to be paid. I can sort the books out tomorrow. The bills are in the folder over there. I've never really enjoyed all the paperwork that comes with running your own business, but I know that is your forte. Perhaps you can help me with my accounts,' she says.

'Okay. Let me take a look.'

In the folder Tara has all the financial stuff carefully handwritten in an old notebook. She certainly is old fashioned with keeping records. This could all be computerised. I tell her it would save so much time. A pile of bank statements are tucked in at the back of the folder showing a balance of millions of euro in investments.

Why is she slogging her guts out in the bookshop when she has all this money?

At this stage in her life, she should be putting her feet up and relaxing. I go over the sales records.

'Something is up with the sales, Tara. They've decreased since you gave me the cards. I think something weird is happening,' I say frowning.

'I asked the cards to make my bookshop a roaring success with a hint of magic. But since I gave them to you perhaps that wish has worn off. The books don't whisper anymore. They used to tell me what customer they wanted to go to. I didn't know the magic would wear off. How could I have known … the note never mentioned this.' She looks worried.

'Does that mean everything you asked the cards for will now go?'

'Perhaps. It seems that way, but I really have no idea.'

'Ah, that's not good.' I'm really worried for her; I bite the inside of my mouth. What if everything she asks for disappears? 'I can ask them for anything you want.'

'Not at all. I'll be fine. I don't need the cards to run my life anymore and sales will pick up again, it's only a matter of time,' says Tara.

I'm impressed by her composure, but a weird feeling comes over me as I realise that this could happen to me too. I could potentially lose everything I asked the cards for if I give them away.

Ah, feck.

I could lose Jay and my job. I get panicky, but then tell myself to get a grip. I don't need to give the cards away and I won't. They are mine now forever. I never want to lose them. I can't imagine a life without them. I wonder if there's any way of finding out who had the cards before, and what happened to them.

'Don't look so scared, Jane,' Tara says, interrupting my thoughts.

'I want to know where the cards came from.'

'I don't think we should go down that rabbit hole, but I do have something to give you.'

She walks off upstairs for a few minutes, and when she comes back, she hands me a black and white photograph. The photo shows two men and four women sitting close together smiling.

'This photograph was down the side of the armchair when I found the cards. I've done everything I can to find out who they are. I even hired a private detective, but it was no use. It's like they disappeared off the face of the earth.'

'I could try and find out. I can post it online.'

'I don't think that's wise. Who knows what you might drag up? It's not the right time yet. You can keep the photograph though. It may be useful at some stage.'

'But Tara, I think it's important we know what happened to these people—'

'No more, Jane. Leave them alone,' she said, rattled. 'And don't even think of asking the cards who the people in the photograph are because I tried that before and they wouldn't tell me.'

I don't want to upset her anymore so I drop the subject.

'You should hire a manager to help you out,' I say later on in the day to Tara. 'It will take some of the pressure off.' The look on her face tells me she's horrified I've suggested that. 'Until you get your strength back …'

I want to tell her that I asked for the cards to make her better and the advice they gave, but something stops me. I get the impression Tara wouldn't like me meddling in her life.

'I don't want a stranger coming in and reorganising things. I have my own system and it works for now. I'm perfectly fine. I've something to do. I'll be back shortly.' She walks off up the stairs.

I wonder if I can change things so Tara gets her wishes back. It's worth a try.

'Hello cards,' I say as I shuffle the cards. 'Can you give Tara back everything she wished for?'

I shudder as I feel a strange sense that I've done something wrong. I'm waiting for something to happen. Like the weather to change drastically – heavy rainfall or a thunderstorm, but it doesn't. Everything is quiet. Eerily so.

I pick a card. It's blank. A big blank card of nothingness. The room isn't vibrant either like it normally would be when I hold them.

Tara arrives back to the shop floor twenty minutes later with a dreamy expression on her face. I've been wondering if her mind is wandering a bit too much lately. Most of the time she's sharp, but there's been a few moments where it's as if she's in a different world.

'You know, Jane, after Harold died, I was lost but my shop gave me a purpose. I never want to give this place up, even though I tire easily.'

'I'll help until you feel better. Who was Harold?'

'Harold was my late husband. He was my one true love.' She smiles at his memory.

'Is this him in the photo on the desk? The guy on the motorbike? Wow, he's handsome,' I say. 'My dad mentioned to me you had someone close to you who died.'

'Not a day goes by when I don't think of him. I can still remember his face as clearly as if it were yesterday. I've never met another man as good as him since. His shoes were too big to fill.'

'You must really have loved him,' I say as an image of Jay pops into my head.

'I did. I loved him with all my heart. After he died, I went to a very dark place, Jane.' She coughs again. 'It was only when I bought the bookshop that I began to get a glimmer of light again.'

'Did you have any children?'

'Yes. A daughter. She's still nearby.' She smiles and her eyes gleam.

'That's nice. That's handy she lives close by. I'd love to meet her sometime.' I imagine a younger looking version of Tara. Someone in their fifties maybe.

'That might not happen.'

'Ah, well maybe one day. I'd really like to meet her,' I say, slightly taken aback.

Why does she not want me to meet her?

'When you used to come here with your dad, you reminded me of her. You were only a child then but seemed older. Old beyond your years.'

'I couldn't understand why I wasn't as talented as Gillian. She was amazing. A true star and I was well … well, I'm not sure exactly, but because of the cards my career is taking off. Anything is possible,' I say. 'I'm even getting used to the noises, they don't bother me as much anymore.'

'I found this the other day when I was looking for something else.' She hands me a sheet of paper from a shelf overhead. Her eyes light up and sparkle. 'It's an old drawing. Imagine after all this time I still have it.'

I stare at the colourful picture I made many years ago. It's of myself and Tara stacking books together in the bookshop. I have my hair in pigtails and I'm smiling up at her. *By Jane McAlister. Age 9 and ¼* is scrawled in crayon at the bottom of the page. I remember the day I made the picture. My mam had spent the last few days in bed. My dad took me to the bookshop, and I told Tara I thought my mam was sick. I asked her if she could give me medicine to make her better.

'I can't make your mam better, but I can give you a book to take your mind off all your worries,' Tara had said.

She gave me a book about a girl who became a superhero with lots of special powers. 'Jane,' she said. 'You have so much potential, never forget how talented and creative you are. You have untapped potential.'

After she said that I created the picture, and imagined I had special powers to make all the customers' problems just disappear and my mam better.

'My dream was to have my own bookshop one day, just like this one, and to help others, but I got older, and life got in the way,' I say now.

'I really looked forward to your visits. Do you remember the red coat I gave you once for a Christmas gift?'

'No, but I've seen a girl in a red coat here at the bookshop.'

Our conversation is interrupted by a loud bang. The photo of Harold in the frame falls to the floor and smashes into tiny pieces. Tara lets out a quiet moan.

'Your photo of Harold is ruined. What happened to make it fall?' I say. The banging sound is getting louder and it's not just in my mind as Tara can hear it too.

'I have no idea,' she mutters and shakes her head. 'This has never happened before.'

There's a scuffle sound outside. We both turn and look at each other at the same time. The air is clammy, and my skin is prickly.

'You stay here. I'll go outside and check,' I say trying to act all brave, but inside I'm trembling.

I peek through the window instead of going outside and then I see her. It's the girl from before. She has her face up against the glass window.

'Jane, Jane please help me. I'm lost,' she says anxiously. The rain is pouring down, and her pigtails are soaking wet.

I feel a hand on my shoulder. I scream. Tara. It's only Tara.

'What are you looking at?' says Tara.

'The girl. I've seen her before. It's like she's following me around. Why is she outside on her own in the rain?'

'There's no one there, Jane,' says Tara.

I try to open the front door, but it's locked. Tara is nowhere to be seen. I find a key at the top of the door frame and use it to unlock the door. The girl runs away. I don't even try to catch her this time. Tara appears with a sweeping brush in her hand and the photo of Harold.

'Ah, there you are, I just went to get the brush to clear up the glass.'

'The girl … she was really there … she ran away once I got the door open. She knows my name, Tara. How does she know my name? She needs me to help her. She's lost,' I say.

'What girl? I don't see anyone there, Jane. Now, I must get a new frame for the photo of my Harold. I have some spare photo frames here somewhere.'

CHAPTER 13

BEN

Now that Jane's not sitting beside me anymore, I'm losing interest in working in the bank. I've been lying awake at night wondering why I'm still working there. The only thing I like about work is having lunch with her.

Sarah knows something is up with me and she's been getting on my nerves. During our latest breakfast date, she was quite intense.

'Where do you see our relationship going, Ben?' she said. 'Are you happy with the way things are?'

'Yeah, I'm happy. Things are grand,' I said.

'Just grand.' She looked shocked. 'Ben, you can give me more info than that. Do you ever think about what the future holds? Like our future together. We can't just live together forever. We need to think long-term. We've both invested so much into this relationship and I'm not getting any younger … what if we want to have kids?'

'I don't know, Sarah. I haven't given it much thought.'

'Why not?'

'Because things work the way they are. We get on well. We have a good life … and I …'

'You what, Ben?'

She looked like she was going to thump me.

'… and I love you,' I said. I held her hand tightly and kissed it. 'Why all these questions? You know I love you, don't you? What else can I say?'

'I love you too, Ben,' she said as she squeezed my hand.

Even though she didn't say it I know she's at me again to propose to her soon, but the thought of it unnerves me. I'm only twenty-five and my folks weren't exactly the best role models for a healthy marriage. Marriage to me feels like being trapped. I wasn't lying when I told Sarah I loved her. I do love her, but all these feelings I have for Jane keep coming up. I've never done the dirt on Sarah before and I don't intend to, despite all the opportunities I've had with other women, especially Emma.

I think back to when things began to get even weirder with myself and Emma. It was when we took part in a mentor programme through the bank and Tim, who was our director at the time, was Emma's mentor. I got to know him pretty well when I joined the bank's rugby team. He's a sound guy and not a bad rugby player either. We've had many great nights out after matches. Emma got lucky getting Tim. He's big into bringing people along and helping them reach their potential. The next thing we know she gets promoted and she's now the manager of the whole department, including myself and Jane.

One day she calls me into the boardroom and tells me I'll be next up for promotion, if I play my cards right.

'I'm not interested in being promoted,' I said.

'Why not? There could even be a few more quid in it for you. We made a good team once; stick with me and we could be running the bank soon.'

'I might be leaving soon,' I said, 'My old man has plans for me to take on some of the family business. Lately he's been harping on about wanting me to manage a new line of business to distribute Irish food stuff abroad. Jane's your best bet. She's in it for the long haul.'

'Jane's not the right fit. Think about it, Ben. This promotion would be a good move for you, and we can spend more time together.' She rubbed my chest. That's Emma all over. She's always been very touchy-feely with me even after we split up.

'Just do the right thing and give the promotion to Jane.' I moved her hands away.

'Anyway, are you sure working for your dad is a good idea? If you took this promotion it would be the perfect excuse not to have to work for him.'

The truth is I don't ever want to work for my old man, for many reasons and I told her all about them before when we were close.

Mainly because I can't stand the sight of him. I used to idolise him. It all changed, though, the day I was playing rugby in the Leinster Senior Cup final with my secondary school, Blackrock College. That was the day my illusions of my old man were shattered into pieces.

I went to his work early – expecting him to give me a big pep talk before we went to the match. His business was called Cakes of Ireland. It was one of the family businesses that was passed down to him from my grandmother who had developed some famous soda bread and scone recipe and turned it into an international success. People across the world went mad for it. Since my old man took over, he made it more gimmicky – now it's stuff like cakes and buns in the shape of leprechauns and four-leaf clovers.

The door to his office was closed when I got there. I knocked, but there was no answer, so I just walked right in.

My dad's face was in a right state. All hot and sweaty. It was the face of a cheater. I had caught him in the act.

His secretary didn't even notice I was there. She had her back to me as he sat on his swivel chair.

'Jesus Christ, Ben,' he says. 'I wasn't expecting you this early.'

His secretary, Miranda, I think her name was, jumped up. 'Oh my God. I'm so sorry,' she said as she avoided eye contact. She fixed her skirt and her blouse before she scurried out of the door.

'Keys. Give me your keys,' I shouted at him. 'I'll wait in the car.'

I slammed the door as hard as I could.

We sat in silence as he drove me there. The blood was rushing through my veins, and I wanted to rip his head off. He caught my eye in the car mirror.

'Your mother doesn't need to know anything about this. It would only upset her,' he said. 'And you wouldn't want to do that, would you?'

What an asshole.

I bulldozed my way through the match. I crushed anyone on the other team who looked at me the wrong way. I scored try after try, but all I could think of was how much of an asshole my dad was. We won the Leinster Senior Cup, and our win went down in history, but the victory was bittersweet.

That night when we got home, he kissed my mum before he told her how well I played. Behind her back he handed me a thousand quid with a look as if to say *keep your mouth shut and there's more to come.* I told him to keep the money, but he wouldn't take it back.

After that, everything at home was tainted with what I saw. My mum fussed around packing his case as usual to have everything perfect for his latest business trips. She had no idea though she was packing for her husband to impress his secretary.

After the long-haul business trips, he'd come back all tanned and full of the joys of spring, whistling away to himself and showering my mum with presents. He'd tell her he hated being away from her for so long, but he was doing this for our family.

When he wasn't travelling, she'd complain that he worked late all the time. They argued constantly.

'All these long hours and work stress isn't good for you, James,' she'd say.

'I'm doing it for us. To make sure we all have a good life,' he'd reply.

He kept throwing cash my way as a reminder to keep my mouth shut despite my protests. The night of my twenty-first birthday he surprised me with the keys to my own swanky city centre apartment. There was no mortgage on it. All paid for in cash. Later on when I mentioned I was thinking of applying to work for Becker Bank International, he goes ahead and talks to his mate, CEO Walter Becker, and just like that I had a job there. I didn't even have to do an interview.

I told my mum that Dad was having an affair with his secretary, but no matter what I said she brushed it aside.

She told me Miranda had a crush on him, but he dealt with it. 'She doesn't work with him anymore. She's been transferred to a different department. Your father loves this family, and he would never jeopardise what he has with us for some floozy,' she said.

'I know what I saw, Mum, you must believe me,' I said.

'Leave it Ben, I don't want to hear any more about it.'

There was nothing I could do to change her mind; all I could do was wait until she found out for herself.

CHAPTER 14

JANE

THE NEXT DAY I shower in my apartment during my lunch break. I'm sweaty after a long run on the treadmill.

When I get out of the shower, I hear a shuffling sound. My body tightens in fear. I'm sure there's someone in my office.

Is this the cards messing with my head again?

I tiptoe out of the bathroom and peek through to the office area. I get a glimpse of a man. He has dark hair and is wearing a suit with his back to me sitting on the couch. I freeze.

He turns around. His tie is loose, his shoes are off and he's relaxing watching football on the TV.

'Jane, I knocked on the door for ages and when you didn't answer I came in. The door was open. We arranged to meet for lunch—'

'I forgot … I was in the shower,' I say.

'I can see that,' says Ben.

As the water from my hair drips down onto the floor I realise how shocking I must appear. I haven't seen Ben as much as I normally would lately. My life is so full now between Tara, Jay, and my new job, I've hardly thought about him.

'So, I'll just go get dressed and put some make-up on,' I say.

He stares at me for what seems like forever. I feel my face get hotter and hotter. Any minute now he's going to start teasing me. I'm just waiting for it. I've never let Ben see me in a bathrobe or without my make-up on.

'Put make-up on if you like, but you don't need to. You look … well … different, but in a good way.'

'Thanks,' I say as I stand there. This is awkward, way too awkward. I'm not sure what to do next so I just walk off to change into my clothes.

'So, lunch … are you hungry?' he says when I come back and sit down on the couch opposite him.

'Yeah. Shall we order food from an express delivery service? I have a room service menu somewhere. I just need to find it. I think they even have your favourite. Meatballs,' I say as I search my office. 'I remember thinking of you when I saw the spaghetti and meatballs. Ah, there it is. Meatballs *are* your favourite, right?'

'Jane, this office is more like a five-star hotel. You have seriously landed on your feet.'

'I know, it's unreal.'

'Show me the menu. Perfect. Yeah. I'd love the meatballs,' he says as he spreads out on the couch.

A moment passes as we both sit in silence. Ben is engrossed in the footie.

'You're really making yourself at home,' he says as he turns to look at me. 'So, what have you been up to lately? Hope Becker hasn't been working you too hard.'

'It's not all been about work,' I say. 'I've been seeing Jay most nights.'

'Who's Jay?'

'Oh, I forgot to tell you. I met a new guy.'

'Spill the details.' It's obvious he's shocked.

'He's staying at the cottage on Gull Island. It's so lovely there … magical almost. I like him … a lot.'

He narrows his eyes and does this thing with his body where I can feel coldness pour out of him.

'What's wrong?'

'Magical? Really …'

'Everything feels that way when I'm around him. He's totally broke and is obsessed with getting rich, but apart from that he's perfect.'

'Broke?'

'He doesn't have much money because he's put it all into his business. He's working on a new cryptocurrency.'

'His own crypto business ... huh. A bit risky. I wouldn't want to waste my trust fund on that, but he's in safe hands with you.'

I catch Ben's eye and we both smile. I remember how I loved the way his eyes crinkled when he laughed. I want to tell Ben how ridiculous I find Jay's cryptocurrency obsession, but I don't. Instead, I find myself looking at him in a new light as I realise, I don't fancy him anymore. I haven't dreamt about him in ages either.

'The thing is, Jay is really clever when it comes to stuff like this. Like super intelligent but he's a bit extreme when it comes to how far he wants to take it—'

'I miss you,' Ben says, interrupting me. 'Work's not the same without my sidekick sitting beside me.' He gives me a nudge and I smile while my heart melts a little. When the food arrives, I'm grateful for the distraction it provides.

'So how did you meet Jay?'

'Oh, that's a funny story,' I say.

'Tell me.'

'Well, I fell asleep at a sound bath and rolled onto his mat and kissed him by mistake. I was mortified, but it all worked out in the end. He didn't mind.'

'Of course, he liked it. Most guys would.' He looks at me as if I've just grown two heads.

'Things are moving fast.'

'I can see that. I can't put my finger on it, but you seem different. You haven't known the guy that long so don't get in too deep. He could be just an ex-convict for all you know.'

Oh God. If he only knew the truth. I get an urge to tell Ben about Jay's past, and the cards, but I don't. I doubt he'd believe their magic, and he may think I'm losing my mind.

'Any news about Emma?'

'She's been fired. She stormed out of the building today and hasn't been back since.'

'No way. Seriously, never in a million years did I think she'd get fired. I can't believe it.'

'I know. It's true though. The three musketeers are definitely no more.' He looks at his watch. 'Is it that time already? I got to go. Let's do lunch again tomorrow.'

'Ben,' I shout after him as he walks away. 'I miss Emma. What about you?'

'I don't. This power trip she's on is wrecking my head.'

I put my iPhone on loudspeaker as I file my nails. I lean back on my leather chair listening to Emma. Not long after Ben left my office, she rang me.

'Jane, I tried so hard to get you the promotion, but Tim was insistent that it should go to Ben. Now I've been fired, which is so unfair.'

'I felt like I had no other option but to leave,' I say. 'I thought I was going to have a panic attack. I had to get out of there.'

'You can't imagine how bad I felt when I was delivering the news. It broke my heart in two. I need your help to get my job back.'

'I don't have the power to do that,' I say in what I hope is a serious voice. I don't want Emma to think it's okay to completely ignore me like she did after the appraisal. I don't want to be a pushover.

'You do. I know you report directly to Walter. He'll listen to you. Tell him it's not my fault.'

'I'm not sure that will work—'

'It's worth a try. It's not right that Tim gets away with this especially when he didn't even value you in the first place. I do.'

'I'll have to think about it.'

'I'm … eh, sorry I haven't been in touch earlier. I just felt foolish that I couldn't help you at the appraisal. It was awkward. You're still one of my best friends. Congratulations on the new job, by the way. I can't wait to hear all about it.'

CHAPTER 15

I PHONE WALTER, BUT THERE'S no answer so I go to the kitchen to get a snack. It's filled with pastries, bagels, cream cheese, smoked salmon, and donuts. Donuts are my biggest weakness. The smell of freshly baked food gets me every time. I take a bite out of the first one. It has vanilla frosting with sprinkles and a nice yeasty flavour. Custard oozes out onto my tongue tantalising my taste buds. As I walk around my apartment, I realise how lucky I am to have this place. It seems such a waste not to move in. I know Ben said it's not a good idea, but I'll get more work done as well as living in luxury surrounded by all this food.

I lick my fingers which are covered in vanilla frosting. Heaven. I'm about to take another donut when my desk phone rings. It's Walter. We chat about general work stuff and then I ask him if he could give Emma her job back.

'So, what you're telling me is that Emma should not have been fired,' he says.

'That's right, Walter. I don't think she should have been fired.'

'Who was responsible for not promoting you before? Was it Tim?'

'I'm not really sure, Walter,' I say in between mouthfuls.

'I need to know. A name, please.'

'But I can't give you a name ...'

I really don't want to land Tim in it.

'I need a name right now,' says Walter, raising his voice.

'I can't. I don't know. I ... I—'

'A name now, Jane,' he shouts.

'Eh ... I'm told it was Tim.'

I feel awful saying this. I hope it was really Tim's fault like Emma said.

'I'll need to investigate this,' he says.

This is my first time meeting angry Walter. What a stressful conversation. I didn't think he would be so cut-throat about the whole thing. I don't want to point fingers at anyone. Is this the crazy Walter that Ben goes on about?

I move over to the couch and bring my cards with me. I shuffle them as I wish for my friendship with Emma to be back to the way it was before any of the work stuff took over.

The word *Moths* is engraved on the top of the card I pick. There's a picture of a group of people drinking through straws from one big pitcher.

> *Because your light is now shining at its brightest, you*
> *must beware of attracting too many moths. Some of*
> *your loved ones are here to support and lift you, others*
> *however only have their own interests at heart. You are*
> *encouraged to get together with friends closest to you.*
> *Listen to your intuition when something seems not right.*

A get-together … huh? Who should I invite? Well, definitely Jay, and Ben. Perhaps we could do a double date with Sarah too, and Emma.

I'm full of energy for the rest of the day. I get so much work done that I decide to leave work a bit early and bring a load of my stuff from home to my office apartment so I can move in properly.

Afterwards I go to the bookshop to see Tara.

'Tara, what sort of stuff did you ask for when you had the cards?' I say as I dust some first editions.

'Ah, now that is an interesting question,' she says, lost in thought. 'I was quite foolish at first with my choices. I still wasn't happy though. Something was missing.' She gives me a look as if she can read my mind. She can't of course. It's just the impression I get from her.

'What happened then?'

'I couldn't sleep, I'd lay awake at night and long for Harold to be beside me.' Her voice becomes low almost like a whisper.

'What did you do?'

Tara picks up more books and places them on the shelves.

'I'd hear noises. Night-time became something I dreaded.'

'The noises … that's just like me.'

'Yes … something similar.'

'Then what did you do?'

'I wanted him back, Jane. I really did, but I knew he had to go. It was his time. You can't bring back the dead. So, I didn't ask for him back. I asked for something else, something worse than that.' She shakes her head. 'What a waste of time that was.'

'What did you ask for?'

'I was very foolish back then, Jane.'

'Please tell me. I want to know.'

'I asked the cards to bring me someone that was just like Harold.'

'And did they?' I gasp in surprise.

'Shortly afterwards I met many different men. There was John who had Harold's smile. Tom had his laugh, while Gary and Robert both looked very like him.'

'Did you fall in love with any of them?'

'I tried to tell myself I was in love with Robert, but it was a lie. The fact is no one could ever replace Harold. Our marriage wasn't perfect. We had our ups and downs. A lot of tragedy too, but we got through it because we worked at it.'

'You must have so many fond memories of him.'

'I do. But I have regrets too. I have many regrets. Especially with Candice. My advice to you would be don't waste time. Not a single second. When you find the one you love, tell them.'

'Who was Candice?'

'Candice was …well she was… I'm afraid I can't say.' She coughs loudly and turns her back to me.

'I'm sorry. I didn't mean to upset you.'

'I need to get some rest. I think I'll shut the shop up now. It's time for you to go. You've done enough for me today as it is.' Tara walks away.

Why will Tara not tell me who Candice is?

It's strange now to realise that Tara may not have the answers to everything. When I was younger, I thought she was the wisest person in the world. Any problem I had she could turn it on its head with just a few words.

I remember when I was about twelve years old, I had a big argument with one of my best friends at the time, and I was devastated. I don't recall what we fought over, but I poured my heart out to Tara over how bossy I thought this girl was and how she tried to get her own way all the time.

'Jane, anyone would be lucky to have you as a friend. Don't change who you are for anyone, and don't be afraid to stand up for yourself. What's meant for you won't pass you.'

I listened intently to her every word and wondered who her friends were. She didn't like talking about herself so I knew it was best not to ask.

The next morning in the office I'm engrossed with work when I hear the click of my office door opening. A smell of strong aftershave like a fresh sandalwood aroma tickles my nostrils.

'Ben, what are you doing here?' I say breathing in his scent. I can't help it. Despite the fact I don't fancy him anymore he still smells so good.

'I was chatting to Tim earlier; I'm going to be promoted. How about we head out for a drink after work to celebrate?' he says smiling.

'A drink … that sounds lovely.'

'It will be good to just hang out outside of the office,' he says.

When he says this, I realise how much I miss hanging out with Ben. Just being around him and the fun we had together. Pre-Jay and the cards, every encounter I had with Ben I turned into something major in my head. Like the times we'd go watch the rugby in the pub together. Baggot Street was our usual haunt. I loved how he got so into it. He'd touch my arm or hug me when he was excited about the match and my body melted at his touch. I find it hard now to know where I stand with him or even act around him. Our relationship is different.

'What's this?' he says as he stares at the boxes of my personal stuff I brought over from home.

'Oh, I've still to unpack those. I've decided to move in.'

He frowns.

'It just makes more sense you know. To stay here when I'm not in Jay's. I'll get more work done,' I say lowering my voice.

'You're living in a bank now. I hope you realise how bizarre that is. Who lives in a bank? What are the cards for?' he asks.

On the floor beside him my cards are scattered around. They must have fallen to the floor without me realising it.

'Oh, just a game I was playing for a bit of fun, that's all.' I rush over to the cards and crawl around picking them up. I'm so nervous in case he looks at them too closely.

'Really, what sort of game?' He picks up a card, shakes his head and then puts it back. 'These things look mad. Where did you get them?'

Now's my chance to confide in Ben about the cards. I want to tell him so much, but I can't. There's no way he would believe me if I told him about their magic. I want to change the subject fast before he asks any questions about the cards.

'So, I was planning to organise a little get-together and was wondering if you're free tomorrow night.'

'I think so. Why? What's on?'

'Can you and Sarah come out for dinner with myself, Jay and Emma?'

He's not answering me. Maybe he's busy and can't come.

'Look Jane, I don't know if this dinner is such a good idea.' He stands up and just as I think he's going to walk away he comes closer to me. His eyes are bluer than usual.

'Why not, Ben?'

'I don't know if Sarah is free, and you don't know this guy very well and after everything that's just happened with Emma, I don't think you should invite her. You need to give up this idea of the three musketeers.'

'Emma deserves a second chance.' I think about telling Ben I asked Walter to give Emma her job back, but then I decide not to. 'How about I text Sarah and check with her if she's free?' I say, to change the subject.

'Sure.' He fidgets with a pen from my desk.

I send Sarah a quick text. She replies straight away.

'Sarah said she would love to go out. So I guess that's sorted then.'

'I might need to work late.'

'But if we are going out for dinner, I need to know numbers to book.'

'It seems like you have your mind set on this,' he sighs.

'It'll be fun Ben. I'll send you on the details once it's booked.'

I'm delighted it's all going to plan. So far, I've followed everything the cards have told me to do, and I dread to think what would happen if I didn't.

My iPhone rings. Jay asks me to see him tonight. He's so persistent, but I say no as I don't want to let Ben down. When I finish my call, I can tell by Ben's face he's heard the whole conversation.

'It doesn't matter now. Let's just cancel our plans. You're too caught up with Jay,' he says.

He turns around without saying another word and slams the door behind him. I hate the awkwardness between us recently.

The next morning, Jay pulls up outside the bank and I get off his Vespa. I stayed in his cottage the night before. As I take off the helmet my hair blows in the wind and sweeps all over my face, tickling my nose.

'It's not fair, you don't have a hair out of place,' I say.

How does he look so perfect all the time? He doesn't seem to have any idea just how good he looks. His eyes are bright and alert despite the fact he's only had a few hours' sleep. The way he's standing with his shoulders back and one foot up against the wall, he look like he's posing for a modelling shoot. As people pass by, they turn to stare at us.

'You look beautiful to me. Any chance you can take the day off?' he says.

I laugh. 'I'm flattered. Really, but I've so much work to get through today and we have the dinner date with my friends later, remember. I'll see you then.'

'Hmm … I'd forgotten about that. I'm not sure I like the idea of sharing you.'

'Haha! Listen, I better go. I'll meet you later at the restaurant.'

'So, where is your office? This place gives me the creeps if I'm honest. It's all the glass and the size of it. So restrictive. I'd feel trapped working in there. Office work is not for me.'

'Most of the top floor of the bank is mine,' I say as he leans in to kiss me.

His lips taste like ripe strawberries. I don't want to leave, but I have to. There's a bit of a crowd starting to form around the reception area. They're all looking at us through the glass doors and pointing at me.

'Come closer, I need one more kiss before you go. I love you. I can't wait to see you later,' he says as he grabs me again.

We finally say goodbye and I walk into the bank. Emma and a group of girls I recognise are laughing. Emma races over and puts her arm around me. Her short tight red skirt and blazer highlight her slender frame. The bright red firecracker lipstick matches the colour of her high heels that make a loud clip clop sound against the tiled floor.

'I'm back, Jane! I have my old job back. I take it you asked Walter to give me my job back.'

'Yeah, I had a chat with him. I'm glad it all got sorted out for you.'

'I knew I could count on you. Who's the guy you were kissing?' she says as she gawps at me.

'That was my boyfriend.'

'You have a boyfriend! I saw you from my office and my jaw just dropped to the floor. He's gorgeous. I just had to tell the other girls to come and look. Good on you getting a guy like that.'

'I'm mortified to think I was being watched kissing Jay.'

'Ah, don't worry about it. You'll be the talk of the office for a while, but then it will someone else's turn. I heard Gillian got engaged. Will she have an engagement party? I'd love to go. I missed the last two. Can you set me up with one of Jay's friends?'

My friendship with Emma is back, just as I asked.

CHAPTER 16

BEN HAS HIS BACK to me as I approach. When he turns around to face me, his eyes look troubled.

'Emma's telling everyone you got her her job back. Tim has been fired. He's a good guy, and he shouldn't have been fired.'

I walk into my office. It's spotless. The windows have been washed. The coffee mugs I left on my desk have been removed. The place smells like fresh laundry and disinfectant. The cleaners came in when I left. All my clothes in my apartment have been freshly laundered. My every need is catered for.

'Look Ben, Emma told me it wasn't her fault and I believe her. I feel awful that Tim got fired, but I didn't tell Walter to fire him. He just wanted someone to blame.'

He turns away from me. 'If Walter senses anyone is lying to him, he fires them. That's the type of guy he is.'

'I'm starting to understand that now,' I whisper. 'I can tell you're angry but please sit down so we can talk about this properly.'

He moves to sit beside me. His legs are touching against mine and his arm is slung over the couch, but I don't feel anything. Nothing. No butterflies. The cards really did their job when I asked them to help me get over Ben.

'I can't believe you listened to that girl. She's not a real friend to you,' he says.

'Everyone deserves a second chance. It wasn't her fault she couldn't promote me,' I say.

'You need to change this.'

'I can't change it. I've already spoken to Walter, and he's made his decision.'

'That's a big mistake.'

His words are like a bright red noise, on a loop that I can't get out of my head.

'I just wanted Emma to be my friend again,' I say.

'I know you look up to her, but it's for the wrong reasons.'

'I don't see her the same way you do,' I say. 'I like her. She's fun.'

'You're a better person than she is.'

'We were so close before – like sisters almost,' I say as I think about our relationship.

'Why do you want to have friends as close as sisters? You have a sister already. You don't need a fake one,' he says.

'My sister and I don't really talk much anymore. Her life has changed a lot,' I say quietly.

'Of course, it's bound to.'

'I know that, but her life is so different to mine.'

'You're both different people. You don't have to do the same things.'

'She has just got engaged. Her career is amazing.'

'Your career is amazing too. Anyway, you're still her sister. None of that changes just because she's getting married. You look like you're going to cry.'

'I'm fine. I don't know what's wrong with me. I'm so emotional lately.'

'I hate to see you like this. I'm sorry if I upset you.'

I move away from him to create some distance between us. Time passes. The only sound is the hum of the air conditioning unit.

'Things have changed between us. What do you think?' he says.

'Well, you don't get a chance to tease me as much as before,' I say.

'No, I don't.'

'You smell better.'

He smiles. 'I always smell good.'

'I guess we were in an open plan office before with lots of people around us, but now it's just us two,' I say.

'I miss sitting beside you in work. It's funny often it's only when someone is gone, we realise how important they are to us,' he says as he turns to me.

'Don't go all soppy on me now!'

'I mean it.' He gently pats my arm.

'That's sweet, Ben,' I say as I feel awkward.

'Hmmm … you're in this big office on your own now with no one to talk to. If you ever need company, just call me.'

I get a sense he's going to kiss me, but then he moves away.

'Why are you yawning so much? Did you have another late night again?' he says.

'I stayed over at Jay's place. I didn't get much sleep to be honest.'

'There's this intensity with you. Can't you just get to know someone first before you turn everything into a big love story? This is not *The Holiday*. You're not Kate Winslet. This is real life.'

'You'll meet him later and you'll understand why I like him so much and you won't be annoyed with me.'

'You need to fix this whole mess with Tim. I mean it, Jane, it's not right.' He turns to leave, but then stops and says, 'Don't you have work to do? I'm sure Walter is piling the pressure on you.'

He's so infuriating. Why does he act so hot and cold with me? The light for the voicemail on my desk phone is flashing an angry red colour. That doesn't look good. I take a deep breath. Ben gazes at the phone and then back to me.

'It's nothing I can't handle. I'm fine. I'll see you later,' I say.

'You should get yourself an assistant. I'm surprised you haven't thought of that already,' he says as he walks out of my office.

As well as the urgent voicemails there are several emails from Walter. The first few are innocent enough. He's asking for financial documents, but then it gets serious. In the last few messages, he's demanding to know why I'm not answering his emails immediately. He writes if he doesn't get an answer back within ten minutes I'm fired. He's turned on me.

What can I say to get myself out of this? I need my cards. They will fix this. I can't get fired. I just can't. I can't lose all of this! My heart is pounding as I hold the cards and talk to them.

'Hello, cards. I really need your help. I'm terrified I'm going to lose my job and I don't want Walter to be angry with me.'

I shuffle the cards.

I take the top card. *The Queen* is engraved on the front of it with a picture of a woman wearing robes with a lopsided crown on her head.

You are not afraid of hard work and are good at business. You need to stop worrying about what others think of you. Spend less time daydreaming and more time doing. Try not to over-react about the little things. Look for ways to get the help you need.

A sense of clarity comes over me and I feel back in control. I think I'll just about pull this off. I open my email.

Dear Walter,
    I am sorry I was not available earlier as I had to take some time away from the office due to personal reasons. I'm sure you understand. Please find attached the financial documents you require. My personal assistant will be in touch with you shortly.

Yours Sincerely,
Jane McAlister

And just like that the email goes off to cyberspace and I feel immediately better.

I hear a shuffle sound first. Then a cough. My office door is ajar. Whoever is there probably heard me talking to the cards. A shadow creeps into the room as the door opens.

'Jane … what are you doing?' he says as he approaches my desk. He's glaring at me like I'm crazy.

'Jay … I … I wasn't expecting to see you. How did you get into my office?'

'The door was open. You left your wallet at the cottage. I brought it back in case you needed it.'

'Oh, that's nice of you. Thank you.'

He doesn't answer me.

'How long have you been there?' I ask.

'Long enough to hear everything.' He picks up the cards from my desk. His eyes light up. His face is flushed.

'They're just a bit of fun. A bit of stress relief,' I say. I'm panicking as I grab them out of his hands quickly.

He leans over and examines them closely. 'What's happening to the room? Everything looks brighter. My aunt was into stuff like this.' He can't take his eyes off them.

I wonder if his aunt's cards are as powerful as mine. Perhaps they are. I'm waiting for him to elaborate more, but he doesn't. He just keeps holding them. Like he doesn't want to let them go.

'Forget about them, I'm more interested in kissing you. That is the best stress relief ever,' I say smiling up at him as I take them out of his hands.

He kisses me quickly and then pulls away. 'I heard you say you were terrified you were going to lose your job.'

'Oh, it's not important. I'm not sure why I said that … I didn't mean it,' I say.

I just want him to leave so he'll stop going on about the cards. I'm not ready to share my cards with anyone yet. There's a knock on the door. Emma walks in.

Now Emma's here, Jay might just forget about the cards. Emma has a knack of knowing exactly what to say. She's usually warm and flattering when she meets people for the first time.

'Jane, I came up to see your new office and to check how you're getting on,' she says in a loud voice. 'It's gorgeous! Well, what have we got here? You must be the lovely Jay. It's lovely to meet you.'

She shakes his hand, takes off her blazer and hitches up her skirt and leans against my desk.

'It's hot in here,' she says as she opens up the top three buttons of her blouse and fans herself with some paper from my desk. 'I'm excited to get to know you, Jay. I'm Jane's friend, Emma.'

The desk phone rings; it's one of my clients.

'Guys, can you move into the apartment so I can deal with this call? It's just over there through that door. Thanks a million,' I say as I point to the door.

The sound of laughter fills the air. They're having a great time. I've never heard Jay laugh that hard before when he's with me. What on earth is so funny?

I stand at the open dining room door once I finish the call. Emma is sitting facing Jay on the oak dining room table. Her head is thrown back, laughing hysterically. They haven't even noticed I'm in the room. I cough loudly to get their attention.

'Jane, you're back. This guy has the funniest stories from when he was a body builder. Not only is he super fit, but he's hilarious too. Did you know Colin Farrell was one of his clients before?' says Emma. 'He helped Colin get into shape for one of his movies.'

'No, I never knew that, Emma,' I say as I notice how he can't take his eyes off her. I start to feel jealous, but then I tell myself I'm just being silly. We're both crazy about each other. He's just a ladies' man.

Emma has always been a big flirt. In the early days, when I was convinced there was something going on between herself and Ben, I asked her about it over lunch one day, and she told me I was wrong to suggest such a thing.

'I'd never go there romantically, Jane, even if he wanted to, because I know how crazy you are about him, and I'd hate to ever hurt you,' she said. 'But you know what I think about Ben. You're far too nice for him. He's a womaniser who'd break your heart. Seriously, move on.'

I thought a few times he was interested in me, but Emma's words stuck in my head. When I found out he was going out with Sarah I was heartbroken anyway.

I need to relax about it and learn to trust Jay. He's my chance to get over Ben. Being his girlfriend has brought out a jealous side to me I don't like. I feel uneasy. My instincts tell me there's some sort of attraction between them and the way Emma is acting unnerves me.

Emma's loud voice brings me back to the present.

'This cryptocurrency you're developing is fascinating. I love working with computers Jay, and I've always wanted to learn how to code. Could you teach me some time? From what you've been describing, it must have cost a fortune,' she says. She flutters her eyelashes and rubs his arm.

'Sure ... any time,' he says. 'What about after the dinner you can both come back to my place and I can you show you how I have my machines set up?'

'When is this dinner on, Jane? I want to come too.'

'Oh, I've been meaning to ask you too, but you can come another time.'

'Just let me know the details and I'll be there. You must be crazy busy with work.'

'Yeah. I need to get an assistant. If you know of anyone suitable, let me know,' I say.

'My cousin works as a PA. She's just back from travelling around Australia and is looking for a new job. She's very diligent. She'd be perfect for the job,' she says.

'Great. Can you send her CV on to me? I'll set up an interview. I need to go to a lunch meeting with a client. Jay, you're welcome to stay in my apartment for a while if you like and I'll see you when I get back,' I say as I give him what I think is a cheeky wink.

'I think you have something in your eye, Jane. I'll take care of him for you. Let's go out for lunch together, Jay, so we can get to know each other. How's Gillian doing? She's having the time of her life lately. Any idea when the wedding will be?'

'The wedding will be pretty soon I think. She wants to be married before she's twenty-five.'

'Well, that's something to look forward to. Perhaps we can all go?'

'Hmmm … I'm not sure who will be invited. That's up to Gillian,' I say.

I wave goodbye and blow a kiss at Jay.

CHAPTER 17

BEN

SARAH GAVE ME A list of websites to go through to book our next holiday, but I can't get into it. They all seem the same to me. All five-star resorts in far flung beautiful places on sandy beaches. The truth is I don't want to go with her.

Something is going on with Jane and I can't stop thinking about her. Whatever it is, I've noticed she has a newfound confidence. There's this look in her eyes I've never seen before, it's like a gleam or a shine even.

There was a moment in Jane's office when I seriously considered kissing her, but when she mentioned Jay, I lost my nerve. I hate the thought of her going out with someone. It's making me unsettled. I've even thought about handing in my notice. The truth is, I don't think the promotion is for me, I don't need the money. It's all beginning to seem pretty pointless. It's obvious to me now that I only stayed there so long because of Jane.

Yesterday I decided to ditch work and just walked along the canal trying to make sense of everything. Hoping answers would come to me about whether I should just pack in my job and end things with Sarah. As I was turning the corner to walk back towards my apartment a homeless guy with a worn-out blanket stopped me in my tracks.

'Hey, man. What's the sad face for?' he said in a thick Dublin accent. I was in a world of my own, it took a few seconds to register he was referring to me.

'Jesus, I didn't see you there,' I said.

'No, but I noticed you. You seem like you have the weight of the world on your shoulders. What are you so worried about?'

'Ah, it's nothing important,' I said. There's no way my problems are any way relative to what this guy must be going through.

'Try me. A problem shared is a problem halved and all that.'

I stared at him for a while trying to decide whether I should just walk away or not. That's what I wanted to do, but he reminded me of myself. We had the same type of hair and build.

'Let me buy you a coffee and we can chat if you want,' I said and I held out my hand to help him up. His hands and fingernails were filthy.

'Sure, but it's on me. My name's Gerard, but my mates call me Gerry.'

He brought me to a soup kitchen where he queued while I sat and waited and thought how bizarre it was that I was surrounded by a load of homeless guys when I should have been working for money-greedy assholes in suits.

He brought me a cup of coffee and some toast, and we sat in silence for a while before I asked him how he ended up on the streets.

'I fell on hard times,' he said. 'Pure and simple. I've never been able to pick myself back up. So, what's your story?'

Fuck me. I wondered what I should do to help him.

'Ah, it's not important ...'

'Tell me why so glum lately, mate? What's your problem?

'Oh, I'm in love ... with someone I shouldn't be,' I said.

'Then just tell her. I see you walk past me most days and there was me thinking it was money you're chasing, but it's not money. It's love and all you need to do is tell her. Just do it.'

'Maybe I will,' I said. 'I'll wait until the time is right. She's still in love with her ex-boyfriend, Colm.'

'Forget about Colm. I'm telling you mate, take my advice. Open up. She'll soon forget about him. I know what I'm talking about.'

'Sure,' I said as I nodded my head. 'Thanks for the advice. Self-sabotage – that's my problem. I've slept with her best friend.'

'You don't need to bring up that. Just tell her now how you feel.'

'But she loves someone else.'

I look at Gerry who is staring into the distance, and I just see a genuine guy who wants to help me, but he has his own stuff going on. The least I can do is offer him the use of my place for a while.

'Do you want to come back to my place and I'll get you sorted with fresh clothes and a shower?'

He smiled at me and displayed a missing tooth. We left the café and headed back towards the apartment.

'Have you ever been in love yourself, Gerry?' I asked him.

He winced. 'Yeah, I was … with a woman named Martina. We were married for three years. She left me though … headed off to India to *find herself*. It was after that the depression kicked in, and I lost my job. I couldn't keep up with the mortgage repayments. The bank repossessed the house …'

'Ah, sorry to hear that, mate,' I said. My heart went out to the guy.

'I'm better off without her, mate. She always trying to change me. Always looking for more. I could never keep up. They're the ones to watch out for. If you find yourself getting involved with a woman like that run for the hills.'

When we got to my apartment, I gave Gerry clean clothes and he had a shower. I made him food, and we sat and chatted. I saw him for what he truly was. A nice guy who was down on his luck. I really wanted to help him get back on his feet. I suggested he stay with me for a while until he sorted himself out.

'Nah, I have a place to stay in a hostel. If I don't take it tonight, I could lose my spot. You've done enough, mate. You've given me a boost with the shower and the designer gear. I feel human again, now I've the courage to start looking for a job.'

I told him about my dad's bakeries in the city centre. 'I'll ask my dad to give you a job. If you call in and mention you're a friend of mine, it's a done deal,' I said.

His face lit up. He shook my hand. 'Thanks, mate,' he said. 'You're an awfully nice fella. You deserve to be happy. Make sure you tell that girl how you feel. She could be one of the good ones. Not like Martina.'

'I will,' I said.

We sat and had a few beers and watched the footie together. I dozed off, and when I woke up he had gone. It was clear now what I had to do about my feelings for Jane, and I called my dad and asked him to give Gerry a job.

CHAPTER 18

JANE

I FINISH MY MEETING AND go back to the bank. I read the latest emails from Walter. He thanks me for emailing the financial documents earlier. The tone of the emails aren't as angry. I breathe a sigh of relief, pick up the pack of cards and kiss them.

Crisis averted. I think I may have kept my job intact. The mulled wine I drank earlier has put me in a great mood. I send an email to Walter to impress him with the work I've completed so far. The cards were right, I am a hard worker and good at my job. I don't know why I was so worried earlier. I really thought I would get fired but obviously I was just over-reacting. I've noticed when things are going well with work, I feel on top of the world, but when things aren't I get this dreadful feeling that something dangerous is going to happen. As long I have my cards, though, I know I'll be okay.

I'm at Mamma Mia's Pizzeria in Dublin's Italian Quarter, waiting for the others to arrive for dinner. The smell of tomatoes, garlic and oregano makes my mouth drool. I'm starving, as I forgot to eat lunch. I order a Christmas cocktail and decide what I'm going to order – a ham and mozzarella pizza. The delicious dough with the slowly simmered sauce is to die for. The food here is fabulous. I've been here a few times with Ben and Emma for dinner before.

I can't concentrate on anything, so I just fidget with the cutlery on the table. I'm worried about how tonight is going to pan out with Jay meeting my friends. I've only met his friends once before when we went for drinks and Jay was slightly obnoxious in their company. I hope he's on his best behaviour tonight. For some reason I really want Ben to like him. It's almost like I want to show him how happy I am in another relationship. For so long I watched him with Sarah, and it tore me in two.

The restaurant is thronged with diners. The sounds of chatter, laughter and glasses clinking fill the room. A huge white decorated Christmas tree sits in the corner next to me, while the rest of the restaurant is decorated with sparkly white lights, ornaments, and icicles. Christmas garlands and wreaths are strewn all over the place. The restaurant has such a warm atmosphere, but I still can't relax.

What if tonight goes pear-shaped? What will happen then?

I wonder if the cards can make the night go well. I take the cards out of my handbag. 'Hello cards,' I say as I shuffle them, and ask for tonight to go smoothly.

The card I pick has the words **Death & Marriage** engraved on them. There's a picture of a pile of ashes and wedding bells. I read the back of the card.

> *This gathering will be the catalyst for the end and a new beginning. A significant change is coming and how you handle this will determine the outcome. Do not resist these changes, otherwise the outcome will be distressing.*

Death! Does that mean someone here is going to die? This is serious. What have I done? I pace up and down the restaurant, counting over and over again. Maybe I can fix this. If I ask the cards to change the outcome maybe this will all go away, but then I remember the note. It said I must take the advice. This is it. I've no choice but to see what unfolds.

I'm shaking when Ben and Sarah enter the restaurant. I wave over to them, and they make their way towards me. Sarah gives me a hug. She's wearing a sparkly long-sleeved dress with ballet flats. Her long black hair frames her pretty face. Standing beside Ben's tall build, she looks tiny.

'Well, where is he then? Where's this guy you really wanted us to meet?' he says as he pushes out the chair to sit down on it. He's wearing jeans and a shirt.

'You could at least say hello to Jane first instead of speaking so abruptly,' says Sarah as she nudges Ben. They're on edge, I can tell. I'm trying to push everything about the cards out of my mind and just focus on Ben and Sarah, but I wonder who's going to die.

Am I?

'Oh, Jay's not here yet, but he'll be here soon. He's looking forward to meeting you both,' I say. My voice is shaky. I feel queasy.

'Are you alright?' says Ben. 'You look like you've seen a ghost.'

'Yeah, I'm fine,' I reply quietly. I'm not fine though. I don't know how I'm going to get through the night after getting that message.

'I love your dress, Jane. Ben told me about your new office apartment. It sounds amazing.'

'Thanks. I love it. It even has a four-poster bed. The cleaners even come in and scrub it from top to bottom every day. No more housework for me. Ha-ha!' I sound more normal now; perhaps if I just focus on enjoying myself, I can get through this.

'You work so hard,' she says.

'She sure does,' says Ben smiling at me, 'but Jay doesn't even have the decency to turn up on time though. Why is he so late?'

He storms off to the bathroom and Sarah moves closer to me and lowers her voice.

'I must apologise for his behaviour. This past while he has been in awful form. By the time he gets home from work, after stopping off at the gym, I'm lucky if I even get a word out of him.'

'That's not like Ben,' I say.

'I know. He doesn't even want to eat dinner with me in the evenings anymore. He tells me he's eaten a big dinner in work which he never did before. I'm sure all the girls in the office fawn over him. Do they?'

'I don't know.'

'Your face is very red. It's hot in here, maybe we could turn the heating down.'

'No. I'm fine,' I say, quieter this time.

'You know, I think Ben has lived such a charmed life. Everything comes so easy to him. Sometimes he needs a bit of a push to figure things out.'

'A push. What do you mean by a push?'

'I want more of a commitment. I believe he wants more too, but he's scared to ask me to marry him in case I say no, and that's why he's in such a bad mood all the time. Or maybe he is questioning what he wants out of our relationship. I'm a lot older than Ben. I know I don't look it but I'm nearly thirty. What do you think?'

'I think … hmmm … what do I think? I really don't know, Sarah.'

Marriage! That must be what the card relates to. Ben and Sarah are going to get married … this means the death part might come true. I hate to think of Ben getting married, but at least that means he's not going to die. Sarah's not either. I feel sick. Physically sick.

Who is going to die?

I'm panicky and count quickly to myself.

'Do you think I should propose to him? Then I'll know either way. I'm so ready to get married. Ben's coming back from the bathroom. Please keep this quiet, Jane. Don't mention our conversation to him.'

Don't propose to him, I want to say, but I don't. Instead, I just say nothing and keep counting to myself in my head.

Ben walks back to the table and taps his watch.

'Still no sign of this guy. He's forty minutes late now. Let's just go ahead and order. I'm starving,' he says.

I'm afraid I'm going to have a panic attack, so I go outside and breathe gulps of air. Perhaps no one will die. Maybe the card means something else. Whatever happens there's nothing I can do, otherwise I'll make it worse. I check my watch, willing the time to move faster so I can leave soon.

I go inside and then Jay and Emma stumble into the restaurant. Jay sits beside me. I can smell the alcohol off him. Emma puts her hands on Jay's chair to hold herself up. She's swaying.

'Guys, I'm so sorry. This is my fault. We ended up having a few drinks over lunch and one drink led to another and we lost track of time. Sarah, Ben, it's great to see you … how about I order us some shots,' she says slurring her words. She stumbles off to get a waiter's attention.

I can feel Ben's eyes piercing through me. The good impression I thought Jay would make on them obviously hasn't happened.

'Jay, these are my friends, Ben and Sarah.'

'Hi guys,' he slurs and waves his hand in the air. He kisses me on the forehead and then presses his forehead against mine. His eyes are red and bloodshot, and he reeks of a sweet whiskey like the one my mam used to drink.

'Emma sure knows how to party. She was piling the drinks into me over lunch. I've no disposable cash so do you mind paying the bill for me tonight?' he shouts as he picks up some slices of my pizza and shoves it into his mouth. Some pieces of mushroom fall to the floor and land on my shoes.

'No worries,' I say although I'm fuming inside.

Not only am I annoyed with Jay and Emma, but I'm particularly mortified by Jay's carry on. Ben is horrified, I can tell by the look on his face. He hasn't said a word yet to Jay which isn't a good sign.

'When I'm a millionaire I'm going to give you everything you want. I'll look after you. You know that, don't you?' He squeezes my two cheeks with his fingers and rubs my head, messing my hair and leaving two bright red stinging marks on my cheeks. 'So how do you know my girlfriend?' he says staring at Ben with his mouth full of my pizza.

'I work with her in the bank.'

That's it. There's no *it's nice to meet you, Jay*. Ben hates him, I can tell.

'I'm going to wipe out the banks, just you wait and see.' He points his finger at Ben and Sarah.

'How are you going to do that exactly?' says Sarah, fascinated by his statement.

'When I take over the world with my cryptocurrency. Isn't that right, Jane? You'll never need to work again.' He slings his arm over my shoulder, drawing me tightly towards him. 'I was telling Emma all about it earlier. She agrees with me. I'm onto something special.'

'What exactly is cryptocurrency?' says Sarah.

'It's a digital currency that's stored on a computerised database with strong cryptography. The beauty of it is that it's not reliant on any central authority, such as a government or a bank to maintain it.'

'Wow! That sounds complicated.'

'There's nothing more you need to know apart from the fact that my cryptocurrency will be smoother, faster and easier to use than any other one out there. If you invest with me you'll double your money.'

'Double. That's amazing. What do you think, Ben? How much should we invest?' says Sarah.

'No thanks, mate. Cryptocurrency is not my thing,' says Ben.

Jay bangs his fist down on the table which makes everything on the table shudder. Sarah's cocktail glass falls to the floor, shattering into pieces, just missing her leg by half an inch. The drink splatters up her legs.

'Watch yourself there, Jay,' says Ben raising up from his seat.

'I don't know what you're on about, mate. Can you sit back down, eat your food and let me enjoy my night with my girlfriend and her friends please?'

He reaches out and holds my hand. A moment of silence passes. The tension starts to build. It's really awkward. I wasn't expecting Jay to act like this. He's coming across like a fool over his cryptocurrency.

'Be careful … you made Sarah's drink fall,' I whisper to him, but he just looks at me blankly. 'I'm sorry, Sarah. Here let me try to get someone to clean this up,' I say as I get up from my seat. Jay pulls me back down and kisses me again.

I want to tell him to stop, but I don't want to cause a scene. I'm hoping Emma knows how to smooth over the situation. Hmmm … maybe not. She looks just as wasted as Jay. I pull Jay away from the group and try to talk some sense into him.

'He was slagging off my cryptocurrency. How fucking dare he …'

'Stop, Jay. Ben's a nice guy. He didn't mean anything bad. It's just not his thing.'

'I'll show him. When I take over the banks he'll be sorry he missed out.'

'Come on … stop.'

Another glass is slammed down on the table, but this time by Emma. She's carrying a tray with ten tequila shots and drops the tray on the table over the rest of my food. I glare at her, but like Jay she's oblivious to what she's just done.

'Guys, you need to lighten up a bit. Jane and Ben, you look like two boring old accountants. Nothing a few drinks can't fix. Get the shots into you and I'll organise some more cocktails. Hey waiter, over here.' She wolf-whistles at the waiter. 'I want a pitcher of your best Christmas cocktail with five straws please.'

Once the pitcher arrives, she makes us drink through the straws. She pushes our heads together until we drink it all in one go. The image from the card I picked earlier flashes through my mind. Emma wraps her arms around Ben and wiggles her hips in front of him. Sarah's disgusted.

'Let's have some fun. I wanna dance with somebody. Did Jane tell you about her sister Gillian?' Emma shouts over to Jay. 'She's a professional dancer as well as actress. Come on, Jane, show us how you can dance like your sister.'

'I can't dance. I have two left feet.'

She grabs our hands and drags us off to a small dance floor in the restaurant next to the Christmas tree. She takes my handbag and swings it around over her head. Then she dances around it. I rush back to the table where Ben and Sarah are sitting. This night can't get any worse.

'Ben, Jay's not normally like this. I guess he just had too much to drink.'

'It's okay,' says Sarah. 'He's just drunk. I'm sure he's a nice guy. He's gorgeous looking. He can't stop kissing you. We can meet him another time.'

'Your boyfriend is a gobshite, Jane. An absolute gobshite,' says Ben shouting.

'Ah, Ben, don't be like that. Will you both come out and dance with us once you finish your food?' I say. 'I'm going to leave then.'

'Sure, we will. When was the last time we danced together?' says Sarah.

'Dance? I wouldn't call what those two crazies are doing dancing. The state of them. Emma has your handbag on her head, Jane.'

'Ben, you need to lighten up. You're dancing with me after we finish our food, and we are going to have some fun tonight.' Sarah kisses him.

My stomach turns sour, and I feel off. It must be all the drink on an empty stomach.

CHAPTER 19

I WAKE UP IN BED, alone. My mouth is dry, and my head is pounding. Water, I need water, I croak. There's tinsel in my hair and around my neck. I'm still wearing my clothes from the night before. So, I didn't die. I'm alive even though I feel like death. I've never handled hangovers well.

The last thing I remember is dancing around the Christmas tree in the restaurant and then drinking more shots. Emma kept buying them for me – to show me how grateful she was that I got her job back. I've no recollection of how I got back to my old apartment.

What time is it even? Nine am. I'm going to be so late for work. I need to get moving.

As I grab my phone, I notice a load of text messages from Sorcha.

> Jane. A new guy started working at the hospital. He's a neurologist called Matt. He's known for being the best in his field.
> Anyway ... I got chatting with him yesterday and he told me he's just moved from Perth. He knows no one in Sydney, so I offered to show him around the city.
> At the end of my shift there was a bouquet of flowers waiting for me in the office from him. What a nice guy.
> I think I'm in love! And it's all thanks to your cards.

> I'm delighted for you, I reply. Will call you soon. X

This is major news. Sorcha has found it hard to meet guys before, she hates nightclubs and prefers quiet drinks with a few friends. She's never really had a proper boyfriend.

After I get dressed for work, I check in my handbag for my cards, but they're not there.

This can't be happening. I need my cards. I want to find my cards – and where is Jay? I call him, but there's no answer. I try again and again, but no luck. My iPhone rings. It's Emma.

'Well Jane, how's the head? You were drinking shots like water last night.'

'Hmm … last night was a bit of a blur. I can't get through to Jay. Do you know what happened to him?'

'No. I thought he was with you. I still can't get over how Ben was with him.'

'He's not with me,' I say as my voice rises. 'What did Ben do to Jay?'

'He was so rude. At one stage, Ben threatened to get him kicked out of the restaurant. They almost had a bust-up.'

'I don't remember that. Where did Jay go?'

'You and Jay went off in a taxi at the end of the night about half past eleven.'

'He's not with me. I've tried calling him, but there's no answer.' I'm slightly hysterical now. He must be dead. That's the only explanation.

Where else could he be?

'That's weird, but I'm sure he'll call you back. Listen, my cousin really wants to be your assistant. She read the *Forbes* article and was really impressed. How about I tell her to come in today, and I'll set her up so she can at least answer your phone until you get in. It will take the pressure off you a bit.'

'Sure. Thanks Emma. I'm worried about Jay. Something really bad must have happened to him. Why else is he not answering my calls?'

'Relax. I'm sure he's fine. I'm in work now so I'll pop up to your office and get things sorted for Adele.'

'I need to get moving. I hope Walter isn't looking for me.'

'Here's Ben, coming in. I still can't get over the nerve of him yesterday. Sarah must be a saint putting up with him.'

'I got to go.'

I can't listen to her giving out about Ben. I just want my cards. I could wish for Jay to call me back and tell me he's okay.

What if he's dead?

He can't be. He just can't be.

I ring the restaurant, and they tell me the cards aren't there.

CHAPTER 20

WHEN I GET INTO work, Emma is on the phone with her feet up on my desk. The drink from the night before is seeping through my pores and my face feels itchy and sore. I'm dressed down. She's wearing one of her power suits and is acting all bright and breezy.

'Jane, you owe me one, big time. That was Walter on the phone looking for you. I didn't know Anderson & Co was one of your clients. Anyway, Walter needed some of their financial reports and I found them in a file in your desk drawer. So I saved your ass, big time.'

'Thanks. I've a pretty bad hangover.'

'Oh, right. Well, do you want to go have a shower and fix yourself?

'No. I'm grand. I've so much work to get done today. I'll just crack on with it. It will take my mind off everything.'

'I can look after things here. Walter seems to really like me. We had a great chat earlier.'

'What did you say to him? Did you tell him where I was?'

'He just asked for the Anderson files. I told him I was helping you for a while.'

'Was he angry?'

'No. He was lovely.'

'Great. Thanks. Still no word from Jay. He must have about ten missed calls from me at this stage. What if he's dead lying in a ditch somewhere? I'm so worried about him.'

'I'm sure he's just asleep with a dead phone battery.'

Maybe she knows where my cards are. If I don't find them soon I'm going to explode.

'I lost something when we were out last night.'

'What did you lose?' She frowns.

'I lost a pack of cards.'

'A pack of cards? Right, so just get yourself another pack.'

'I can't just get another pack. The cards mean a lot to me. They have meaning. They're magic.'

'Magic! Are you still drunk, Jane?' she says.

'No … the cards are important. Very important. I need to find them.'

'Jane, you need to get a grip of yourself. Seriously,' she says as she holds on to my arms tightly, 'you're over-reacting. I've got a meeting to go to. I can't be late. I'll leave you to it.'

How can I get a grip of myself when my cards are missing? She has no idea what they mean to me. I stare at my iPhone willing it to ring, to prove to me that Jay is not dead.

A glamorous twenty-something-year-old comes out of the dining room area. She holds out her arm to shake my hand and her bangles jingle. She's wearing an off-the-shoulder yellow top and skirt. Her bronze tan glistens and glows. She has a large cup of coffee in her other hand.

'Hi Jane, I'm Adele. Emma's cousin.' She licks her lips and flicks back her long brown curly hair.

'Hi Adele. Thanks for coming in at such short notice. Let's get straight to the interview.' I'm trying to come across as a sane person.

'Can I get you anything? You look a bit … well … under the weather,' she says.

'No thanks,' I say, and settle into the interview.

I'm getting more and more anxious as the day goes on and the fear starts to kick in. By the time Ben knocks on my door for lunch I'm close to tears. Adele leaves to take her lunch break as Ben walks in the door. His dark hair is gelled back, and he's wearing a light grey trouser suit with a white shirt and grey tie.

'Who's that girl?' he says as he sits on the couch beside me.

'Ah, that's Adele. My new assistant, she's Emma's cousin.'

'Emma's cousin?'

'Jay's gone missing. Emma told me he left in a taxi with me last night, but he wasn't there when I woke up this morning.' My voice is rising, and my speech is getting faster with every breath. 'I think he might have di—'

'He didn't go home with you in a taxi,' he says.

'How do you know?'

'I know because I brought you home.'

'What? Why did you bring me home?'

'Emma and Jay disappeared off somewhere and you were so drunk. You got a taxi home with me and Sarah. We helped you get into your apartment.'

'I don't get it. Emma said—'

'She's lying, Jane.'

'I don't remember any of this, Ben. It's like I had a blackout.'

'Emma was piling the drinks into you. You could hardly walk towards the end of the night.'

'But I woke up in my bed this morning. How did I get there?'

'Sarah and I put you to bed.'

'You did?'

I'm noticing a side to Emma now that I never knew. I need my cards and I want to know where Jay is.

'Where did Jay go? I need to know he's okay.'

'I have no idea.'

'I want to talk to Jay, but he won't answer his stupid phone.'

'Jane, calm down. I'm sure he'll call you soon.'

'There's something else. I've lost something … something very valuable, and I have no idea where they are.' My voice is shrill, almost hysterical.

'What did you lose?'

'Something that means a lot to me and if I can't find it – well, I don't know what will happen.'

'What did you lose?'

'Maybe Jay has them, maybe he found them and is keeping them safe. If only he would call me back.'

'Jay has what exactly? Tell me what's going on.'

'I lost my cards, Ben and I need them back,' I say as the tears flow.

'I know you're hungover, but this is a bit of an over-reaction.'

'You don't understand. No one understands. I need my cards back.' My tears land on his suit jacket.

'There's no need to cry. You've been under a lot of pressure lately, with your new job and Jay. It's all happened so fast.'

'I have to find them.'

'Jane, listen to yourself. A pack of playing cards can be replaced.'

'No, they can't. The ones I had were special. Tara, the owner of Hidden Secrets, gave them to me.'

Tara. Tara will know what to do. Maybe she has another pack of cards she can give me that I can use to get my old ones back.

'I need to go see Tara.'

'Let me come with you. I want to help.'

'No. It's probably best I go on my own,' I say as I grab my stuff and rush out the door.

When I get to Hidden Secrets, it's different to the last time I visited. There's a long queue of people at the till. People are agitated and irritated. There's no smells of Christmas drinks or mulled wine anymore. I find out from Gus that Tara is sick. She collapsed earlier that morning and was brought to the hospital in an ambulance.

'I don't know anything else, Jane. I called the hospital to get an update on how she is doing, but they won't tell me anything as I'm not family.'

'I need to speak to her urgently. Please tell me what hospital she's in. I need to see her.' I get down on my knees in front of him and grab his arms. 'Please, please Gus.'

'There's no point, they won't let you in. Jane, seriously you need to calm down. You're in a right state.'

'You don't understand—'

'I have to go. We're short-staffed. I'm rushed off my feet.'

I leave the bookshop in a daze. All I can think about is finding Tara. I decide to call all the hospitals in Dublin and maybe I'll find her then. Someone behind me puts their hand on my shoulder.

'I know you told me not to come, but I was worried about you,' says Ben.

'Tara's sick. She's in hospital somewhere. I don't know where, and I need to track her down. She can help me find my cards,' I say.

'You need to relax about the cards.'

'Can you help me call the hospitals? If we both do it, it will be quicker.'

He grabs my shoulders and looks me directly in the eyes. 'Maybe your drink was spiked last night. I think you need to take the rest of the day off work and just go for a sleep. Sleep this off, whatever it is. Did Jay give you something?'

'No. How can I sleep when my cards are missing? Jay is missing and now Tara.'

'Did you take any funny stuff last night?'

'Jay has gone. I think he's dead. Tara's gone. She could be dead. My cards have gone,' I shout, 'and you're going to get married and then you'll go too.'

'I'm not getting married. I'm hardly marriage material. With parents like mine … they've put me off marriage for life.'

'The cards are bigger than me. They are bigger than all of us. I am nothing without them.'

I scream in the middle of the street.

'I WANT MY CARDS BACK.'

CHAPTER 21

BEN

A PACK OF CARDS IS just paper. It doesn't have any power, but something is making her act crazy. Her screaming attracts a crowd that gathers around us. People are whispering and staring. Pointing at us. I'm afraid someone will call the Gardaí, so I hold onto her until her screams became raspy. A group of passers-by stop and ask if they can do anything to help.

'She's just upset. She'll be fine,' I say to anyone that asks, but that doesn't stop them from staring.

All I want to do is to get her home. Once she's home, I know I can calm her down. All the people coming up to us are putting me off.

'I'm worthless without my cards, Ben. I can't cope without them,' she says, over and over again.

'No, you're not,' I reply.

'I had my cards and then puff, like magic, I got everything I asked for.'

'They're not magic. They can't be. We need to go.' From the corner of my eye, I see a Garda car. I grab her hand and we move down a side street.

'The cards made me feel powerful and strong.' She stops and leans against a wall.

'You're powerful and strong even without the cards. Here's my handkerchief to wipe your eyes. We need to go now.'

'I thought no one carried these around anymore.' She sniffles and takes it from me and wipes away her tears.

'For what it's worth, do you want to know what I think?' I say.

'Go on, tell me.'

'The Jane I know is smart, hardworking and logical. Which are all qualities that would attract a promotion. I'm surprised you didn't get one sooner. I can also see how Jay was attracted to you.'

'I'm flattered Ben, but you still don't get it. You don't understand what my cards mean to me. I can't be without them. I can't—' She shakes her head. 'I think Jay's dead.'

'Dead? Where are you getting that from?'

'The cards told me someone is going to die,' she says. A shiver runs through me, but all I can think of is calming Jane down.

'Look, you're not thinking straight. I'll take you home, and call Walter and tell him you're not feeling well.'

'He won't like that. He likes me to be on call 24/7. I'm never sick. I need to go back to work.'

'You can take a day off. One day won't matter. He can do without you for one day—'

'But Emma's cousin, she'll be left on her own.'

'I'll deal with it. Anyway, it's starting to rain. Let's go.'

I'm delighted for the rain as the crowd start to walk away and there is no sign of the Gardaí anymore. We arrive back to Jane's apartment and the mess is the first thing that I notice when we walk in. For someone who is organised in work she doesn't take care of herself at home. She's a total workaholic. She goes straight to bed and hands me her spare key.

I take off my jacket, roll up the sleeves and clean. After that I stock up on a few groceries. A few hours later Jane wakes up and I make her a cup of tea and toast.

'You were out like a light. Did you sleep well?' I say as she slumps back on the couch and sips her tea.

'Yeah, but I heard noises. Really loud noises … they woke me up, but they're gone now.'

'That's weird. There's no one here. Only me. I didn't want to leave until I knew you were all right.'

'I hear noises sometimes when I'm asleep. They wake me up.'

'Does it happen much?' I say.

'Only since I got the cards. I wish they would go away. I wish I had my cards so I could just make it all stop.' She places her hands on her forehead as if she has a migraine. 'I thought I was being followed, but I'm not. At least, I don't think I am …'

There's no way these cards are magic. There were no noises the whole time I was here.

'Have you ever talked to anyone about the noise thing?' I say.

'Only Tara. It's just one of my fears. As well as the good, the cards bring out people's fears. I'm afraid of loud noises.'

'Maybe someone might be able to help you figure it out. Like a professional. Instead of using the cards. I've heard hypnotherapy is good—'

'So, you think I'm a raving lunatic now who needs professional help. I'm not. I just want my cards and to get Jay back.'

I sit down beside her. I lean over and nudge her with my elbow. That never fails to make her laugh. 'That's better. A smile. It's great to see you smile again,' I say.

'You're not as funny as you think you are Ben.' She laughs.

'You could just be paranoid about being followed – as you live alone. Or it might not mean that at all, Jane. I'm just speculating, but you'll be able to solve this without the cards.'

'But the cards are the only thing that have helped me get what I want.'

I'm exhausted as this point, and she's going on and on about the cards. She's still not herself. Her hands are shaky, and her eyes are watering up. I'm convinced she's coming down from some hallucinogenic drugs.

'Do you want me to stay with you for a bit? It might take your mind off the noises and the cards for a while.'

'Sure, okay. I'm starving.'

'I'll make you something to eat. I bought lots of food. Let's see what I have got here. Ham, mushroom, and mozzarella pizza? You never got to eat yours at the restaurant yesterday. Or I could just order us a takeaway if you prefer …'

Before I can finish my sentence, I hear a bang and then we're both engulfed in darkness. I can't really see. We try to turn back on the lights, but the electricity isn't working. I check to see if it was a fuse that blew out, but they all appear fine. I use the torch on my iPhone to search in a kitchen cupboard for some candles. I find six small tea light candles and light them. Jane's facc is slightly visible to me.

CHAPTER 22

JANE

I'M GRATEFUL THAT BEN is here right now otherwise I would be seriously spooked out.

'Why is the electricity gone?' I say.

'I've no idea, but I'm glad you had candles.' His voice is low and soft.

Someone knocks on the door. A loud insistent knock. We both stand there in silence. A face appears at the window. The air feels cold. I shiver. There's another loud knock.

'What do they want? I don't want to answer the door. It could be anyone. What should we do?' I grab hold of Ben's arm.

'Calm down,' he says as he touches my arm. 'It's probably just the takeaway delivery guy. I ordered a takeaway for us when you were on the phone trying to get through to Jay.'

'Can you check?'

He opens the door and I hear muffled voices as I wait for him to return. It feels like he's gone for hours even though it's probably been a few minutes. He brings in some pizza boxes and sits beside me.

'I had a look outside. All your neighbours seem to have lights on. Your place must be the only one without electricity,' he says.

'I wonder why I'm the only one,' I say.

What if my cards did this? I don't know how or why; I wonder if they are trying to communicate with me. They could be trying to tell me where they are.

'Let's just wait and see what happens. Let's eat. You must be starving,' he says.

We sit close with a blanket wrapped around us and eat. Sitting in candlelight feels surreal. His iPhone keeps beeping. He frowns each time he checks it. I hope he doesn't need to leave soon. There are shadows in the spaces where the light of the candle doesn't reach. I've always hated the dark ever since I was a kid. Is that a face in the mirror? It's gone now. Maybe it's just a trick of the light.

'That was Sarah, she's wondering where I am,' he says.

'Do you have to go now?' I ask crossing my fingers.

'Well, that depends on you. Do you want me to stay?'

'Yeah … can you stay with me a bit? The candlelight is a bit off-putting.'

'How about I stay the night? You've had a tough day and your electricity is gone. I'll sleep on the couch.'

'I'd like that, but will Sarah mind?'

'I'll text her and tell her I'm staying over in Tim's place.'

'Tim, who worked with us?'

'Yeah, I've stayed there before after nights out. She won't mind if I say I'm staying there. I just don't want to worry her …'

'Sure …'

I wake in the middle of the night by the usual noises that torment my mind. I stumble into the living room. Ben's asleep on the couch. He wakes up when I sit on the edge of the couch. He's naked apart from his underwear. It's pitch black in the living room. I tell him I heard the noises again. He lights a candle and checks the apartment, but there's no one there.

I get back into bed and Ben sits beside me on top of the duvet covers and reassures me. He holds my hand as he touches my hair.

'You're safe, Jane,' he says. 'Try to get some sleep. There's no one else here.'

He leans over and kisses my forehead, but I move, and our lips meet instead. He lies down beside me as we kiss. It's fast and deep. He wraps his arms around me and then his hands move up and down my body with urgency.

I turn away and cry out Jay's name.

'I'm sorry.' He stops. 'I don't know what I was thinking. You're in love with Jay.'

'I wasn't expecting that,' I say.

'I shouldn't have done that. You don't need this right now. I'm sorry ... Jane. I'm an idiot.'

'You're not an idiot.'

'The timing is all wrong.'

'We're just friends. You have no idea how long I liked you, but I've moved on.'

'Friends ...' He laughs. 'You have no idea how long I've wanted to kiss you.'

'I ... I love Jay.'

'You're in love with Jay ...' He lies on his back and stares at the ceiling avoiding my eyes. 'I wish I knew you liked me before. It would have changed everything.'

'I couldn't tell you. Every time I tried to, I chickened out. I thought you'd never be interested in me.'

He looks at me with such intensity I avoid his gaze. 'I've loved you ever since the first time I met you.'

Is this true? He's also in love with Sarah. I frown trying to make sense of everything.

'I only came here to help you. I don't want to confuse you or hurt you—'

'You did help me. You've always been a good friend to me, Ben, but you and Sarah, I thought you were happy together.'

'We were happy, but not anymore.'

I've so many questions to ask him, like is this just a one-night thing to him. What am I to him? Is this the first time he has cheated on her?

My iPhone rings, interrupting my thoughts. I'm about to knock it off to just focus on Ben, but then I realise it's Jay.

He's alive.

Thank God for that.

'Jay, thank God. It's you. I was so worried about you. Did you see all my missed calls?'

'Yeah. I saw your calls.' His voice has an awful coldness to it.

'Where did you go last night?'

'I didn't call you back as I needed time to think.'

'You don't sound like yourself. Where are you?'

'I'm at home.'

'So, you're not lying in a ditch somewhere.'

'No. I'm not.'

'There's a voice in the background. Is there someone there with you?'

'No … ehm … it's the, the TV,' he says.

'What did you need to think about?'

He's going to break up with me. I know he is. I need to change his mind. I need to tell him everything will be okay.

'Us. I need time to think about us.'

'What does that mean?'

I wait for his reply but there's none.

'Jay …'

'Do you trust me, Jane?'

'I … I don't understand what's going on.'

'I want to know, what do you think of my cryptocurrency idea?'

What does his cryptocurrency have to do with our relationship?

'I don't know, Jay. I told you already what I thought.'

'I took your advice. You know your stuff.'

'Yeah, but I deal with big clients with multi-million-euro investments, I don't deal with cryptocurrency.'

'So, you have access to a lot of their information.'

This conversation is getting bizarre. Why is he so interested in my work suddenly?

'Yes, I do, but it's confidential – and what has this got to do with us?'

'How did you get that job?'

'I told you before, I got promoted recently.'

'And before that Emma told me she was your boss.'

What is this leading to?

'What has Emma got to do with us?'

'Where did you get the cards?'

'I … I … I can't remember,' I say.

'I've had a breakthrough with my cryptocurrency business today. I'm on the cusp of making millions. I just need people to invest and build confidence in my brand. Will you come and work with me and help me get clients to invest?'

I don't want to give up what I have in the bank. Anyway, I think cryptocurrency is as risky as hell. There's no way I would ever invest in it.

'I'm not sure,' I say.

'So, you don't trust me?'

'I'm not saying that.'

'Are you with me or not?'

'I want to see you.'

Once we are together everything will be okay again.

'Will you help me with my crypto business?'

'Sure, I'll help you, but I'm not leaving my job.'

'I need space. We need a break.'

'A break?' He can't be serious. This conversation is knocking me sideways. 'A break from what?'

'A break from us. You and me.'

'So, you're breaking up with me ... you told me you loved me.'

'I did love you. I do love you. I just need time alone.'

'We were meant to spend Christmas together. We had plans made.'

'I need to focus on my business now. It's all I can think about. I'm asking you to come and work with me and we can still be together, but you're not interested.'

'So, if I worked with you, we would still be together.'

'Well, it would change things. We would be working towards a shared goal.'

'Jay, none of this makes any sense. This doesn't even sound like you.'

I need my cards back. They're the only thing that can put this right. I wonder if Jay knows where they are.

'I have other priorities now.' He coughs.

'I had my cards in my handbag last night. Did you see them? I've lost them.'

'No. I didn't.'

'There's nothing left for me to say then, apart from have a nice life. Goodbye.'

'It doesn't need to be this way—'

He's still talking but I cut him off mid-sentence. My hands are shaking, and I want to throw up. I am panicky. Disoriented and dizzy. My mouth is dry, while I'm sweating.

Ben is lying beside me, he's heard every word. I wonder how he can appear so calm and relaxed when my whole world is falling apart. How can Jay dump me over the phone like that? I've done nothing wrong, but he still broke up with me. I feel like he just tore out my heart and stepped all over it. Did he really love me like he said? Maybe it was all in my head. Did I misunderstand something or come on too strong? He asked me to spend Christmas with him, though. Why would he do that if he didn't mean it? That's a big thing to ask someone. If I could just see him, I know it would be okay.

I want to just get up and go to his cottage. What if he doesn't answer the door?

He might think I'm stalking him.

My mind continues to race with my thoughts. Ben puts his arm around me.

'That was Jay on the phone,' I say, shaking.

'I gathered that. Does he have your cards?'

'No. He doesn't. He broke up with me. It's over between us,' I whisper as I take his arm away.

'You're better off without him.' His voice is soft and tender. He searches my eyes. 'You're too good for a gobshite like him.'

'I don't get why he ended this. He told me he loved me. He only wants to see me now if I work on his cryptocurrency business.'

'Jane, that's not real love. He's a selfish prick.' He raises his voice and narrows his eyes.

'He blindsided me. I didn't see that coming. I wonder what I did wrong.'

'How could you know that was coming? He was all over you at the dinner last night. He couldn't keep his hands off you.'

'I loved him, Ben. I still do. I believed him when he told me he loved me.'

'That wasn't love.'

'How do you know what I felt?' My voice is rising with anger. I want to lash out. I want to shout and scream.

'I could never treat someone I love the way he has just acted towards you,' he says.

Lucky Ben. Not everyone is as perfect or as privileged as him. I turn to him in fury.

'Apart from last night you never saw us together.' My expression softens once I notice he's upset. Why is he upset?

'I'm sorry. I just care about you and hate the thought of anyone hurting you.' He coughs to clear his throat and the room is filled with silence.

'Let's just get some sleep,' he says eventually, and then he turns his back to me.

'Was this just a one-night thing to you?' I sit up on the bed. 'What are you looking for from me? You already have a girlfriend.'

'Nothing … forget about it. I don't want anything from you.'

'Fine then.' I turn my back to him and try to go to sleep.

CHAPTER 23

I WAKE UP TO THE bright sunlight shining in through the windows. A warm glow runs through me, but then I remember Jay broke up with me and I'm brought back to earth with a jolt. There's an empty space beside me. Ben left while I was asleep. There's no traces of him left in my apartment. Not even a note. My electricity is back on. I don't want to be on my own today. I call Ben several times, but he doesn't answer. I go back to bed and wonder what I'm going to do today. I'm in no frame of mind to go to work. Not when my cards and Tara are missing. I try to formulate plans to find them, but everything in my head is muddled and makes no sense. I send an email to Walter to tell him I won't be back in the office today. All I want to do is to go to the bookshop to get answers as to Tara's whereabouts. Tara is the only one who can help me find the cards and get Jay back.

As I leave my apartment on Clanbrassil Street the rain is lashing down. I don't mind the rain. I actually enjoy walking in the rain. I hear loud footsteps behind me, but every time I turn around there's no one there. It's like I'm being followed. I can almost hear someone's breath on my neck. I walk quicker to see if that makes a difference. The street is empty as I quicken my pace, yet I get the eerie sense that someone is close to pounding on me. I remember hearing before that if you think you're being following you should turn four corners and see if that deters them. On the fourth corner someone brushes against me. The girl from before, wearing the red coat, runs past me. Her coat hood is up, but from the back I can see her pigtails sticking out of the hood.

The rain gets heavier, and I realise I'm completely lost. It's lashing as if sheets of glass are crashing down from the sky. I'm soaked from head to toe. I turn another corner and at the bottom of the lane I recognise Hidden Secrets. The atmosphere changes, as does the rain. It becomes misty and cold. A face appears in the rain. An unusual face. It's like the face of the girl. I hear someone call my name.

'Jane, Jane, help me,' says a child's voice. I look around, but no one's there.

I walk towards the bookshop and the girl is sitting on the doorstep of the shop. She has her arms clasping her knees and her head drawn in towards them.

She calls out to me.

'Help me, Jane. Help me.'

I run over to her. She's soaking wet.

How does she know my name?

When I get to the doorstep, the girl has gone. It's like she disappeared into thin air.

Through the large window I see Tara. She's sitting in the red armchair staring out at the rain with a soft pale blue blanket around her knees. Although she's looking out the window, she doesn't see me. She's glancing at something far away in the distance.

I rush over to her. I wrap my arms around her and hug her tightly. She's fragile and thin. I stand back, afraid that I might break her if I hold her too hard.

'Tara ... I missed you so much,' I gush.

'I was sick for a while, but it was my own fault. I'm afraid I've been overdoing it a little. I need to take it a bit easier ... I collapsed.'

She has dark circles under her eyes and her hands and face appear to have more wrinkles than usual. She's not as well dressed as she usually is. Today she is wearing a long plain black dress. It seems the last few days have taken their toll on her. She's sicker than ever.

'Why are you working today? You should be home in bed.'

'I couldn't stay away from the place, I'm afraid. I want to keep busy. Anyway, they ran some tests when I was in the hospital, and

I'm as fit as a fiddle. Well, as fit as you can be for an old fogey. They have given me bags of medicine to help with my cough. I need to shift this thing.' She shakes her head as she wheezes. 'For some reason or other this cough just seems to linger. I have no idea why.'

'You should slow down, Tara. You do too much. If you don't start looking after yourself, you'll get burnt out. Your mind, body and soul need to be balanced—'

Tara laughs at my rambling. 'Where is this all coming from?'

'The cards. I asked them to help you get better.'

'You didn't need to do that for me. The cards are to change your life not mine.' She shakes her head crossly. 'I don't need you to meddle in my life. I'll be fine.'

'I was only trying to help,' I say. 'You've been so sick, and I feel partly responsible because you gave me the cards.'

'That's a load of rubbish. My sickness is not your fault. Now, tell me how you've been.'

'The strangest things have started happening and I was worried you would go, just like everything else. The cards said something that you needed to let go and move on—'

'I'm not going anywhere, Jane. You're stuck with me for a bit longer I'm afraid, whether you like it or not.' She laughs and I catch a glimpse of the old Tara for a few seconds. 'Now do tell me, what's been happening with you?'

I've so much I want to tell her, but I don't want to overwhelm her. I don't want this to be all about me, but the words just come gushing out.

'My cards are missing. They're gone and I don't know how to get them back. My boyfriend has just broken up with me. I don't know what to do.'

As I listen to the sound of my own voice, I become aware I sound hysterical. To an outsider it must seem ridiculous that I'm getting so wound up about a pack of cards. Tara is the only one who could truly understand. I wait for Tara to speak her words of wisdom. Perhaps she has a spare pack somewhere hidden in the shop and all my problems will be fixed just like that. Maybe something like this has happened to her before.

Tara purses her lips and cocks her head to the side. The silence in the room is deafening.

'I see, and tell me, have you learnt anything from this?'

All I've learnt is that Ben might have feelings for me. That kiss was so unexpected. As I think about the kiss, I can't help but touch my lips and relive the moment in my head. After all this time fantasising about Ben I finally get a chance with him, but I'm still in love with Jay and he doesn't love me anymore. Tara coughs again bringing me back to reality.

'Tara … if you could just get my cards back … I'll never leave the cards out of my sight again. I'll guard them with my life. I promise.'

Tara walks to a big high pile of books close by and starts placing them on some empty shelves. She gestures to me to hand her more books. I stand beside her, and we work in tandem stacking the books on the shelves just like we used to when I was younger.

'Gillian chose what made her happy. Don't you think you deserve to be happy too?

'Of course I do, Tara, but what has this got to do with Gillian?'

'These high expectations you place on yourself don't do you any favours. You work too hard for that bank. Hoping to be a success, just like Gillian.'

'I'm not sure what else I'm supposed to do.'

Tara just continues stacking the huge pile of books. I stop picking up the books and slump to the ground.

'How do I get my cards back? Do you have any idea what I should do?'

'There's no need to do anything. They will come back to you, and only you. All in good time.'

I breathe a sigh of relief. I relax a little now I know they will come back. I glance around the bookshop. Even after all those years it still gives me a great sense of comfort.

'Sometimes I feel like everyone else's life seems so together. Like they have their lives sorted. Everyone apart from me,' I blurt out.

'Everyone has their own timeline. It's not always a race. Some things just take time,' she says. 'Just focus on yourself, and ignore what everyone else is doing.'

If only everything was that simple. I should hang out here more often; anyway, she really could do with the help. She's out of breath already. I insist Tara sits and rests. I take over stacking until the huge pile of five hundred and sixty-three books are all placed on shelves. I find it soothing.

My mind clears and I focus completely on the present and then the image of the young girl pops into my head.

'Tara, did you see a girl on her own outside the bookshop today?' I say.

I glance over at Tara who is asleep on the red armchair. She's snoring. I place the blue blanket over her knees and kiss her gently on the forehead. She must be exhausted. The poor thing. I'll call in again tomorrow and check if there is anything else I can do to help.

I remember when I was younger, and I fell asleep once on the same chair. I was up late the night before with Gillian having a midnight feast. We had stashed a few bags of jellies and crisps during the week so we could munch on them. We woke up at midnight and stayed up for what felt like hours eating and giggling under the bed covers until all the food was gone.

I couldn't stop yawning at the bookshop the next day, so Tara played some board games with me to keep me awake. She introduced me to *Scrabble* which I loved. She didn't let me win like she normally did. I guess she wanted to keep me on my toes. I still found it hard to keep my eyes open, so she let me curl up on the red armchair and put a soft blanket over me until my dad was ready to bring me home. I felt so comforted and cared for.

CHAPTER 24

TARA

I LOVE TO SIT IN my garden and watch the seasons come and go. It reminds me of the circle of life. Life, death and everything else in between. I enjoy listening to the ebb and flow of water from the water fountain with the sun on my face. There's nothing more powerful than nature. It could wipe us all out in a second if it wished to. And then there's the cards. Their power is outstanding. I spent many hours researching their origin and I still haven't figured it out, but I believe they come from a source of a higher being. One with more capabilities than humans will ever have. Once the group in the photograph are discovered it could be like opening a can of worms. I never thought I would be the type of person that would come into contact with something so powerful; it still amazes me that the cards chose to come into my life.

Before I bought my shop, I was a teacher for twenty years. Students often came to me for advice not just with school work, but with stories of angry parents or problems with friends. I heard it all and helped where I could, without getting too involved of course. That never does any good. And now I watch my customers find peace while reading a good book. I have a knack for picking out the right ones – books that can change their lives or transform them in a small way. Just like I did with Jane when she was younger. I never set out to give her the cards though. There's no doubt in my mind that they chose Jane for a reason too. She has many lessons to learn. I realise that it all boils down to her sister. She compares herself to her too much. Until she learns what truly matters, she will never be happy, but she needs to learn that herself. I can't get involved.

As I sit here in my garden with my face turned to the morning sun I can feel how rapidly my skin is ageing. I've been stuck in time for too long and my body is feeling the impact. It's almost as if my veins and bones are protruding from my very being. I'm concerned about the mysterious girl that Jane keeps seeing. It unnerves me. I've been looking out for her everywhere, but there's no sign of her. I've been spending more time in my secret room. It's so peaceful there. I don't care about my wishes going as long as I have that, I'd even go as far as to say it's my favourite place in the world. My secrets are kept safe there, but I must get all my affairs in order soon. Death is knocking on my door, and it's calling my name.

CHAPTER 25

BEN

I'M READY NOW TO break up with Sarah. It's not right being in a relationship with her when I'm in love with Jane. I'll give Jane time, and then tell her how I feel again.

I met Gerry again; he's happily working away in one of my dad's bakeries. He asked me if I told Jane how I felt about her yet, and I gave him a vague answer. He reminded me that I really need to get my act together, and to stop the self-sabotage. If he can get his life back on track then so can I.

Sarah's up and dressed early, drinking a large mug of coffee when I walk into the living room. This is unlike her. She's usually still in bed by now. Her face is wet with tears. Something is wrong. Did she find out I didn't stay with Tim?

I reach out and hold her in my arms. 'I'm sorry,' I say.

'It's not your fault, Ben. There was nothing you could have done. There's nothing anyone could have done. The warning signs were there, but he didn't listen.'

What is she talking about? It's not about us.

'But who?'

I stay silent, waiting for her to tell me what happened. Terrified I'm going to say something wrong and make her more upset.

'I always thought he was invincible, Ben. But I guess every girl thinks that about their father. I need to go see him and find out what's happening. Please come with me babe. I can't do this alone.'

She wraps her arms around me, and I hold her while she sobs. Through her tears she tells me her father had a fall earlier and they believe it's a stroke. He's in hospital.

'Of course, I'll come,' I say. 'I won't leave you. It's all going to be okay.'

I breathe deeply as I get my car keys and drive her to the hospital. I try to push any thoughts of Jane out of my mind.

But I love her.

But what is love?

Love is chaotic. Fucked up. Love makes you hurt people. Love makes you lie and cheat.

I ask myself, am I ready to succumb to this?

I stay for an hour with Sarah in the hospital and then she tells me she'll be fine on her own until her mum comes in. I leave and drive along aimlessly for hours. With no end destination. I drive through hundreds of traffic lights in a blur. Pass by millions of street signs, housing estates and people until I realise, I need to stop this shite and just go home. But then I see her. I'd know that face and body anywhere. It's etched in my mind. I stop the car and run after her.

'Jane … Jane,' I shout. She turns and glances at me up and down.

'Excuse me,' she says. 'Do I know you?'

'Sorry,' I say as I realise it's not her. It's just someone that looks similar.

I get back into my car. As I drive, I see her again and again. She's everywhere. Except it's not her.

I end up outside my folks' house. I'm not sure why. I didn't intentionally mean to come here.

I walk into their kitchen; my mum is slamming pots and pans while my old man is sitting at the kitchen table with his head in his hands beside some spotty teenager.

'Meet your new brother, Ben,' says my mum spitting fire.

'Is this true?' I say to my old man. The look on his face says it all.

The teenager gets up to leave. 'I can see this isn't a good time,' he says. 'I'll go, but I'll be in touch soon Dad.'

My mum just breaks down in tears.

My old man comes back after talking to the kid outside for a while.

'I've never met this boy in my life, Therese. He's lying,' he says. 'I'm telling you he's lying.'

'But why did he come here? Why would he make this up, James?' my mum says.

I can't keep quiet anymore.

'Don't believe him Mum. He's been cheating on you for years. I told you I caught him with his secretary years ago.'

'You don't know what you're talking about Ben. Stay out of this,' he roars.

'No. Mum deserves better than being married to a scumbag like you.'

He gives me this look and then says, 'I'm selling your apartment. I want you out of there today. It's going on the market tomorrow. Now get out of my house.'

'No, James. Ben won't be going anywhere. You get out of my house.' My mum grabs his car keys and throws them at him. 'Go. Before I call the guards.'

My dad leaves without a word and slams the door on his way out.

'I'm sorry, Ben,' my mum says. 'I should have believed you.'

We sit and talk, and she tells me their marriage was probably over years ago, she just never had the courage to end it.

'Ben,' she shouts at me as I'm walking to my car. 'Whatever you do, promise me you won't end up like your father.'

CHAPTER 26

JANE

THE NEXT DAY I catch up on emails. It's nice to be back in work to take my mind off Jay. I missed the place. I touch my lips and think more about Ben. An image of him kissing me again pops into my head. I need to talk to him and figure out what's going on. I wonder is he still with Sarah.

Adele asks for a list of my clients.

'You don't need that yet,' I say.

'Oh, but I really want to phone them to introduce myself. That's why I'm asking for the list,' she says.

'My client information is highly confidential so you need to sign some NDA's, non-disclosure agreements, before I can give you any of their details.'

I take out the NDA's and hand them to her. 'Have a good read of the paperwork before you sign anything.'

She reads through them at her desk and within the next ten minutes she's signed them, and I pass her my client list.

'Great,' she says with a smile. 'I'll get straight to work on this list.'

There's a knock on the door and then Emma walks in. Her hair is wavy today and it hangs down around her shoulders. She has a pair of sparkling diamond earrings and a matching diamond ring on. They must be new. She comes bouncing into the room and stands beside my desk.

'Jane, I was so worried about you. Ben told me you were sick. I wanted to call you, but I didn't in case you were sleeping.'

'I'm okay. I'm glad to be back at work to be honest, to take my mind off everything.'

'I can imagine. Especially with Jay breaking up with you. That must have hurt,' she says.

'How did you know Jay broke up with me?' I ask.

'Oh, Ben told me.'

'Ben! How is he? I've been trying to get in touch with him. He kissed me, and I've been going around in circles trying to figure out what I did to make Jay break up with me.'

She raises her hand and interrupts me. 'The best thing you can do is move on. Sometimes you just need to let certain people go. It wasn't meant to be. Forget about Jay... and Ben.'

'But ... but I'm not like you. I can't just forget about the guy I love with a click of my fingers.'

'I mean it, Jane. It's not good for you to dwell on this. You need to get over Jay. And if you and Ben were meant to be together you would have hooked up by now. I don't think we should give this any more of our energy.' She gives me a faint smile.

Ouch, that hurt. That was a bit much. She really doesn't want to talk to me. I had forgotten how abrupt she can be.

'Adele, how about I take you out to lunch today?' says Emma as Adele enters the room.

'I'd love that. Thanks,' says Adele. It's obvious she idolises Emma.

'I'd ask you, but myself and Adele have some family stuff to talk about. We'd probably just bore you. Best we just go on our own,' she says to me.

'Right. See you later so,' I say, frowning.

This isn't how I imagined things would be between us. Maybe Emma's just having a bad day.

I take out some of my client files and prepare some financial reports that are due. I plan catch-up meetings with my clients to check in with them all. I really don't want to be on my own. I text and call Ben, but there's no answer.

Hours pass and there's no sign of Ben. I spend my lunch break on my own thinking of him. I handled the kiss all wrong, I don't want to lose Ben as a friend. Something tells me I've made a huge mistake.

I email Sorcha to get advice.

Hey Sorcha,

An email from me is well overdue. I've tried calling you a few times, but we keep missing each other, you're probably in a loved-up bubble with Matt. So much has happened in the last while – I don't know where to begin. First of all, Jay dumped me. My heart is literally broken in two. I don't know what I did wrong. He told me he needs time alone to work on his cryptocurrency, which makes no sense at all. I could never imagine dumping him for that reason. He is that type of guy though – so single-minded about making money. My cards have gone missing so I can't use them to help me fix this mess. I just wish I knew a way to get back with Jay. I badly need some of your wisdom and advice. Emma is no help to me at all. She suggested I just get over him. You know what I'm like – I don't just get over things that easily. If I had my cards I know everything would be okay. When I realised they were gone I was so upset. You know the way I suffer from panic attacks? Well, this was worse – I had some sort of breakdown and if it wasn't for Ben being there at the time, I dread to think what would have happened. God, Ben. There's been drama with Ben too. He kissed me when he stayed over in my apartment. We ended up in bed together, don't ask why because I don't even want to get into the reasons, but basically the electricity went off and I've been hearing weird noises – that are to do with the cards. I'm used to them now so please don't worry. This probably makes no sense to you as it's like a stream of my thoughts pouring out, but basi-cally Ben was there and he helped me through everything and I was so grateful that he was there as my mental state would have got a hell of a lot worse. He made me feel safe and he was so kind and lovely. He was basically just being Ben – looking out for me like he always does. I've messed it all up though. I've hurt his feelings which is the last thing I've ever wanted to happen and I feel bad. If I had my cards back, I could fix everything so that's what I probably need to focus on next – finding my cards. I was hungover too so that makes it worse. I wish you were here, and we could curl up on the couch together and eat ice-cream and set things right just like old times.

Love you,
Jane xxxx

CHAPTER 27

GILLIAN

ICHAEL AND I WENT to a private members' club again last night. That's all we seem to do nowadays – go to clubs or parties. When's the partying going to end? It has to end at some stage. Right? I'm in-between movies at the moment and that's when things get messy. I need something to focus on as I get bored easily, and just end up going out with Michael. To be honest I'm just happier staying in, ordering food and watching a movie, but Michael persuades me to go out in the end. He's setting up his own production company and wants us to network as much as possible.

Last night in the club I remember clearly when he sat beside me and nuzzled into my neck. He kissed my ear before he moved his lips closer. 'The good stuff is coming,' he whispered. 'It's the best there is, Gill. You and me, baby, are going to get so high. We'll be on fire. Tonight is about to get a hell of a lot more interesting.'

But the night was already interesting enough for me. I took in the Parisian floral carpet and the dim chandelier lighting. The decor was all sublime. Leonardo DiCaprio sat in the corner and when he noticed me, he gave me a nod of the head. I nodded and smiled back. Despite how famous I am, I still get starstruck whenever I meet my idols.

Michael grabbed my hand as he put his other one on the small of my back. I think he saw Leonardo staring at me and he didn't like it. 'Come with me, let's go. There are some people I want to introduce you to,' he said.

We swayed in time together as we moved across the room. All eyes were on us. Everyone wanted to be us. Everyone wanted to be around us. Being in the same room made them feel like they were someone. I glanced around, I knew how to play the game. Give them what they wanted to make them feel like they were worthy of my attention. I am an actress after all, and a damn good one at that. People looked at us and saw money, success and power. Although I'm more famous than Michael he is so good-looking – in a tall, dark and handsome way, he commands stares wherever he goes. We were the most attractive couple in the room.

I wanted it all and I had it all; well, that version of me did. The version that was externally beautiful and obnoxious. That's the version people were expecting and that's what I gave them. The real me was kept hidden – where it needed to stay. No one needed to see that. If the layers underneath were peeled away, I would have been just me. The scared young Irish girl who wanted to find her place in the world. To have someone to love her for who she really was.

Michael turned to me. 'We are so good together. We make the best couple. Together you and I, baby, ARE DYNAMITE. Are you ready? Are you ready for the best thrill of your life? Give me the cash you brought and I'll make it all happen,' he whispered.

I hesitated. *Why was it always my money?* I wanted to say. *Why was I expected to pay for everything?* But I didn't, because that would have made me seem cheap and I couldn't be cheap. I was Oscar-winner Gillian O'Hara. I was successful, brilliant and loaded. What was a few drugs between lovers?

I shrugged my shoulders as I passed the money over.

'Thanks baby. I'll pay the next time,' he said with the brightest, most dazzling smile.

I nodded my head and gave my brightest smile back. I knew right then he wasn't going to pay me back, because he never did.

Later on, I giggled while I was in the bathroom as I watched the sparkles on my red floor-length dress change colour. They moved from light to dark – a kaleidoscope of colours. All the colours of the rainbow for me to reach out and touch.

'Gillian. Gillian. Are you all right? You've been in there for ages,' I heard.

Of course, I'm all right. I'm living my wildest life, the life of my dreams, I thought.

'I'm ready,' I said. 'Just give me a second.' I swaggered over to open the bathroom door. It was Rose. One of my girls. One of my best friends.

'Michael is looking for you. He wants to go to another party,' she said. 'The car is waiting.' She wiped the white powder from my nose before I grabbed my coat and bag.

I looked in the shell bathroom mirror and reapplied my lipstick.

'First let's dance,' I said as I held her hand and led her out onto the small dance floor.

Everything was heightened – it was light, bright and glittery. The music flowed into my veins. Each beat hummed through my body, moving of its own accord – like it was interpreting every single sensation from my movement and reacting effortlessly. Rose and I were connected, our bodies moved in synch with one another. In dreamy circles.

'We need to go now Gillian,' she shouted loudly over the music. 'Michael will be looking for you. I told him I'd bring you to him.'

I followed Rose and grabbed a bottle of champagne on my way out. The giraffe with his neck and head rising out from the floor stared at me. A rush of love for it came upon me as I patted it on the head. How soft and fluffy it felt. In my head I named it Harry. It was as if I was in a fairy story. A never-ending fairy tale where I played the lead role and Harry the Giraffe was my prince. I laughed hysterically.

Michael appeared beside me and threw his arm around me as we descended the steep flight of stairs. We came out of the unmarked maroon door onto the street. He cheered and posed for the paparazzi as I covered my eyes from the glare of the flashing lights.

'Gillian ... Gillian. You're beautiful,' I heard as my bodyguards put me into the car. 'Show us some leg Gillian. Give us a smile. Give me some love Gillian,' the paparazzi roared.

This morning when I woke up I wracked my brains trying to remember the rest of the night, after I left the club, but I couldn't. Michael told me I knocked back a load of champagne in the car and that I was so wasted he dropped me home. 'You were lucky I was with you,' he said.

He's right. I dread to think what would have happened if he wasn't there. I've been in too many situations that haven't ended well.

Today, social media is full of pictures of me walking out of the club looking wasted. I'm so ashamed of myself! I don't know why I get myself into messes like this. I hope my dad doesn't see any of these pictures.

I'll never forget the first time he saw pictures of me wasted coming out of some club – he was furious.

'I don't want you turning into your mother,' he said. 'You're too talented for that. Lay off the booze, Gillian and just focus on being professional.'

I wish I had taken his advice, but I can't stop myself. He gave up trying to talk sense into me and that's probably why we don't really have a relationship anymore. He never liked me as much as Jane. In his eyes, she can do nothing wrong. Jane would never approve of this lifestyle either. That's why I'm selective about what I tell her.

Michael was full of life when he woke up. His arms reached out for me ready to make love, but I just wasn't in the mood. I haven't been in the mood for a long time. He brought me breakfast in bed this morning. After we ate he gave me a massage and tried to entice me again to make love. I couldn't think of anything worse. All I wanted to do was throw up. I got up later and went to see my friend Maria's baby. She's a few weeks old. I didn't think it would be my thing really so I've been putting it off for a while. It was such a strange experience, I surprised myself with the reaction I had when I held her.

At first, I was afraid to hold her, but Maria convinced me it would be okay. The child just stared up at me with the bluest eyes I've ever seen. A rush of something came over me. It's hard to describe, but the thoughts of holding something so dependent and vulnerable brought tears to my eyes. I imagined Maria's baby was my child and my heart soared. I realised then that there is no pretence with babies. All you need to do is just love them and they love you back. Unconditional love. I've never experienced that in my life. Being loved for just being me. No strings attached. That thought rocked me to the core and at that moment my mind was made up. I wanted to have my own child. I needed to have my own child. It was all I could think about.

Michael's out again. He's always out. He's been so emotionally distant with me lately, but having a baby would change all that. Having a baby will bring us closer, and he won't leave me like the rest of them did. I'll move my wedding forward so my bump isn't visible in my wedding dress.

I just got off the phone from my accountant. He makes every conversation we have about my money so complicated, and I don't want to come across as being stupid, so I told him to go ahead with whatever he was suggesting. Perhaps if I had asked Jane to be my accountant, I wouldn't be in this mess, but realistically that was never going to happen. She would have been horrified to know what I spent most of my money on. She'd think I was deranged. There was something different about her the last time we were in contact. A quiet confidence. Whatever it was, I'd like to bottle it.

At the beginning of my career, I was high and drunk at all the parties and I spent way too much. It was fun and exciting. Not that I did anything too mad, but I threw money around like it was no big deal. I found out pretty soon though that people loved my generosity and they expected me to pay for everything.

I never had many friends growing up, because I was so obsessed with becoming an actress. Mam became more of a best friend rather than a mother. I think kids my own age found me too intense, too much. I had no interest in any of the games they wanted to play at break-times. All I wanted to do was to sing or dance or act out plays. I got annoyed with all of their questions: 'Why won't you play something we all like?' 'Why do you dance so much?' 'Why can't you just have fun?'

Every day after school and weekends I had no time to play with kids my own age as I was too busy with stage classes. I grew up entering every competition going and wearing fancy costumes and hairstyles, while my classmates would talk about doing simple things: going to playdates or family days out.

Was there something wrong with me? I used to wonder. And every time I confided in my mam about how I was feeling, she assured me I was perfectly fine. I was star material and my class-mates were probably just jealous of me.

'They spend their time doing pointless things. Even your sister and father waste time reading books or going to that second-hand book shop. What good is that going to do? Your time is spent wisely – working towards stardom, and you are going to be a star,' she said.

I knew my mam was lonely and her relationship with my dad was all wrong. They fought too much and our home was filled with tension. There were times when she didn't know I was watching her but I knew she would often cry. I used to watch people a lot then. I still do, I take everything in. I could tell I made Mam the happiest. Way more than my dad or Jane ever could. Apart from when she drank. When she drank she would be on a high, or could be sad. Sometimes she'd ask me, why didn't my dad love her as much as she loved him? My heart broke for her. I just wanted my mam to stop crying and just be happy.

Mam told me many times that her life didn't turn out the way she wanted it to because her parents didn't have the resources to turn her into a serious performer, but she was going to make sure I had every opportunity in life.

Sometimes when she picked me up from school, if I was tired I'd ask if I could skip lessons and just go home, but she would refuse.

'No, Gillian. You can't give up. Giving up is for the weak,' she said.

'Ah, please, Mam. I'll get back into it tomorrow.'

'Every lesson you go to, you improve. Do you hear me? Better than anyone else. You will be a star. But you must focus all your energy on it. Every ounce you got.'

Most of my childhood was taken up with lessons to make me the best: ballet, tap dance, piano, speech and drama. You name it, I did it. I kept going even in the summer with my mam by my side. The two of us were on a mission to make me famous. Apart from when she went on drinking binges. When that happened she could go away for days at a time and I'd have no idea when she'd be back. While I waited for Mam to come home my dad was there to take care of me. I knew Jane was his favourite, and I could never have that same bond with him and that hurt. They had so much in common, they both loved books, and spent a lot of time in a second hand book shop.

Sometimes I wish my relationships could be more straightforward – like what Jane has with my dad.

CHAPTER 28

JANE

MY MAM CALLS WHEN I'm least expecting it. She never calls me just for a chat. It's always for a particular reason or when she's had a few drinks. It's usually to do with Gillian.

'Hi Jane, I'm checking in to see what your plans are for Christmas. Will you be joining us this year?'

'I'm not sure,' I say quietly.

'And if you do come, will you be bringing a guest? You know your sister will be there with Michael. Oh, he's such a lovely fella.'

I should have known this would come up. My love life is a great concern for her.

'No guest for me Mam. I thought I would be spending it with someone else, but it … well … it didn't work out,' I say.

'That is disappointing. Can I ask what happened?'

I wish I had a crystal ball to know the answer to that one. I bite my nails just like I used to when I was younger.

'He dumped me, but I'm not sure why?'

There is silence on the end of the line. I wait for my mam to speak, but I can't hear a word.

'Mam, are you still there?'

'You haven't been very lucky with men. Have you, Jane? You really need to get some advice from your sister. She'll be able to set you off on the right track. She can set you up with one of Michael's friends.'

I was wondering when she would bring Gillian into this.

'I don't think that's a good idea—'

'Well, you'll never get anywhere in life if you don't at least try. I don't know what else I can do to help you.' My mam sighs.

How about nothing. I don't need you to meddle or involve Gillian in my love life.

'I'm sure Michael has some nice friends. I'll ask Gillian after our call. She knows so many eligible men-'

'That's not necessary. I really just want time to figure out what happened with Jay-'

'I'm only trying to help. You don't need to get so cross with me.'

I really need to change the subject before this gets silly.

'So have you heard from Dad lately?' I say.

'No ... I haven't heard from your father. Have you?' she says.

Conversations with my parents have been few and far between since they split. I'm the only one in my family who has regular contact with him now.

'Dad asked me to come and visit him once I can take some time off work,' I say. 'I'm not sure when that will be though. I don't want to be away from the office for too long because of my new job.'

'And what about myself and your sister. Has he asked after us?' she says.

The truth is he hasn't, but I don't want to hurt my mam's feelings, so I try to think of an excuse for him not getting touch.

'He's been busy with ... work, and Kate is in the middle of a big case at the moment. A high profile one. I'm sure once things settle down, he'll be in touch with you and Gillian.'

'Oh, I see. Well, I won't hold my breath. He never had time for me when we were married. Why would he change his behaviour now? He never wanted me to push Gillian into stardom and look how wrong he was. When I think about all she has achieved now ... just look at the man she is going to marry ... I was right all along. He doesn't care though.'

'Come on Mam. Don't be like that,' I say.

'It's true. All your father cared about was work and you. You were always his favourite.'

'There's no point in dwelling on the past Mam. It just didn't work out between yourself and Dad despite how hard you both tried.'

'I tried. Your father didn't.'

Mam seems to have forgotten about the times she'd just up and leave and go off on drinking binges.

'That's enough talk about your father. I can't wait for Gillian's wedding. Gillian wants you to come to London to see her very soon to look at wedding dresses. She's anxious to get things organised. She's brought the wedding forward.'

'Hmmm ...'

'Vera Wang. Can you believe it? Her wedding dress will be designed by Vera Wang. Some people would sell their soul for a custom-made dress by Vera. It just shows you if you work hard enough you can achieve anything. Isn't she wonderful? I'm so looking forward to the wedding despite the fact that your father will be there.'

'He's not that bad, Mam. I need to go. I'm in work,' I say before she rants any more about how great Gillian is and puts down my dad any further. I don't even want to get into a conversation about bridesmaids.

'Of course, your job at the bank. How's the promotion going? I hope you're able for all that new responsibility,' she says.

My mind starts to wander. I put my phone on speakerphone. I imagine I'm having a different conversation with my mam. One where I tell her that I won't be home for Christmas as I'm going to be spending it with Jay. She will be shocked of course, but she will think I'm doing something with my life. That I am lovable, despite not being as famous as Gillian. I think of Jay and try to picture his face, but the profile I conjure up is slightly blurry. I make a note to search for him on social media, but then I remember he's not on it. Instead, I end up checking out Gillian's Facebook account. There's a picture of her engagement ring. It's huge. She has nearly two million followers now.

Another image pops into my head. Of the girl sitting on the doorstep of *Hidden Secrets* asking me to help her. This one is clear, crisp and sharp. Something clicks in my brain. I picture her asking for my help again. I can still hear my mum talking. It sounds like background noise, but it brings me back to reality.

'Mam, do you remember that red coat I had when I was younger?' I say.

'I do. You loved that coat. It was a present from the owner of that old bookshop you liked. What was her name again? I can't remember. She was always so kind to you. You insisted on wearing your hair in pigtails whenever you wore that coat.'

That little girl reminds me of myself when I was a child. The hair style, the coat is just like what I wore. I wonder does Tara know more than she's letting on. I need to get to the bottom of this.

'Mam, I have to go. There's something I need to do,' I say.

I shut down my laptop and scribble a note for Adele to let her know I'll be back soon. I grab my coat and bag and rush out the door. There's a thud sound and then I realise I've walked straight bang into someone who was bending over slightly. Everything falls out of my handbag. My make-up, keys, receipts and a load of other bits and bobs. He steps back to avoid getting hit again. He's rubbing his eye.

'Ouch. I wasn't expecting that,' he says in pain. 'I dropped my keys. I was bending down to get them.'

'I was on my way out and I'm so sorry … let me help you …'

'It's okay, Jane. I'm grand.' He looks down at me and smiles sheepishly. 'I've had worse bangs than that before. I'll survive.'

'Your eye. Show me your eye. Take away your hand. Oh, Ben, that was some bang you got.' His eye is swollen and bruised. 'Come in and sit down, I'll see if there's any ice I can put on it. Ah, there it is. Stay still, let me help you. That's some knock you got.'

Ben sits and lets me take over. He winces in pain.

'I could get used to this,' he says as he leans back on the couch and rests his arm over the top of it. His arm touches against my shoulders.

'It's my turn to look after you now,' I say. I push back a piece of his hair that has fallen over his eye. 'You left. That morning in my apartment. After we kissed. I wanted to see you-'

'I know. I felt awful about what happened. I went to see Sarah; her dad was sick. I should have phoned you early-'

'I tried calling you, but you didn't answer.'

'That's why I'm here … to explain. Can you take the ice off now so we can talk?'

I take off the ice pack and underneath his eye is still very swollen.

'Is her dad okay? I think you might need the ice on longer. It's very bruised.'

'He's over the worst of it. He had a fall ... a mini stroke they think it is.'

'Oh, the poor man-'

'Jane don't fuss.' He takes my hand and holds it tightly.

I don't move a muscle. I'm enjoying the closeness between us.

'I've waited so long to tell you this,' he says.

'Tell me what?'

'I like you. I like you a lot. The fact is-'

'Ben, I don't know what to say. I-'

'Please, hear me out. This isn't easy for me.' He faces me with a serious look, the one that means business. I've seen it so many times in work. 'You have no idea how long I have waited to tell you this. The fact is ... I care about you ...' His face softens and he grabs my other hand then clasps them both in his. 'You're my friend. You're more than a friend. What I'm trying to say is. I want us to be together. Me and you.'

'But Sarah. What about Sarah? You're with Sarah. You live together.'

'I don't love Sarah.'

'What?'

'I tried, but I can't shake off the feelings I have for you. I can't get you out of my head. You're under my skin.'

'I thought you loved her. You have been together so long. I just—'

'I thought I loved Sarah, but I've had a thing for you since the day I met you, Jane. What I feel now is even stronger. You moving offices and then hooking up with Jay made me realise how much you mean to me. I took for granted you would always be there, but you won't be unless I do something about it.'

'You never said. You never told me. If only I had known, back then. It would have changed everything. I was mad about you for so long.'

'I tried to tell you so many times, but I couldn't go through with it.' He strokes my cheek gently. 'I love you. I love everything about you. The other night when we were in bed together ... well that was a wakeup call for me.'

'Oh, I didn't know what that was about. The kiss.'

'I'm going to call it off with Sarah. Now I know her dad is better. I want to be with you, Jane. I need to know how you feel about me.'

'Ben, I'm flattered I really am, but this—'

'I get it. I've taken you by surprise. You'll probably need time to process this. So, take some time. I can wait. I've waited a long time already. I thought you were in love with your ex-boyfriend, Colm, but you're obviously not,' he laughs. A nervous laugh.

Ben loves me. He just said he loves me. He doesn't love Sarah. He loves me. I don't know how long I've wanted this to happen. What does this mean? How did I miss this? I wanted this. Why would he think I was still in love with Colm? He's so helpless looking, sitting there with his black eye. How do I feel about him? The kiss … it was nice. It was more than nice. He makes me feel safe and warm. Do I still love him? I tried to forget about him, and the cards guided me to Jay. I still love Jay … I know I do.

My phone rings and I jump in shock. I sit at my office desk with my head in my hands.

'Oh, I wasn't expecting that,' I say to Ben. 'It's Jay. He's calling me …'

I wonder what he wants. Is this a sign? I was just thinking about him, and he called.

I press the speaker phone button by mistake and Jay's voice fills the room, loud and clear.

'Jane, Jane. Is that you? I miss you. I've done it, Jane. I've hit the jackpot with my cryptocurrency. I've named it Jewelcoin …'

'Don't listen to him,' Ben whispers.

'I need to hear what he has to say. I want to know what happened,' I whisper back.

'No. Just hang up,' Ben says.

'I bought you a gift. It's a red dress. I want you to wear it for me while we make love. Red looks so great on you.'

I'm stuck to the spot. I'm mesmerised by Jay's voice. We both stand in silence listening to Jay spout on about how much he misses me and wants to me to come over so we can make love all night. That he should never had let me go. I take the phone off speaker.

'Don't believe him,' says Ben. 'The guy is a gobshite. He's not right for you. He's not good enough for you.'

'I don't know,' I say. 'I just don't know. My cards said ...'

'I know you have it in your head that Jay is the one, but what if he's not?'

'My cards work. I met him because of my cards.'

'I've just poured my heart out to you, but you don't seem to give a shit.'

'No, Ben. It's not like that.'

'You don't need those cards. I think they're causing more harm than good,' he says as he turns away from me.

I try to think of something to say. To let him know I care, but I can't think of anything. Nothing. I open my mouth and close it again. If it wasn't for Jay being in the picture, there would be no hesitation.

He walks slowly out of my office. Just as he's at the door he stops. 'Oh, and by the way, I have feelings too and you've just stomped all over them,' he says.

'Stop, Ben. Don't go,' I manage to muster.

It's too late though. He's already left.

I stay rooted to the spot listening to Jay telling me how he wants me back. How he's going to change my life. I don't answer him. I just listen in silence. Eventually he hangs up.

I have a moment where I want to phone him back and say all is forgiven, but I remember that the romance card said I must stay focused to my values and beliefs. If I'm being true to myself there's no way I can take him back after the way he dumped me.

CHAPTER 29

BEN

I WALK INTO MY APARTMENT and drop my keys on the side table. It's in darkness, which means Sarah must have gone out. I breathe a sigh of relief. I vaguely remember her telling me she was busy this evening, but Jane has consumed my thoughts recently.

I click on the light switch and that's when the whooping and cheering starts. My living room is filled with faces, all smiling and cheering. What for? I haven't a clue. I see a few of my mates in the crowd. I look over at Sarah, who's standing beside her parents. She's beaming from head to toe.

'He hasn't a clue,' says a voice from the crowd.

'Haven't a clue about what?' I mutter to Sarah who's walking towards me.

She's dressed up in a long black evening gown and her long curls cascade down her back.

'What's this all about?' I say as I stare at her trying to figure out what she's doing.

'Ben, come here,' she says as she takes my hand and brings me over to the fireplace. A crowd forms around us. 'As you know, I love you very much and I want everyone to know how I feel about you.'

She can't be serious. No. Please tell me this is a dream.

'I love you, Ben and I want to spend the rest of my life with you.'

Shit. She means it. I can't do this. Not now. This can't be happening …

'Ben Arthur O'Malley, will you make me the happiest girl in the world and marry me?' She squeezes my hand.

My first thought is I need to run away and hide and lay low for a few days, but then I look down at Sarah's sweet face and the look in her eyes stops me. She really means this, every single word.

I hesitate for a second and then someone shouts out, 'Come on, Ben, man up. Don't be a wuss.' Everyone laughs.

I turn to Sarah, and she smiles up at me. 'What do you say, Ben … me and you … together forever.'

'I … I … I'm …sorry. I'm shocked. This whole thing … I didn't see it coming. I wasn't expecting it. All I can say is … I …I…'

'Say something, Ben. Anything. Don't just stand there with your mouth open,' she whispers, with tears in her eyes.

There's only one thing to do right now and that's to go along with it. There's no way I'm turning Sarah down like this in front of her closest friends and family. I can't embarrass her like that.

'Yes … of course I'll marry you, Sarah.'

The clapping that follows rings in my ears as I wipe the sweat from my brow. It's okay, I tell myself. It's not like we need to get married today. We have time to figure it out.

I place my arm around Sarah. Her best friend, Joan, comes rushing towards me.

'I told you he'd say yes. I can't wait to go dress shopping. Congrats you two!'

I get clapped on the back all night with congratulations.

'Did you know? Come on, you must have known …,' I'm asked by everyone.

'No … no, seriously I had no idea,' I say.

Sarah has had caterers in and there's a big spread laid out. Every time I glance over at her, she's smiling. I've never seen her so happy in my life.

Later that night when we are in bed, she asks me if I meant it.

'Are you sure you want to get married? I hope you didn't feel pressurised.'

'Of course not.'

'I can't wait to start planning the wedding, Ben. It's going to be amazing. But first we need to go shopping for an engagement ring. Let's do that tomorrow. I want the biggest ring I can find.'

CHAPTER 30

JANE

I STAND AT THE TILL beside Tara, serving customers. I came straight to the bookshop after Jay's call. I didn't know what else to do after both Jay and Ben declared their love to me. Ben telling me he loved me felt nothing like I imagined it would, because Jay kept popping into my head and I couldn't really get into the enormity of it all. I'm still in love with Jay. It must be because of the cards. I'm also worried about the death and marriage card. I wonder when this will come true.

I should be ecstatic and full of happiness, but I'm not. I've lost one of my best friends. Like Sorcha he's always had my back. He even took care of me when I went slightly loopy. It's as if I'm a balloon that's just deflated and has fallen flat to the ground. I figured coming here would take my mind off everything.

Like me, Tara seems preoccupied with something. She tells me she has work to do in her office on the top floor. The shop isn't very busy, so I stack and sort out books. After that's done, I go to ask her does she want a cup of tea, but I can't find her anywhere. I walk up to her office, and I shout out her name, but she doesn't answer.

I settle in and work on the accounts and then she appears in front of me with a dream-like expression on her face. I wonder where her mind has wandered off to this time.

'Where were you, Tara?' I ask.

'Here, in the shop. I was in my office the whole time,' she says, and I can tell by the look on her face not to push it any further.

We sit together drinking tea and eating chocolate digestive biscuits beside the Christmas tree. Her face has more colour in it now.

'Tara, how did you know Harold was the one?' I ask.

'Well, it was quite simple really. When I was with Harold, I felt like I was at home. No matter where we were in the world, I felt complete with Harold by my side.'

'Ah, that's nice.'

'It was, until he was no longer there, and I had to build a new home.'

'That must have been heartbreaking.'

'Yes, I know only too well about heartbreak. My heart has been shattered in pieces many times over.' A tear falls and lands on my hand. Her face has aged significantly in the short space of time that I've gotten to know her again. 'I think you should go home now, Jane. I'm tired.'

I'm worried about Tara. Where on earth did she disappear to?

When I get to the office, Adele is not there, which is unlike her. Since she started working with me, she's been in early each morning.

It's weird because her stationery and her personal photos and everything else she kept at her desk is gone too. She must have come in early and taken her stuff and left.

I get a text message from Emma.

Jane. Adele and I have resigned.

Emma loves her job. Why would she resign?

Maybe she got a new job, but she never told me. Why did Adele leave? The text makes me feel like I did something wrong.

I call Emma, but there's no answer so I text her.

Why resign? What happened?

As I sit at my desk and check my emails my mind is racing. I'm searching for answers to what could make Emma resign. I glance through my emails, not really reading them properly until I come to the one that says urgent in the subject. After that I come across more urgent emails. The first one is from Anderson & Co. They have ended their relationship with the bank. They no longer wish to be a client and have withdrawn all their funds. The rest of the emails are along the same lines. They all wish to take their business elsewhere.

How could this have happened? This is bad. Very bad. I need to speak to Walter. My hands shake as I dial his number and I'm sweating. My fingers tingle. I'm put on hold for what feels like forever. Then Walter's assistant answers and puts me through.

'Walter—' I say.

'Jane,' he shouts. 'Have you read your emails yet?'

'I read the emails, Walter. I know they were addressed to you too. Our clients, so many of them have left us. Why? How did this happen?'

Another email pops up. Another client gone. This is the tenth one. Clients that hold multi-million-euro investments in the bank. They've all left.

'Pack up your belongings and leave immediately,' says Walter, shouting. 'There is no position for you here anymore.'

'Walter, my clients were happy with the service I provided. I don't know what happened. Why are they leaving?' I say as I'm pulling my hair from my head.

'They have found a better service elsewhere.'

'Where though? I have given them the best possible investment rates available. I researched this thoroughly. I know each of their accounts inside out,' I say frantically.

'It seems there is a new competitor in town who has poached our clients. This looks very bad for our shareholders. Once word gets out that our main clients have left, our customers may lose confidence in us. The bank may collapse. We may never recover from this.'

A moment passes, but it feels like an eternity. I feel the lobes of my ears burning.

'There's no position for you anymore,' he says.

My world is crashing down before my eyes. My new job, the thing I wanted so much, has gone. My relationship with Jay has failed. I've messed up everything with Ben. The one person I could rely on. Emma has left and so has Adele.

I float out of my body and look down at someone who looks very much like me clutching the phone. My hair is shocking, I really need to get my highlights done, is all I can think of. Then I realise what an absurd thought to have considering I've just been split in two.

I know it's impossible to be in two places at once, but I am. I'm right at the ceiling now. I'm so close I can touch it. It reminds me of the scene in *Mary Poppins* when Mary and her Uncle Albert float to the ceiling because they are laughing so much. Except I'm not laughing. I'm crying. The me that's clutching the phone is sobbing her heart out. Perhaps this is an out-of-body experience or is it the cards? Have the cards done this to me? Separated me so I can be in two places. Or maybe I just died with the shock of losing my job and had a heart attack. Am I in limbo stuck high up on the ceiling?

'Are you going to comment? Do you have anything to say?' I hear Walter screaming at me. His voice shocks me, and I fall and land straight back into my body that's now sitting on the office chair. I move my hands and stare at them in front of me. I feel my heart beating. I'm not dead after all.

I wish I could get back up to the ceiling and not have to deal with any of this. I liked it up there. It was a nice floaty feeling. Almost like I was bobbing along in the sea. Floating around without a care in the world. Despite my best efforts, I can't get back. I even stand on my desk and try to jump up, but it doesn't work.

'Jane ... Jane ... are you listening to me? Answer me, Jane,' he roars at me.

'All I can say is there must be some kind of mistake ...'

'There's been no mistake. Get out of this building now before I call security,' he says, raising his voice even higher than before.

When I get back to my apartment, I drop my pile of stuff on the floor. I sit on the ground and stare at my clothes, shoes and all the stuff I had brought with me to the office apartment. I remember how happy I felt when I first brought them. My future was bright and full of promise.

If I still had my cards, I wouldn't be in this situation. I'm worse off now than before. Things only started to go wrong once I lost them. I stay on the floor in my messy living room with my thoughts racing. I don't want to be on my own. Another one of my biggest fears coming true.

Why is it I hate being on my own?

I can't tell my mam about what just happened. I can just imagine the disapproving look she would have on her face. She would mutter something about Gillian and how this would never happen to her. She would probably wonder why one of her daughters turned out so perfect while the other one can't get anything right.

What would Ben say?

He would probably say something positive to me. He'd put such a nice spin on it and make me believe it wasn't my fault. I wish I could talk to him now, but I don't think he'll answer if I try to call him. I need to sort things out. I just don't know how.

I ring Sorcha. I'm ready to pour my heart out, but there's no answer. I want to talk to her so much, but she must be busy with the neurologist. Instead, a text comes through.

> You'll never believe this, but we just got married in Las Vegas!! Hope all is well with you! I haven't had a chance to read the last email you sent me as things have been hectic, but I will soon. I promise. I have so much to fill you in on too. I'm going to stay in Australia after all. xxx

Sorcha sends me a photo of her in a plain white dress with a novelty veil over her head. She's beaming. I'm not surprised how fast this has happened. It's definitely the cards' doing. My heart soars with happiness for her, but at the same time I'm devastated because I'm missing her wedding and she's not coming home. There's no way I want to bring her down with my problems. I reply with what I hope comes across as an upbeat text.

> I'm so happy for you. I'm fine. Enjoy your night. X

The only person left who could make me feel better is Tara. I need to get out of here. This overthinking is driving me crazy.

Am I going crazy? It feels like I might be. Another fear of mine.

I make my way to the bookshop to see Tara. It's snowing heavily. I'm not dressed for the snow, but I don't care. I burst into spurts of sprints along the way to silence all the thoughts in my head. I slip a few times on the slushy footpath but I pick myself up and keep going. I need to get Tara as quick as I can. Once I get to talk to Tara, I know I'll be okay.

I get to the bookshop and fling the door open almost knocking a customer over coming out the door. Tara's asleep on an armchair beside the fire clutching the photo of Harold in her hand. Her eyes are closed. It's as if she's asleep. I give her a gentle nudge to wake her up. She stays still.

Why won't she wake up?

I need her now more than ever.

I try to wake her a few more times, but her eyes stay firmly shut. I wish I had my cards back. My cards have the power to fix all of this.

CHAPTER 31

WHEN I WENT TO the newsagents this morning, a familiar face stared at me on the front page of *The Irish Times* newspaper. I rushed home to read the article and then just as I reached my garden my neighbour, Mary, waved to get my attention. I crouched to the ground and crossed my fingers.

'Please, Mary. Not today. Any other day, but not this one. Keep walking, there's nothing to see here,' I whispered quietly as I hid.

'Jane … Jane … where did you disappear to? You were there a second ago. Ah, there you are.'

'I just dropped my key … it's here somewhere,' I said. My face was hot and bothered.

'Do you think you could get me more of Gillian's autographs? I'll need about seven … Jane … where are you going?'

'I'm rushed off my feet today, Mary. Sorry no time to talk,' I said as I tried not to cry. Normally I'd have all the time in the world for Mary, but not then because I had just found out that the death the cards predicted had come true.

The soft white blanket wrapped around me still smells of Ben. I clutch the newspaper in my hand and read over the article again. I can't believe Jay's gone. The whole thing is horrific.

She was in the cottage with him at the time of the fire. It's obvious Jay left me for her.

A Man in his Twenties Dies from a Mysterious Fire on Gull Island, Dublin.

Jay McCabe (Aged 29) was found dead inside the gatekeeper's cottage on Gull Island, which is where a fire started. Emergency services arrived at the scene of the fire at 9:36 pm yesterday evening. The firemen extinguished the fire and removed Mr McCabe, who was pronounced dead at the scene.

Emma O'Brien, who was with the deceased at the time of the fire, was treated for serious burns. Below is her witness report:

'It all started so quickly. Myself and Jay were in the computer room working on our cryptocurrency business when we heard a loud bang. There was an explosion and sparks appeared out of nowhere from the computer equipment beside us. It was like the computer equipment set itself on fire and there was nothing we could do to stop it. We tried pouring water over it, but that made it worse.

'I eventually escaped when emergency services came. Jay refused to leave. He insisted on staying and trying to salvage his computer equipment. There was nothing I could do to save him. It took six hours for the firemen to put out the fire.

'The fire spread throughout the whole island. I have severe scars now all over my face and body, but I'm grateful to be alive.'

The Gardaí believe there was no foul play, and a spark from a discarded cigarette butt was the cause of the fire.

I have a black, sick feeling in my stomach, similar to when my dad told me he was moving to Toronto. I struggle to breathe. Why has the world not stopped turning? How can my life go back to normal? Jay's dead!

This can't be real.

I stare at his face in the newspaper in shock. I gasp until I get my breath back. I want to be a child again. I want to go back to the bookshop, and for Tara to fix this.

But I can't. Tara's sick. She can't help me now.

I need to talk to someone. Anyone. But I can't bring myself to pick up the phone and voice the words, *Jay's dead*. How can I say it and not break down?

I drink vodka. I tell myself to stop after the third glass. I can't turn into my mother. I'd never allow that. I stare into space, my mind racing.

He's really dead. He was alive when I last saw him, and now he's just *gone*. Apart from my grandparents I don't know anyone else I was close to who died.

Later that evening, I stagger and collapse into bed. I cry great roaring sobs to release my pain. I manage to fall asleep around 4:00 am out of pure exhaustion. In the morning, I lie awake considering if it's worth crawling out of bed. My head hurts. I feel guilty. If Jay hadn't met me he would still be alive today. It's my fault because the cards brought him to me. But then I tell myself that's stupid. I didn't kill Jay. Maybe I would have met him anyway without the cards. Some things in life just happen.

I don't recognise myself when I finally get up and look in the mirror. It's as if someone gave me a fright that I can't get over. Like the wind changed, and my face is stuck like this.

Over the next few days, I'm consumed less by guilt and grief and more by shock. Even if he hadn't died, I know we wouldn't have been in contact much, but just knowing he's gone forever is what I can't get my head around.

I get texts from people – mainly acquaintances in the bank – asking am I okay. Some of the girls saw us together outside the bank, and word must have gotten around that he died. Some ask if it's true that Emma was also seeing Jay at the same time.

I reply back, and just say thanks, that I'm doing okay and leave it at that.

I feel like such a fool that Emma and Jay betrayed me. I obviously didn't mean that much to either of them.

A few days later, when I get dressed in black from head to toe, I'm on autopilot. The funeral is in Dublin. I get a taxi over to the church, but I don't even remember ringing for it. It's almost as if someone else is controlling my body. It's me of course, but it doesn't feel like that. The dreams I'm having have been consumed with Jay since his death. I'm chasing after him while he's telling me that I need to go back, because it's not my time. But I want him to tell me he's not dead. That it was a big mistake. He's just somewhere else. He has a few things to sort out and then he'll be back and we'll talk.

The funeral should be a quiet affair as Jay had not many friends or family at the church. At the front two of his friends stand close beside Emma with their arms wrapped around her. She's crying profusely. Another ten or so people are sitting together to pay their respects.

I sit towards the back of the church, alone among the shadows, and listen to one of Jay's aunts speak about his life. She describes him as a self-sufficient and energetic man. A risk-taker, who relied on no one but himself. He was a loner who was obsessed with computers. He was known to spend hours by himself focusing on his computer passion. His dream was to be a millionaire and travel the world.

I can't help thinking about how he had his whole life ahead of him. He could have travelled the world. He didn't deserve to die like that. If only he wasn't so obsessed about that cryptocurrency, he could have escaped the fire.

Jay's aunt proceeds to tells us that Emma was there when he died. She thanks Emma, and asks her to say a few words. I shift in my seat. I'm light-headed and panicky, I shouldn't have come. It was a mistake.

'Jay was a wonderful man,' Emma says sweetly. 'It was love at first sight. Although we were only together for a short time, we were very happy. We talked about getting married.'

I'm shaking as tears stream down my face. Through my wet eyes, I notice Ben standing against the wall behind me. Even knowing he's in the room I don't feel so bad.

I believe everyone has something that makes them special. Ben's something is his eyes. All his emotions can be read there. He even smirks with his eyes. Right now his eyes are swimming with concern, like the deepest rock pools. I want to reach out and touch him, and tell him how much I appreciate him coming for me. To get comfort from his smell, and sob in his arms and forget where I am. Who I am, even. I want to lie in bed for days, with Ben by my side, and for him to take care of me like he did when I went loopy after I lost my cards.

I want to go back in time to before Jay; to when I first met Ben. I was innocent then, full of hope and belief that I'd finally found my soulmate. I believed I could make a difference to the world, if I worked hard enough.

I was naive, but at least I didn't have to face the death of someone I fell deeply in love with.

Ben's eyes change as I gaze back at him. He's troubled. He can see something I can't. He's trying to tell me something. I turn away to the front of the church.

As the service comes to an end, I go to Jay's aunt to give her my condolences.

'Thank you,' she says as she grasps my hand. 'How did you know Jay?'

'We were once very close.'

'Ah, well then you would know how precious he was.'

I nod my head. 'It's unfair that he died in such a tragic accident.'

I turn and walk away to find Ben.

'You have some cheek, showing your face here. Look at the state of me. I only got out of hospital today, I got burnt,' I hear a screeching voice say.

Emma has a burn mark across her face and running down her neck. She's wearing a short black ruffled dress that I bought with her on a shopping trip about six months ago. She has long dangly diamond earrings with a black veil across her face.

'You knew how I felt about him. I was devastated when we broke up, which I understand now you had a part to play in,' I say trembling. All eyes in the church are glaring at me.

'It was your cards that caused this,' says Emma pointing her finger screaming at me.

'My cards! How did you get my cards?' I ask.

'You dropped them on the floor of the restaurant. We wanted to see what they could do, and they worked. They helped us crack the cryptocurrency algorithms. Those cards are evil—'

'No! They are my cards, Emma. You shouldn't have taken them from me.'

'They gave me so much energy, and diamond jewellery. We made millions. We had all your clients lined up as investors, and then those fucking cards, they just started glowing for no reason. The algorithms went haywire and Jay's computer equipment exploded. It went—'

'You stole from me. I gave my client list to Adele. Not you. You took my clients, my cards, and Jay. I lost my job because of you. How could you do this? And now Jay is dead.'

'We lost everything in that fire. All the money is gone because the private key password is lost, everything is gone. I've no way of finding out that password. I'll never be able to get it back. Hundreds of millions of euros are wiped out, just like that.'

That's the issue I have with most cryptocurrency, it's difficult to retrieve missing passwords. The private key password was a 256-bit long number that was picked at random. Jay's software had complex algorithms that made it possible to create bitcoin addresses and associated private keys that were needed to access, spend or send bitcoins to another bitcoin address. Emma's right: now the private key password is gone, the money is lost in cyberspace.

'Where are my cards? I want them back,' I say.

'I don't have them. They're gone. They went up in flames. Like Jay's body. Like everything—'

She caused this. She's toxic. Absolutely toxic. How could I have not seen this before?

'You're supposed to be my friend. How could you go behind my back?'

'Oh, wise up, Jane. You have no idea how annoying it is being your friend, I could never compete with you.'

'What on earth are you on about?'

'The promotion I didn't give you was the only power I had over you and even then, that didn't work out the way I wanted it to.'

'To think I looked up to you. I was so naive.'

'You even have him wrapped around your little finger,' she says as she points at Ben. 'You're far too nice for your own good. You don't even take advantage of the fact that your sister is a major celebrity. All the parties we missed because you're a fuck-ing wimp.'

I put my hands over my ears, unable to listen anymore. Ben puts his arm around me. I turn to him and a rush of warmth hits me. I'm overwhelmed by it. I want to leave right now with him, and forget about the world.

'Emma, I think you've said enough,' he says as he holds my hand tightly and I squeeze it back. 'It was a spark from a cigarette that caused Jay's death, not the cards.'

'I was Jay's girlfriend in the end, Jane, and don't you forget that. He cared about me. He couldn't give a shite about you. He was only interested in getting your clients.'

'That's not true. He wanted me back,' I say.

'As for you, Ben, we had something special. We loved each other, but that's another thing she messed up for me. You could never let her go,' she says.

'Ben … you love Ben …' I say.

'Now's not the time, Emma. Don't go there,' whispers Ben. They look at each other like there's some unspoken secret.

Emma and Ben. No. That can't be right. Emma knew how I felt about Ben. Something happened between them. They kept this from me. Ben has kept secrets from me. My heart slowly shatters as Emma's voice goes around and around in my head. Emma and Ben. Ben and Emma. Were they in love, and this all happened behind my back? Was I right the whole time?

'There's a party for Jay's family and friends later. Don't you dare come, Jane, you're not welcome. I don't want to see you at the graveyard either. Don't ever speak to me ever again. You think you're something special because of who your sister is. I'll get my revenge on you … and your sister. She thinks she's all that, but she just slept her way to the top. Everyone knows it. I was never invited to any of her stupid engagement parties. She'll pay.' She storms off out of the church. The clip clop sound of her heels echoes in the air.

'She's all talk. Ignore her empty threats—'

'Ben, she said she was in love with you.'

'I can explain. I wanted to tell you, but I didn't know how.'

'You and Emma …'

'Let me take you home. We can talk in the car.'

'How could you keep this from me?'

'My car's over here.' He places his hand on my shoulder and directs me to his car. 'It was a long time ago. She kissed me and then it developed into something. She asked me not to tell you. She didn't want anyone in the bank to find out.'

'How long did this go on for?'

'Not long, but none of that matters now.'

But it does matter. All of this matters. Every single lie they kept from me matters. Emma's right, I am too naive. I'm such a fool. A naive fool. All the times I was pouring my heart out to Emma about being in love with Ben, she was seeing him behind my back. And Ben was lying to me the whole time.

What else has he lied to me about?

'None of this matters, Jane … it was a long time ago,' he says as he shrugs his shoulders.

'There's like this whole other side to you,' I whisper.

'I wanted to tell you, I just didn't know how. I'm still the same person. You know the real me,' he says quietly.

'There's been so much deceitfulness and hurt.'

'Please, just let me drive you home.'

We sit in silence in his flashy black Audi as he drives me home. He places his hand over mine, but I push it away.

'Jane, I'm sorry. I'm sorry for everything. I wish the stuff with Emma never happened. It was a mistake and I regret it,' he says.

'I've heard enough for today,' I say, and I really mean it. My head feels like it's going to explode. I physically can't take in anything else. There's nothing he could say or do right now to make it right.

'None of this takes away from the fact that I love you.'

'Please, Ben. No more,' I say, quivering. I stare out the window wishing Emma never told me any of this. 'Can you drop me off here instead of bringing me home?' I say as we get close to Grafton Street.

His lips move as if he's going to say something, but then he just turns and stares at me.

'There's something else I need to tell you,' he says. He stops the car.

'Not now, Ben,' I say. I slam the car door and get out.

He calls my name, but I don't turn back. His eyes burn into my back until I become lost in the crowd.

When I get to Hidden Secrets, Tara's awake and tells me she's well-rested after that long sleep yesterday.

I offer to spend the day working in the shop. She nods and tells me she would appreciate the help. But really, she's the one helping me. I need to have something to do to take my mind off everything and give me time. Time to process Jay's death. Time to figure out my next move. Time to figure out how to sort out my life and work out how I really feel about Ben.

'You're in a pensive mood today, Jane?'

'I was at a funeral earlier. My ex-boyfriend's. He died in a fire. I thought he loved me, but he didn't really. He dropped me like a hot potato once my friend Emma laid her hands on him and then I find out my friend Ben slept with her behind my back, and she knew I was crazy about him. And I'm having all these crazy dreams—'

'One thing at a time, Jane. Acknowledge the pain, and grieve, but don't let it derail you. You've come so far. How disappointing your friend turned out to be. The dreams will pass.'

'The thing is, the cards told me there would be a death—'

Tara's cup of tea crashes to the floor. 'Your ex-boyfriend that died – is this the man you asked for through the cards?' Her eyes twitch.

'Yeah, it is. It turns out he stole the cards from me. Emma played a part in it too. He was obsessed with making money. It was his downfall in the end.'

'I see. And Emma, is she okay?' She picks up her cup. The handle breaks and the cup falls to the floor. She gets out of her armchair and paces up and down the floor.

'She is alive, but got burnt,' I say.

'Was anyone else involved?'

'Not that I know of.'

'The cards backfire if they are not used with the right intent. They don't suffer fools gladly.' She shakes her head slowly and looks ahead into the distance, deep in thought. 'They would never cause a death, though. That was your boyfriend's own doing.'

'I know, he chose to stay in the cottage instead of leaving when he had a chance. Did anything like this ever happen to you?'

'It did with John. Not the same exactly, but along those lines. He was the one who had Harold's smile. He stole the cards and broke up with me. The cards returned to the shop mysteriously afterwards.'

'I know the cards weren't to blame for this. A spark from a cigarette caused the fire. Jay smoked, he wasn't able to quit,' I say. 'I wonder if I'll ever get my cards back. Emma told me they burnt in the fire.' A strong floral smell tickles my nostrils.

'Only time will tell, Jane. They've a funny way of setting things right. One thing I know for sure is lessons will be learnt.'

Later that evening I email Sorcha; I have been thinking over and over again about everything that's happened since I got my cards and about what Tara said about lessons to be learnt and I let just my thoughts flow out of my head and onto the page.

> Hey Sorcha,
>
> A huge massive congratulations to you. I can't believe you are a married woman now. I hope you are enjoying married life. When all the excitement dies down, I want to hear every last detail of what's been going on with you. My life has been a whirlwind since I last emailed. With happy and sad moments. I lost my job, but that's the least of my worries. Jay is dead, Sorcha. He died in a fire at his cottage on Gull Island. He was so obsessed with his cryptocurrency business that he wouldn't leave his computer equipment when it went on fire. It's shocking to think of. To want something so much you would die chasing it. He even stole my cards to get what he wanted.
>
> His death has been a wake-up call for me to be honest.
>
> I spent so long chasing things – a promotion, being as successful as Gillian and finding someone to love me – that I forgot to slow down and figure out what was really important in life. My lifestyle made me oblivious to what was going on around me and what could make me happy.

Like I ignored Tara's bookshop for years despite the fact of how happy she made me feel each time I stepped inside. I was so taken in by Emma's charm that I couldn't see how toxic and dangerous she was. She had a thing going on with Ben when we first started working together and they never told me. Herself and Jay were seeing each other behind my back and it turns out she was jealous of me the whole time because of Ben. He has told me he loved me all along and you know what, I was so stuck with a victim mentality that I couldn't possibly ever get what I deserved. I used to think that I would never be as good as Gillan. Like who was I to step out into the light. How stupid was I. I think we say to ourselves we can't do certain things but in fact we can. I am my own worst enemy at times.

I think the cards made me step out of my comfort zone and take more chances, which was badly needed.

Love,
Jane xxxx

Just before I fall asleep a text comes through from her.

Omg! Jane. You have been through the mill! It's like you've been stuck in a soap opera ever since you got the cards, but lots of insight too. As well as giving you whatever you wanted perhaps what the cards set out to do is show you what you really needed to know. Despite everything you've been through you've handled it all so well. xxx
What's going to happen with you and the lovely Ben?

I text back.

I haven't figured that out yet. I'm still shocked and mourning the loss of Jay. I hope you are well. Can't wait to see you soon. Miss you. xxx

CHAPTER 32

THE DREAMS ABOUT JAY still haven't stopped. Sometimes I wake up at night and lie awake for hours – thinking about our time together. Even though we weren't together when he died, I still can't help replaying our conversations in my head. I've been googling a lot about shock and grief to find out when I should start to feel normal again, but I'm getting no straight answers. Only stuff like, *Time is the greatest healer* or *Time is the only answer.*

I've been thinking a lot about Emma too, and the fact that she had a thing going on with Ben. She must have been laughing at me behind my back that whole time I went on about how much I liked Ben. The fact that I don't have Ben in my life anymore is so hard. I think them getting together was probably more Emma's doing. Ben really is a good guy. He is that and more. He should have told me about his past with Emma but does that really matter now? What matters is looking ahead to a brighter future. One with Ben in my life. I don't want to lose him.

I know I need to stop the overthinking, and move on with my life. I know I should ring Ben, and clear the air, and have a proper conversation once and for all. I keep telling myself I'll do it soon, but I stay in my pyjamas most of the time, only leaving the house to go to the bookshop or to get a few groceries.

When Gillian phones me and insists I go wedding dress shopping with her, I welcome the distraction. Her friend, Rose, was supposed to go with her, but she cancelled at the last minute. Normally I'd dread having to partake in something like that but it's strangely soothing to have someone take over and tell me what to do. I can't bring myself to tell her I lost my job. I'll leave that one for when I feel stronger. For now though, meeting up with Gillian and concentrating on her wedding is just what I need.

'Wear something presentable and remember to smile. A normal smile, not one of your lopsided ones. There's bound to be paparazzi at the airport. There always is when I'm around,' she says.

'Sure. I'll do my best,' I say. I have an urge to tell her about the cards. I don't though, she'll never believe the cards are magical. I dread to think what's ahead of me and what other fears are coming down the line.

'Mam told me you broke up with your boyfriend. He dumped you, she said.'

'Yeah … it's a long story. Anyway he's … he's … I don't want to talk about it,' I say.

'You really don't have much luck with men. Do you, Jane? Do you ever think you might be gay?'

'Gay? Where on earth is that coming from? Seriously Gillan …'

'You can tell me if you are. I won't judge. It would explain a lot though.'

'I'm not gay, Gillian, and if I was I wouldn't hide it.'

'Never mind. Just don't let me down, Jane,' she says before we end the call.

'I won't,' I say.

I kept my promise whereas she forgot.

I think back to the day we made the promise. It was a summer's day, but it was lashing raining which isn't unusual in Ireland. I was about six years old at the time.

'When I grow up, I'm going to be a famous actress and have adoring fans all over the world,' Gillian said as she put on some of Mam's lipstick and wrapped a shawl over her head.

'Do you think so? Really.'

'Why wouldn't I be? I have as much chance as anyone else. Look at me, I was born for the stage.' She glided across the room, doing some sort of ballet move before she sang *la, la, laaaaa, la, laaaaaaaaaaaa. I am the best.*

'And I,' I said in a voice I hoped sounded just like hers, 'I will be your biggest fan.'

'Promise me, we'll always have each other's backs. No matter what happens. That we will still have midnight feasts and sleepovers even when we're older and that we will still be best friends and tell each other all our secrets.'

'I promise,' I said solemnly and we shook on it. I meant it. Every single word of it.

After the call with Gillian, I search for the case I want for the overnight trip. I picture in my mind the exact one I want. I find every other case apart from the Louis Vuitton one. A Louis Vuitton case symbolises power and success, which is the exact impression I need to give.

I find it squashed at the back of my wardrobe. I open the case. It smells a bit musty. I give it a quick clean and take the dust away. I check the size. It should fit perfectly in the overhead locker as hand luggage.

Who knows where we might end up for dinner? The Ivy is one of Gillian's regular haunts. In this instance it's better to be overdressed than underdressed. The press will probably try to make a big story out of a snapshot of us together. I hope they won't comment on how similar we look yet how different our lives are. What if they find out I lost my job? I hope they haven't got wind of that.

I need shoes. I place a pair of Louboutin heels in the case. They represent empowerment. The forbidden shoe. I'll change into them once the plane lands. These are the least comfortable pair of shoes I own, but I can deal with all the pain once I get home. I throw in a pair of red Gucci ballet flats as a back-up.

Now for the right dress. I get the red, off-the-shoulder, ruffled Zuhair Murad dress from my wardrobe. It's still in the bag from the dry cleaners. The last time I wore this was to the Academy Awards when Gillian won an Oscar. I try it on. It's a bit tight, but it still fits. It will give the illusion that I'm graceful, sophisticated, and elegant. Just like Gillian. I place it carefully in the case.

I grab a pair of huge sunglasses, stick on some red lipstick, and practise a few poses in the mirror. I throw both into the case and scan what I've packed so far.

All Gillian's hand-me-downs.

My pyjamas, underwear, a toothbrush, a clutch handbag, and diamond jewellery go in next. The rest of the stuff I need can go in my handbag. I zip up my case. The zipper clicks into place.

The flight to London Heathrow leaves in a few hours.

I wish I had more time to prepare for the trip, but I guess if Vera Wang has a last-minute cancellation, it can't be helped. It's typical Gillian though. She calls and everyone scrambles around to please her.

I remember the last time I went out with Gillian. It was to celebrate my eighteenth birthday somewhere in London. She did my make-up. I wore one of her designer dresses and it fitted my curves in all the right places. Gillian was flirting with the door man of the nightclub, named Ged. He was someone who loved the bit of power he held in his position.

I was annoyed with Gillian for acting so flirty – it meant so much to her whether he let us into the club or not. My wonderful, talented sister cared too much about idiots like this Ged guy.

'I'm an actress, really I am,' she said to him.

'But I don't recognise you. What movies are you in?' he said, smirking.

He knew damn well who she was. He just wanted her to suck up to him. This really got to me, that my beautiful talented sister had to explain herself to him.

Gillian leaned forward and whispered something into his ear. I didn't hear clearly, but it was something about giving him a review on social media.

It embarrassed me that Gillian went on like this. I would have walked away by now.

He nodded and then turned to me. 'Who's this? Another actress?' he asked. He eyed me up and down, waiting for me to flirt with him or something along those lines.

I stood there deadpan.

He wasn't impressed.

'We're sisters,' I said curtly.

Gillian gave him another one of her effortless smiles and he let us in. From the moment we entered the nightclub, The Imperial, I think it was called, Gillian made everything seem bright and dazzling. I was in awe of her. I loved being in her presence. Everywhere she went, she flirted. I followed, just like her shadow. When we danced, men hit on us and wanted to buy us drinks. I never got so much attention on a night out before.

I got compliments all night. I wasn't interested in any of the men, they all seemed obnoxious to me. Gillian got annoyed with me for not flirting back with any of them. She pulled me aside from her group of admirers, and told me to let my hair down and not be so serious all the time. *Have a bit of fun for once in your life. You might even enjoy yourself, Jane,* she said.

I tried hard to relax, to go along with the jokes and the small talk. I laughed when Gillian laughed – tried to copy her body language even – to play the game. There didn't seem to be any rules though, people like Gillian don't follow any. They make them up as they go along.

She got so drunk that night, and went off with some guys to a party. I pleaded with her not to go. I told her it would be all over the newspapers the next morning, but it didn't matter, she didn't listen, and I ended up going back to her apartment on my own.

I take deep breaths as the plane lands. I love travelling and seeing new places but hate flying. I had a bad experience on a plane once where we hit too much turbulence and I feared for my life. I've been a nervous flyer ever since.

It's only after I get off the plane, I realise I didn't need anything to get me through the flight. Normally I'd have at least three vodkas to steady my nerves. I'm more nervous about meeting Gillian, I didn't think about the plane crashing at all.

Does this mean I'm over my fear of flying? Perhaps it does.

When I get to arrivals, I put on my sunglasses and cover my face with as much hair as possible. I wait to hear the screams and the click of cameras, but there's none. Gillian's driver approaches me with two burly security men and brings me to a private carpark where my sister is waiting. She's in the back seat of a blacked-out limousine with the rest of her entourage. They travel around everywhere with her. There's Sophie, her head personal assistant, Mark and Adam, her two bodyguards and Isabella and Ciara, her make-up artist and stylist.

Gillian's face is blotchy and red. Her eyes look glassy. Her hair extensions are a mess. Her hairdresser must be taking a break or gone on strike. She's wearing baggy tracksuit bottoms and a white stained t-shirt.

'Gillian? Is that you?' I say, shocked that she's looking so rough. I can't remember ever seeing her looking this bad.

'I've left him, Jane. I've left Michael,' she says, through tears.

'What! Why, what happened?'

'I caught him kissing some nineteen-year-old wannabe actress yesterday. She's not even as famous as me.'

'No way,' I say, and I mean it. There's no way I would have predicted this.

'It's over between us. I called off the wedding.' She puts her hands up to her face and shakes her head.

'Oh, Gillian. That's awful,' I say. The press will have a field day with this one. I need to make sure she doesn't read anything about herself over the next while.

'I just want to go home and hide, take us home,' she says to her driver.

She places her head on my shoulder and sobs her heart out. I sit in the limo feeling awkward. I pat her head. I'm not used to seeing her vulnerable like this. Apart from when we were little, I've never seen her cry.

'You poor thing,' I say.

'I can never take him back now, Jane. If I did, I'd look like a fool. I just hope the press don't get hold of this.' She blows her nose into a tissue and looks in the mirror.

'I'm sure your team will be able to keep this out of the press,' I mutter. I cross my fingers. I can only imagine the headlines now. More along the lines of the crap people read on social media most likely. She's right though, there is no way they should get married after this, no matter what his excuse is.

'Oh, my good God. I look awful. I cancelled the dress appointment with Vera Wang. There's no point going,' says Gillian.

'Of course not,' I say. I'm secretly delighted I don't need to go through that torture anymore.

When we get to her apartment in Knightsbridge, I trail behind her, and we walk up the stairs. When we reach the landing there's loads of doors. I've never been in this apartment before, so I haven't a clue where to go. It's just like a show home. It's all fancy sculptures, fountains and plants everywhere. When we enter the expensive-looking living room Gillian's yoga instructor, Colleen is standing at the door waiting for us. She is gushing with concern for Gillian as she walks towards us and puts her hand on the small of Gillian's back, but Gillian pulls away and asks for privacy.

I'm afraid to sit down in case I make a mark on the pristine furniture. Everything is spotless. There's not a thing out of place, but there are little personal touches dotted around the room. Family photographs on the walls and some of herself and Michael placed on the baby grand piano. As well as a professional actress, singer and dancer Gillian is an accomplished piano player. Whereas I'm tone deaf. If only I had half of her talents my life would be very different.

'The problem is in my line of work I have men throwing themselves at me,' she says.

Ah here, that doesn't seem like much of a problem to me, but then this is Gillian's world I'm in now. Nothing makes much sense.

'Right,' I say. 'How awful.'

'But so does Michael and he doesn't have the willpower I do.' She flops onto the couch and puts her feet up. The varnish on her toenails is chipped. 'Well don't just stand there with your mouth open, Jane. What are you waiting for? Sit down here beside me.'

'Okay. Where should I go?'

'For God's sake. Just sit.' She beckons me to come towards her. 'It just occurred to me, I never even asked how you are.' She examines me from head to toe. 'You look ... you look different.'

'Right.' I've no idea whether that's good or bad.

'Anything new or strange with you?'

'Well, yeah there is. I lost my job—'

'Oh, Jane. That's just an office job. You'll find another one. What am I going to do? I thought once I got married, I would settle down and have a few kids. Move to the Cotswolds. Stay out of the limelight. It would be my chance to finally retire and live my life the way I want.'

'Retire? But you're not even twenty-five yet!'

'I'm so trapped right now,' she whimpers.

'I thought you loved your life. Do you know how many people would kill to be as talented and successful as you?'

'It's not as good as it looks … it's not all it's cracked up to be.'

'I'd hardly call you trapped. You're the famous Gillian O'Hara. Just look at this place. It's fabulous. You have it all. Anyway, you'll meet someone else. You always do. You'll be fine.'

'You have no idea how exhausting it is being me. I worry constantly about trying to get the next job and being as good as the competition. My schedule is gruelling. I never get a rest.'

'I get that you're busy, but maybe you just need some time off to relax. Take a break and then you'll be refreshed and ready to face the work again.'

'I'm so afraid of letting people down. I wish I could start all over and follow a different path. Then I'd be free. I wish I could be more like you, Jane.' She gives me a look that means she's being genuine.

'What? More like me? Eh, why?'

'You're free. You make your own choices. You have freedom. I envy that.' She reaches over to me and sobs on my shoulder. 'I can't do this anymore. I really can't.'

'Ah Gillian, it's okay. It will all be okay,' I say. I'm shocked. Completely and utterly shocked.

We sit together for the rest of the evening and Gillian pours her heart out to me. She tells me about her insecurities from being in the acting business and how she longs for a quiet life. One where she can walk down the street unnoticed and do simple things like get a coffee or buy a newspaper and sit on a park bench undisturbed. She wishes she knew who she can trust, as now apart from me and Mam, she has no one to turn to. She's afraid of being laughed at once it gets out that she's called off the engagement.

'My problems with men stem from my relationship with Dad, I'm sure of it. Dad showed little or no interest in me after he left,' she says. 'I thought he would be proud of me when I became famous, but he still doesn't care. I'll never have his approval for anything I do.'

'He does care. I know he cares about us.'

'You were always his favourite. You're the clever one and that's what he admires most. I'll never have that same closeness as you do with him.'

'Nah. You just need to see him more often.'

'Perhaps.' She turns and looks me straight in the eye. 'You know, you're one of the few people that never sold a story about me to the press. I appreciate that, Jane,' she says. 'God knows you've seen me at my worst. I can't honestly put my hand on my heart and say that about any of my friends. I know we haven't been close, but I can count on you. It can't have been easy for you when you were younger, and I was away so much. Then there was Mam's drinking ... I hated it when I missed your twenty-first birthday party. I never even made that up to you.'

I smile and my heart starts to melt a little for her. Finally, some of the old Gillian is coming back. That's the first time she's ever apologised to me since she became famous. Our relationship will never be perfect. Our lives are so different, but maybe one day we can find some sort of middle ground and see things from each other's point of view. I feel sorry for her now, but she'll bounce back. She'll be grand. Things always work out for Gillian. She's just that type of person.

'There's something I'd like to tell you,' she says in a childlike voice.

'What ... what is it?'

She's scared.

'The other night after I caught Michael snogging someone else, I was so upset.'

'Of course you were. I can only imagine how devastating it was for you.'

'But the thing is ... well I ... I don't know how to say this the right ... I ... I.'

'Just spit it out Gillian. Whatever it is, you can trust me.'

'Colleen, my yoga instructor was great to me afterwards ...'

'That's good,' I say.

'We had a few drinks and she ... she kissed me, and one thing led to another ...'

'You and Colleen ...'

'Yes. The thing is I liked it. I really liked it. It was better than being with Michael. There was no comparison really. The way she touched me and the connection we had was ... was out of this world.'

'Was that your first time? ... With a woman, I mean.'

'There's been other times. Mainly strangers and I had a few flings before.'

She doesn't make any eye contact and then lowers her gaze to the floor. It took guts to tell me that. So, she's been hiding her feelings for a long time.

'Apart from Colleen, I've never told anyone else this. I've been too scared.'

'Scared of what?' I whisper as I move closer to her.

'Scared of everything going if I admit who I really am. My fans hating me. My career being ruined. My life being ruined. Not living up to people's expectations. Mam's reaction.'

'There's no need to be scared,' I say. I rub her arm and she leans in towards me. 'Other people's opinions don't matter. All that matters is that you're happy.'

'I was projecting earlier ... all the stuff I said to you about being gay. It was about me, not you. I'm bi-sexual and I'm mad about Colleen. I want to be with her more than anything. She's beautiful, caring and so sensitive. She just gets me ...'

'Well, that's what you need to do, sis. Be with whoever you want to be with and start living your life for you. Not anyone else.'

'Thank you ... thank you, Jane,' she says as she breaks down in tears in my arms.

I leave her apartment early the next morning and get my flight back to Dublin. As the plane lands I look out over the beauty of Dublin Bay. No matter where I've been in the world, I love the feeling of being back in Ireland. I'm so lucky to live here. I think about Gillian being trapped in her life and my mind races. Gillian doesn't have cards like mine, that much is clear now. Although she believed in her ability to become a star from a young age, she's struggling like the rest of us. She has a softness and vulnerability to her that I could never see before because I was too wrapped up in trying to be as successful as her.

I wonder if she will ever find the courage to get the freedom she yearns for.

I hopes she does, because I genuinely want her to be happy.

But what about me? Will I ever be happy?

What have I got to go home to? My cards are gone. I've lost my job, my friend and boyfriend and Ben. I'm worse off now than before Tara gave me the cards. I should be devastated.

But I'm not.

In fact, I feel a little lighter and more at ease than before. Happier even. Gillian was right what she said about my freedom. I am free. Free in a way she will never be unless she lets go of the trappings of fame. I have my whole life ahead of me and I can make my own choices.

Things are finally starting to make sense. I haven't really lost Ben. I'm definitely going to contact him soon.

CHAPTER 33

DAYS PASS BY IN a blur. Nothing eventful happens. One day while I'm in the bookshop I broach the subject with Tara about her fears.

'Tara, what sort of fears did you have?' I say.

'I was afraid of spiders, but the cards made me face that fear.'

'How?' I asked.

'I began to see them everywhere in the shop. In places where I've never noticed them before. It was overwhelming.'

'That's awful. What did you do?'

'At first, I thought it was some infestation, so I got an exterminator into the shop, but that didn't work. I still saw them everywhere. Like on the street or in my car.'

'Oh my God. Did they ever go away?'

'Yes and no.'

'What do you mean?'

'I got used to seeing them so much I soon realised there was nothing to fear. They weren't going to cause me any harm.'

'Do you still see them, Tara? Like the way you did before?'

'No. I believe because I faced up to my fear of spiders they just went away.'

It hits me how weird this conversation is and how calm Tara is. I get this sense of calmness off her, but at the same time a vulnerability. She's fascinating. I could spend all day talking to her.

'And what about your other fears? Tell me about another fear you had.'

'I was afraid my nearest and dearest wouldn't be around anymore ...' She stares ahead into the distance and purses her lips. '... and that I would be left on my own.'

'Like dying you mean …' I whisper. 'I can understand why you would think that after Harold passing away so young.'

'No, it wasn't that. I'm not afraid of my loved ones dying.' She frowns and her eyes look troubled. 'I'm afraid of them not being close by anymore.'

'Oh sorry, Tara. That's so sad. I shouldn't have said that. For mentioning the dying piece. I didn't fully understand what you meant. It's sad about Harold's death, but you still have your daughter. It must be lovely for you to have her close by.'

'What do you mean by that?' she says, slightly startled.

'Your daughter … you told me before she lives close by.'

'Yes, you're right. She's still around. I have yet to face that fear though. I have work to do in my office, Jane. Can you please look after the shop for a while?'

'Of course,' I say.

I'm puzzled by what she said about her daughter, but I know better than to ask. She walks away, leaving me in the shop on my own. I smell lilies all around me.

Late afternoon the next day, I'm in my pyjamas updating my CV. The thought of going through the interview process fills me with dread. Who's going to want to hire someone who has just been fired from their job?

Once Christmas is over, I'll need to really focus on getting a new job, but at least I can still help Tara out in the bookshop until then.

The news comes on the TV. Walter is on the screen being interviewed by a news reporter outside the bank.

'Becker Bank International has closed its Dublin branch today due to the loss of many of its high investment clients, resulting in 22,890 job losses rippling through the bank worldwide,' says the news reporter.

Some very pissed-off looking colleagues appear on the screen exiting the bank. The camera focuses on Ben. He's frowning, holding a box of his belongings in his hand. I can't believe everyone has lost their jobs. This is all because of Emma and Jay taking my clients.

'It's a sad day we close the doors here at Becker Bank International. This branch will be the first of the five hundred branches we have across the globe soon to close. This bank has been in my family for many generations,' says Walter.

The news reporter turns to some distraught employees, and they give their thoughts on having no job the day before Christmas Eve. The stories are heartbreaking. Some people discuss not being able to afford to buy Christmas presents for their kids and the worries they have about not being able to pay their mortgage or rent.

'It won't feel like Christmas in our house this year,' someone being interviewed says. Another employee shouts, 'Walter Becker is nothing but a scrooge. To fire us just like that when we did nothing wrong, well it's criminal.'

The camera turns to Ben who walks away from the reporter just before he says, no comment.

I pause the TV, so his face covers the screen. He's genuinely upset. My eyes well up. The anger I had felt towards him after Jay's funeral has gone. It's been gone for a while now. All I can think about is the kiss with Ben. My fingers touch my lips. My stomach churns. I hope he's okay. It's odd seeing him upset. He looks like he could do with some help. It's about time I stopped messing around. We both deserve to be happy. He needs to end things with Sarah once and for all and we can start a relationship afresh. I want to give it a go with Ben.

I dial his number as my hands shake.

I need to hear his voice. Please pick up Ben. Please pick up.

'Ben, Ben – is that you?' I say.

'Jane, it's Sarah ... so, I take it you heard the news. Has Ben told you everything? Everyone was working as normal and then the next minute he was told to pack up his stuff and leave. Just like that, everyone lost their jobs.'

'I just watched the news. That's why I'm calling ... I just wanted to see how Ben is ... I mean ...how you both are. How are you?'

I hear voices faintly on the phone. It's like Sarah and Ben are having an angry conversation, but it's hard to make out. I hold the phone closer to my ear and can make out an argument of some sort. I imagine Ben rolling his eyes at Sarah.

'Ben, are you there? Hello. Hello,' I say. I'm desperate to hear his voice.

'Hey, Jane. Sorry about that. Sarah just popped into my apartment, to get some of her stuff, but she's on her way out now. So, you heard the news. It's fucked up. Becker just walked in with a load of security and that was it. We were told to drop whatever we were doing and pack up our stuff.'

'I am sorry, Ben. I really am—'

'It's a messed-up situation, but you have nothing to be sorry for.'

'It was my clients that left the bank and I feel like I'm somehow responsible—'

'Nah. There's no way this was your fault. Emma and Jay are responsible for this, they shouldn't have taken your cards. Hold on a sec. Sarah's on her way out,' he says.

'Okay. Sure.' I place the phone down on the table and I breathe slowly. My heart is pounding, and I feel panicky. Ben's acting as if Sarah doesn't live with him anymore. They must have broken up.

Why am I so nervous? I wish I could talk to him in person without all the interruptions on the phone. I can't gauge what's really going on. I want the bad feelings between us to go away.

'Sorry about that,' he says when he comes back.

'I missed you. I really did,' I say. 'I kept meaning to call.'

'You too, Jane. I missed you too.'

'Can we meet? I think it would be good for us to talk and … well I want to see you.'

'Sure. How about tomorrow? You could come over here. There's something I need to tell you.'

'What about today? Are you free now?'

'I don't know, Jane.'

'Can you meet me at St Stephen's Green in an hour … beside the ice-skating rink in front of the food stalls? We can get a hot chocolate and talk then?'

'That's not a good time.'

'How about half past five? We can get a bite to eat …'

I've got this urge now to tell him it was always him I loved. That I've moved on from my obsession with Jay and I'm not under his spell anymore. I love him, and I always have and always will. I don't need the cards.

'Not today.' He lowers his voice softly.

'What you said to me in my office. Did you mean it?'

'When?'

'When you told me you loved me.'

He hesitates. 'But … but … I mean yes. I did. I meant it at the time, but we can't keep going around in circles like this.'

'If you meant what you said you'll be there. I'll be in front of the ice-skating rink at St. Stephen's Green.'

I wait for Ben to reply, but all I can hear is his breath against the phone.

'Ben, are you still there? Can you hear me?'

'I'm still here. I heard you. I … I have to go.' I hear a sharp beep … beep … beep… beep sound. I stare at my phone confused. Ben has hung up.

Does that mean he'll be there?

Until I see him, I won't know what's going on. He won't let me down. He's never let me down before. I wish I knew what he was thinking. I think back to all the good times we had working in the bank together. He's always made me laugh or given me a boost, even when I wasn't feeling good. The bank closing symbolises a chapter of my life ending and a new beginning. Gillian was right. I am free. I have the freedom to move on and decide what I want to do next on my own terms. I don't need to try to be as successful as her. I can be successful in my own way, whatever way that is. Ben had been telling me this all along, but I couldn't see it at the time. I wasn't ready then to listen, but I get it now.

I feel high. I get a burst of energy. I tidy my apartment as I think about Ben. My wish to meet someone new to get over Ben seems so insignificant now. That was stupid. It's always been about Ben.

He's on my mind as I spend the next few hours shopping for food for Christmas and decorating my apartment. Maybe I won't go to my mam's house for Christmas this year at all. The thought of having a relaxed Christmas day in my apartment with Ben seems perfect.

I'm humming Christmas carols as I walk to meet him.

I get a sense that I'm being followed again. I shiver as I feel like eyes are upon me. Then I see her. The girl with the pigtails. She runs past me. I follow her. I want to finally get a chance to talk to her. As I turn the corner, she's sitting on the ground not far from Hidden Secrets.

I sit down beside her, and she looks at me directly. I get the feeling of déjà vu and then something inside me clicks.

Maybe in some weird way she is me as a child.

Am I face to face with myself as a child? Have the cards done this?

Is this where I have a chance to change the path of my life?

I turn to her and smile.

'I know what it feels like to be lost. I was once lost like you, but it doesn't need to be this way. You don't need to run anymore.'

'I need to keep an eye on my mum. She still needs me. She misses me too much and I can't find my dad. I want to see my dad,' says the little girl in a soft, sad voice.

I think back to the time when my dad was minding me at the bookshop. He was so pre-occupied with work. There was one day I lost him. I was stacking books with Tara and when I went back to the snug he had been sitting in, he was gone. I was terrified at the time. I searched everywhere for him. When he came back, he told me he left to take a work call and he couldn't get a signal in the shop. I had nightmares for years afterwards. Nightmares where I'm lost and I'm all on my own. Maybe all of this is somehow connected to that experience.

I focus my attention on the girl and search to find the right words to help her, but she's not there anymore. She's standing in the middle of the road up ahead.

'Dad, Dad, you came for me. I missed you, Dad. Bring me with you, I want to go now. I don't need to stay here anymore,' says the girl.

She walks off down the street holding a man's hand, skipping happily. The man's appearance is faint, but his outline shows a tall man wearing a hat.

That must be her dad. She's happy now. The happiness is radiating from her.

I close my eyes and contentment washes over me. The girl and her dad disappear, and then white feathers fall from the sky. Lots and lots of soft beautiful feathers. They float along towards the open door of the bookshop.

Something shifts inside. Is this what true happiness feels like? I think it is. Almost. Perhaps I've faced all my fears now and let go of whatever was blocking me.

I'm late to meet Ben, so I run towards St. Stephen's Green. I have butterflies in my stomach as I think about what to say. I want to articulate it with such meaning that Ben will have no doubt how strong my feelings are.

I search ahead for signs of him, but I can't see him anywhere. My heart beats fast and loud. So loud that it almost deafens me. I see him. I smile. A huge smile.

He came. I knew he would. It's time. I'm ready now. Ready to start a new chapter of my life with the man I love.

'You have no idea how much I wanted to see you,' I say as I take his hand. It feels soft and warm, but strong. It's like the perfect fit.

CHAPTER 34

'YOU CAME. I KNEW you would,' I say. My heart soars so much it's as if it's going to jump out of my body.

'I can't stay long,' he says.

'Just listen to what I have to say.'

'Before you say anything I need to tell you something.'

'All that stuff you said to me in my office, well, I feel the same way. Like when you told me you loved me. I want to give it a go. I'm ready now, Ben. Being rejected was a big fear of mine for a long time, but I've finally found the courage to tell you.'

'But things have changed.'

'I know you're upset you lost your job, but we'll both get new jobs.'

'That's not the only thing that's changed.'

'I don't need my cards anymore. I've figured it all out. I know I'll be fine without them. I'm not as obsessed about work like I used to be. It's a fresh start for me. Gillian helped me see how lucky I am. You told me this all along, and I get it all now.'

'Good. Good. I'm glad, but I can't do this anymore, Jane,' he says as he steps back from me.

'What ... what's going on?' I move towards him and wrap my arms around his neck.

He takes my arms away. 'I can't do this, I've moved on. I had to. Sarah and I, well, we are ... we're engaged.'

'Engaged!' I say as my stomach lurches. The marriage card. This is what the cards were referring to. It's come true.

'She proposed to me and I said yes. At first I thought I had to go along with it for a short while, but everyone wants this to go ahead. Our family and friends are so excited ... and I thought you hated me. We keep going around in circles. I don't want to hurt you and I don't want you to hate me anymore.' He walks further away making the distance between us like a big hole I can't fill.

He avoids my eyes and gazes down at the floor. A group of teenagers comes between us. Their laughter is loud and carefree. They have no idea how significant this moment is in my life. If only I could be a teenager again, I'd do things very differently.

'You told me you loved me. You said you didn't love her.'

'I did love you, but I have to move on. The things Emma said to you … she hurt you because of me and I don't want to hurt you anymore … I need to give it a proper go with Sarah. She's already started planning the wedding … I bought her a ring. A very expensive ring.' He raises his eyebrows.

'You say you don't want to hurt me. You think this won't hurt me?' My voice cracks.

'I want to move on. I'm trying to move on. I need to get you off my mind … out of my head.' I wish the ground could just swallow me up. I stare down at the ground and see cracks everywhere. 'I didn't know you cared. You were so wrapped up in Jay. I thought you still loved him …'

'His death has showed me I need to stop wasting time. His life was cut too short, but we could have a future together. I was so excited, but now…. now you tell me you don't want me.'

'It's for the best. Believe me, it is.'

'So, this is it. You're just going to give up on us.'

'There is no us. I mean we can still be friends. I don't want to lose you as a friend.'

'I feel like you've closed your heart to me.'

'I have to, Jane.' His eyes tear up.

'No, you don't.'

'I do. Believe me, I do. It's for the best.'

'So that's it. Best of luck with your new life.' I walk away backwards to get one last look at his face.

'I wish things were different. I wish I never got involved with Emma.'

'That's just an excuse. You're throwing me aside just like you did with Emma.'

'It's not like that. I never threw her aside. I just … moved on.'

'Congratulations on the wedding. Pass my regards on to Sarah. Have a nice life.'

'Don't go … Jane … come back. We can't leave it like this.'

I walk off out of St. Stephen's Green in shock. Complete and utter shock. Never in my wildest dreams did I imagine this is how things would play out.

Tara is busy with customers as I enter Hidden Secrets, she doesn't even notice me, so I just sit down in a snug by myself. I came straight here after the disaster with Ben. Snow falls from my coat, and I stomp on it with force as it lands on the ground. I imagine it being my heart shattering to pieces.

My past with Ben flashes through my mind, like clips from a movie. Memories come back: colours, vivid images and feelings. Moments of time that are so hard to watch. The way he looked at me when we first met. Times when he teased me as we sat next to one another. How his eyes changed with intensity when we were together. Him being kind to me when I went crazy. Kissing me in my room. Me taking care of his bruised eyes, and him telling me he loved me, that he loved everything about me. Him being there for me at the funeral.

Some of the sweet things he said to me, race through my head: *I think I'm going to miss you sitting beside me. The Jane I know is smart, hard-working and logical. Which are all qualities that would attract a promotion. I'm surprised you didn't get one sooner. I can also see how Jay was attracted to you. You have no idea how long I've wanted to kiss you. I love you. I love everything about you. The other night when we were in bed together … well that was a wakeup call for me.*

The more I think about him, I'm brimming with anger. He's engaged!

Why did he tell me he loved me before?

I sit in silence and just let the rage wash over me. Despite being so angry with him, I know I still care about him. God, this is so hard. Too hard.

How will I recover from this? This morning, the world seemed full of hope and possibilities, but now I feel like I'm dying inside. My life has changed completely in just a few hours.

I try to block out all thoughts, but the next memory knocks me over like a tidal wave, almost drowning me. I'm brought back to when I told him how I felt, but he rejected me. Complete and utter rejection. Ben's voice comes into my head, *I can't do this, I've moved on. I had to. Sarah and I, well we are … we're engaged.*

That moment of rejection will play on my mind forever. When my heart was ripped open, sucking the life out of me.

Every Christmas, I'll remember this day and shudder.

Tara approaches me. The white feathers from earlier surround her. She's glowing inside, and looks years younger.

'What good timing this is. I have some news,' she says smiling. 'You're very pale. Why, whatever is the matter?'

'I hope it's good news. No bad news please.' I place my hands up over my face. I don't think I could take anymore disappointment.' My stomach churns. 'I just poured my heart out to Ben. I finally told him I loved him, but he turned me down. He's engaged, Tara! I just made a fool out of myself.'

'There's no harm done there, Jane. You were right to tell him how you feel. You should have done it sooner.' Her voice softens.

'But Tara, I can't see him ever again. Not after what happened. This is the whole reason why I never told him in the first place … in case he turned me down. Which he just did … I faced my fear, and he rejected me.' I cover my face in my hands in embarrassment.

'Jane, my dear, come with me,' she replies as she takes my hand.

We sit at the café section and Tara hands me a brownie and ice-cream with sprinkles.

Her eyes twinkle as she watches me eat. 'You still like it, after all this time,' she says.

'Of course, who in their right mind would say no to this? Apart from my crazy sister, that is.' I smile at the thoughts of my sister.

'Love is so hard, Tara.'

'Yes, but you did the right thing. You should be proud of yourself. You need to let him go now. If he truly loves you, he'll be back.'

'God … I doubt he'll be back … I've lost Ben. I can't be his friend now; I can't go to their wedding. I hope he doesn't expect me to.'

'You will get over this. You are stronger than you think.'

Can I really do it? Just let Ben go, like Tara said? I have no choice, I have to.

'I'm afraid I have more news to break to you. I've decided to spend some time in Florida to live with my sister, Chloe,' she blurts out. 'I had an epiphany today when the feathers arrived. I'm wasting my life and it's time to move on.'

'Why?'

'My doctor has been urging me to take things easy and get more time in the sun. It's time I took his advice. I was worried about leaving my daughter, but I don't need to worry anymore.'

I've no idea what she means about leaving her daughter, but I don't ask as she didn't want to talk about her before.

'But the bookshop. You told me you could never leave it.'

'I need to give up control. I've decided to get a manager in place to take care of things while I'm away. Once the person is in place I'm off.' Tara smiles.

'If that's what you need to do. I'm happy for you but I'll miss you so much.' I hug her tightly as tears stream down my face. I don't want to let her go.

'I'll miss you too, but it's not the end. We can still stay in touch.'

I love this place, but it won't be the same when Tara leaves. It's Tara that makes this shop so wonderful. I don't want to lose her. I wish she could stay forever. Sorcha not coming home was tough, then Ben rejected me and now Tara is leaving.

I don't bother even turning on the light when I get home. I sit on my couch and think about my fears and how I've been made to face them. It feels good knowing I did. Everyone leaving me doesn't feel as soul destroying as I thought it would. I hear Tara's voice in my head: *You need to let him go, Jane. He will come back to you if it's meant to be.* I know she's right – there's nothing else I can do. It's time to let go. Although it didn't work out with Ben at least I tried, and Tara's not gone forever. We'll keep in touch.

When I get up to get ready for bed, I realise I've been sitting in the dark for quite some time and it didn't even bother me.

When I awake the next morning, something feels different. I can't put my finger on it. I stretch out and yawn and then I realise what it is. The noises are gone. For the first time since I got the cards, I've slept through the night.

But why? Does this mean I've learnt my lessons?

My phone rings, interrupting my thoughts. It's my dad. I tell him that I lost my job.

'This is just a blip. With your talents you'll be snapped up in no time,' he says. 'You should make the most of your time off now, Jane. Before you know it, you'll be working God knows how many hours again.'

He asks me to come and stay with him. He's going to pay for my flight.

To be honest the thought of just getting on a plane away and leaving my life behind is so appealing right now. Even if it's just for a week.

I tell him I'll go as soon as I can. He's going to book the next flight which is an overnight flight on Christmas Eve that will get me there early in time for Christmas Day. When I mention to him, I've been spending time in Hidden Secrets again, I feel his smile through the phone.

'She was a lovely lady – the owner. She really took a shine to you. It was sad what she went through,' he says.

'What exactly happened, Dad?' I ask.

'All I know is there was some sort of traffic accident right outside the bookshop. She lost someone close. She bought the bookshop after it happened … to keep herself busy, she told me.'

I call Mam to let her know my plans to spend Christmas in Toronto with my dad.

'How could you do this to your sister? She needs your support more than ever. She needs you here. Christmas Day is going to be so difficult for her,' says my mam. 'We need to be there for her.'

'I'll be back for New Year's Eve—'

'That's not good enough. Poor Gillian.'

'What about me? Have you ever stopped to think about me? I'm sick of feeling like I don't matter. I'm sorry I'm not as successful in your eyes as Gillian, but I'm living life now on my own terms. Like it or lump it. Gillian may have broken up with her boyfriend, but mine DIED!'

'Oh … well. I didn't know that. You never told me. How was I to know? You should have said.'

'Hence why I won't be home for Christmas.'

'But … how did he die?'

'That doesn't matter, Mam. The fact is, he was someone I cared about, and now he's gone.'

'But I didn't know.'

'I've been through a lot in the past while. Gillian's not the only one suffering right now. And if you ever took the time to ask Gillian what she wants, you'd realise that she doesn't want any of the fame that you pushed her into.'

'Don't be ridiculous. Your sister loves her life.'

'No, she doesn't. She wants to move out of London and give up her career.'

'No more of this nonsense. Stop making up lies. I don't believe Gillian would throw away everything we worked so hard for. All you had to do was tell me about your boyfriend. You never tell me anything—'

'And you never ask.'

'I'm so sorry, Jane. I'm trying my best. I really am.'

She hangs up before I can reply.

But I don't care. It felt good. Very good.

My only regret is that I should have done it sooner.

I go for a run. The sound of my feet against the pavement spurs me on to go faster. When I make it to Trinity College, Ireland's oldest university, I consider walking around the campus or just going into the library. The Long Room houses two hundred thousand of the library's oldest books which I could count to my heart's content. Sitting around masses of books and counting them may be just what I need. My thoughts turn to Tara. I feel bad the way I left abruptly. I decide to just make my way over to Hidden Secrets to say goodbye to her properly.

She greets me at the door with a big smile. Memories come flooding back to me. Memories from when I first walked through Hidden Secrets. They hit me like a ton of bricks. My eyes well up. We have become so close over the past while. Like my love for Ben, this is another chapter of my life that will close.

'Jane, my dear friend. I've something I want to ask you,' she says as she grasps hold of my hands.

'What is it? I'm sorry I walked out yesterday,' I say.

'You were upset. But all is not lost. We'll stay in touch. True friendship never dies. You're more than welcome to stay with me in Florida anytime.'

'Ah, Tara. Thank you. I'll miss you so much. I may take you up on your offer. What did you want to ask me?'

'Well, it's about this place,' she says. 'I think it could do with a new lease of life. A new owner even.'

'Oh, that's hard shoes to fill. Any idea who the lucky person will be?'

'Well, I was hoping you could tell me that.'

'Me?'

'Yes, you. I want to give you the bookshop, Jane,' she says as her grey eyes fill up with tears. 'I know it will be in safe hands with you.'

'No way … I mean … I … yes … but I'm going to Toronto tomorrow to see my dad.'

'A visit to your father is well overdue and the shop will be here waiting for you when you come back. I'll talk to my solicitor and get all the paperwork drawn up. There's no one else I trust with this place, only you.'

We hug for what feels like forever. She knows me better than anyone. Our bond has grown so strong it will never be broken.

It's early in the day on Christmas Eve and I'm in the bookshop cleaning out some cupboards while Tara is resting. A book falls to the floor. It's a scrapbook busting at the seams. It's full of newspaper clippings. Photos of the girl with pigtails and the red coat cover each page. She's Candice – Tara and Harold's daughter who died in a traffic accident when she was only eight years old. The accident happened just outside the bookshop. The exact same girl who told me she was ready to move on.

I shiver. Poor Tara. She has suffered such loss. At least I know she's happy now.

Tara walks into the room. Her face is glowing, she seems so happy and carefree about her decision. She sees me with the scrapbook in my hand.

'Candice,' she whispers. 'My darling Candice.'

'Candice ... was your daughter. I'm so sorry for your loss, Tara,' I say as I give her a hug.

'I felt closer to her here than anywhere else in the world,' she says. 'I caught glimpses of her smile and her sweet floral smell tickled my nose. Everything about her lingered here. But something has shifted. That's how I knew it was time to give you control of this place.'

She's shaking as I hold onto her. 'I met her,' I say. 'She was the one that was following me around. She's moved on to a better place. She's with Harold now.'

'But how ... I don't understand.'

'The cards must have allowed me to see her. I asked them to show me more about you and then Candice appeared. I thought it was me as a child, but it was Candice all the time. She was hanging around to keep an eye on you.'

Tara gazes at me for a few moments before she takes my hand. 'Harold blamed himself. He was minding her while I was getting my hair done on Grafton Street. He bought her a red ball in the toy shop.' She points in the direction of the shop next door. 'They were going to go to St. Stephen's Green to play with it. The ball fell from her hand, and she ran after it. A car came speeding around the corner and hit her and that was it. She ... she ... died instantly. There was nothing anyone could do to save her. It was a hit-and-run.'

'Ah, Tara. That's shocking—'

'Harold blamed himself of course. He was never the same afterwards.' She lowers her voice. 'But then neither was I ... ever since her death ... I've spent too much time in my mind reliving every single memory I have of her ... in my mind she was still alive.'

'Harold,' I say. 'What happened to Harold?'

'He died not far from the spot where Candice ... he had a motor-bike accident. He crashed into a wall.'

Poor Tara. I'm lost for words. I search my mind for something to say to give her comfort.

'Come. Follow me to see my hidden secret,' she says interrupting my thoughts.

She brings me to the top floor of the shop. We walk into her office and over to a large bookcase. She takes out a book and the bookcase moves. Behind it is a hidden door. Through the door is a huge room filled with light. A playroom. Full of toys and boxes, upon boxes of clothes. Photos adorn the walls of Candice and Tara together. Smiling. Laughing. Just hanging out. Tara opens up one of the boxes and takes out a child's polka dot dress. She brings it to her nose and breathes in its scent.

'She wore this to her eighth birthday party,' she says. 'I remember everything. I could get over losing Harold, but not Candice. Not my precious girl. When life gets too much for me, I come up here and she feels real. In my mind's eye she's dancing. Sometimes we danced together or just hung out. I sang to her. So many songs. Sometimes I relived her last birthday party.

'Not anymore though. It's time. I've let go of the past. You've helped me, Jane, more than you'll ever know.'

I go home after helping Tara sort and clean Candice's stuff to go to charity. I'm on my own, but I'm happy and content. I'm drinking some homemade mulled wine and watching *The Holiday* when the doorbell rings.

I open the door to find Ben standing there with my blue velvet drawstring bag in his hand. The snow is belting down. He has snow all over his hair and snowflakes land on his long eyelashes.

'I had to see you,' he says. 'I found these on the doorstep.'

I take the cards from Ben. 'You ... my cards ... I have my cards back.' They smell like burnt paper, but they're all still intact.

'Everything becomes brighter ... more vibrant when I hold them ...' he says.

'I told you,' I say, 'they're magic.'

He looks from me to the cards in shock. 'Well, they must be magic to survive the fire.'

As I hold them in my hand, I wait for the rush of excitement to flood through me like it used to. But it doesn't. 'Hello cards,' I say to them, and I try to think of something I want, but my mind goes blank.

The thing is I've gotten used to being without them now. Dare I say it, but I really don't need them anymore. I place them in my handbag and put them out of my mind.

CHAPTER 35

BEN

JANE INVITES ME IN and gives me a glass of mulled wine. We sit on the couch and watch *The Holiday*. Everything worthwhile in my life comes down to this moment. My heart races. I'm full of adrenaline, I feel like I could run a marathon.

'My engagement to Sarah is off. We had a huge argument and she ripped up my clothes before she left,' I blurt out.

'What was the argument over?' she asks.

'You,' I say. 'I told her I can't be with her anymore … because of my feelings for you. I understand if you hate me. I acted like a dick because I was scared. But the truth is I can't be without you.' I put my head on her shoulder. 'I'm not expecting you to make a decision now. Take your time. I can wait. I've waited long enough.'

I sound calm about breaking up with Sarah, but there was nothing calm about it. At first Sarah was devastated. She threw her engagement ring at me and told me I ruined her life. I felt so bad I nearly backed down, but I didn't. I couldn't let my chance with Jane slip away from me again. When I told Sarah about my trust funds being wiped out with Becker Bank, she was horrified and said she was only interested in me for my money, then became deadly quiet before she took my car keys and drove off in my Audi.

'I'm leaving in a few hours to fly to Toronto to see my dad.'

'Let me come with you,' I say as I take her hand. 'Please Jane, I just want to be with you. I'll book a flight online. If there's any seats left, I'll go. I don't care how long it takes.'

'Okay,' she says quietly. 'Only as friends though, I need time to get my head together.'

'If that's what you want.'

Friends will do for now. As long as I'm with her.

I tell her my father's business went bankrupt. All the family money was lost once Becker Bank International went bust. My trust funds were wiped out, but all I care about is being with her. She doesn't bat an eyelid. I love the fact that me having no money doesn't faze her.

'What matters most is that you're okay,' she says.

CHAPTER 36

JANE

LTHOUGH THERE IS SNOW everywhere when we arrive in Toronto, the city feels yellow. The colour of positivity. The thought of spending time with my dad again makes me feel so happy and having Ben by my side makes everything twinkly and bright.

My dad and Kate bought a new condo since the last time I was here. They now live in a three-bedroom place in Yonge and Eglinton. They show us around. It's simple, but elegant. The kitchen and bathroom are tiny, but functional. They have few personal possessions. The communal areas are fab. There's a roof-top pool, party and media room and barbeque area.

Completely different to my mam's mansion at Abington.

It's Ben's first time here, so we do a load of touristy stuff. Everything in Toronto is huge compared to Ireland, like the subway, buildings and even the shopping centres or 'the malls' as they call them.

Our days are spent exploring the city. We visit bookstores to get inspiration to add some new life to Hidden Secrets. In the evening we go out for relaxed dinners with my dad and Kate. From spending time with Kate, I can tell she's a practical, no-nonsense type of person. She's beautiful, but in an understated way. She's probably in her late fifties with grey hair. She wears no make-up and simple but stylish clothes. One evening while we are having dinner at the local pizzeria she comments on how close and happy Ben and I are together.

'Karl,' she says to my father. 'Why did you not tell me Jane had a boyfriend?'

'Oh, we're not going out,' I say.

I blush. I hate being put on the spot. There's silence and I can feel Ben's eyes upon me. My dad breaks the awkwardness.

'Well, I know that you've been sleeping in separate rooms, but Ben has my seal of approval, that's for sure,' he says, and we all laugh.

Since we arrived in Toronto, Ben hasn't pushed me into making any decisions about us. The thing is, I know exactly how I feel about him, but I don't want to rush into anything.

My dad and Kate head off after the meal to meet friends and Ben and I walk home from the restaurant holding hands. I tell him I wish the holiday didn't have to come to an end. I feel like we are suspended in time here. There's no drama or pressure.

'Yeah, I know what you mean,' he says. 'But aren't you looking forward to getting home? You have the bookshop waiting for you and not just that, there's more. There's us ...'

'Us.' I smile.

'At some point you're going to have to take a chance, Jane.' He frowns and a look comes over him that I can't quite make out. 'You need to give me a chance. I'm going to prove to you how much I want this to work.'

We walk back in silence. Ben follows me into the kitchen when we get to the Condo.

'I love you, Jane,' he says with such intensity. 'I've never been so sure about anything in my life.' He kisses me and it feels like the most natural thing in the world.

I put my fingers through his hair to get close to him. 'I'm so fucking happy right now,' he says and we both laugh. The room spins as he carries me over to my bedroom and lays me on the bed.

He kisses me with such passion I crawl onto him so I can get lost in him. My eyes stream with emotion – all the love for him I've kept inside, for so long, is finally released. Afterwards when he has fallen asleep with his arms wrapped around me, I realise I've found where I belong.

The next morning Ben tells me he's going to spend the day with my dad as there's some historical exhibition on that they both want to see. He's booked dinner at the CN tower for the four of us later, for our last night in Toronto.

Kate and I go to Yorkville and browse around the shops before dinner. We get there early to do a tour of the CN tower and when we meet up with my dad and Ben, I can sense something is wrong. Ben's jumpy and on edge. He's on his phone a lot talking in whispers. I hope it's nothing serious.

I take him aside and ask him what's wrong.

'Nothing. I'm grand. Everything is fine,' he says as he grits his teeth. 'My stomach is a bit off, that's all. Probably just something I ate earlier.'

Are we going to go our separate ways once we get home?

During dinner, Ben is the perfect gentleman. He's attentive and good company, but I can't relax. His hands keep shaking and his voice sounds weird, kind of crackly.

I go to the bathroom and when I come back, I can't find my seat. The restaurant is revolving. My sense of direction is off. When I eventually figure out where they are, there's waiters surrounding them.

'What's up?' I say trying to sound as casual as possible.

'Oh, we're waiting for you to try a new signature dessert. The waiters have just brought it out. We've had a piece already,' says my dad.

'Where is it?' I ask.

'Under the platter,' my dad says. 'Come. Sit down and try some.'

Ben pulls out my chair as the waiter takes the lid off the dessert platter. Underneath is a big sparkly ring.

He gets down on one knee and all the diners in the restaurant surround our table. Now both my stomach and the restaurant are spinning.

'Jane McAlister, make me the happiest man in the world. Will you marry me?' he says.

This is it. There's no running away anymore.

'I do ... I mean ... yes. I will,' I say.

He places the ring on my finger and the crowd around us cheers.

'I told you I meant it,' Ben whispers to me.

'Champagne. Champagne,' my father shouts. 'Get me a bucket of your finest champagne.'

Kate's eyes tear up as she says, 'I knew it. I knew it, Karl. I could tell there was something special going on with these two.'

When we land back into Dublin airport, I get a call from Tara.

'The paperwork is all sorted, Jane. Everything is in order with my solicitor. It's all yours now to do as you please,' she says.

'Thank you. I'll take good care of the place. How's Florida? Hope it's treating you well.'

'Florida is even better than I ever dreamed it would be. I'm having a great time. I'm either on the beach or the golf course with my sister.'

'That's the way it should be. It's your time to relax now and rest. How's the cough? Are you all cured yet?'

'It's completely gone. I feel marvellous.'

Ben and I go straight to the shop once we get the keys. I'm worried he's going to hate it like Jay did. What if he thinks it's just a dusty old shop?

'Wow, Jane. This place is amazing. Not what I was expecting at all,' he says as he wraps his arms around me. 'There's definitely something special about this place.'

'Come on,' I say. I take his hand. 'Let's explore.'

I'm sure Ben will love it here just as much as I do. We come across many empty rooms that I never knew existed. Rooms within rooms. Empty rooms just waiting to be explored to become part of something special.

There's a wonderful small garden out the back of the shop that I never knew about. Full of apple and pear trees and a fabulous water fountain and sculpture.

'You've landed yourself a goldmine, Jane,' Ben says. 'Such potential.'

'I know and I have plans. Big plans for this place.'

When we go back inside, I sit on the red armchair. Tara's favourite chair. I take the cards out of my handbag and wonder what I should wish for. But I can't think of anything. Nothing. I have everything

I could ever possibly want. This must be it. The end of my journey with the cards. I'm ready now to give them up. I place them on the highest shelf where I first found them.

A card falls to the floor.

Inner Strength and Confidence
You had all the inner strength and confidence you
needed to achieve what your heart truly desired all
along, you just needed some reminding.

I smile as I put it back on the shelf.
Another card falls.

White Feathers
White Feathers were a sign from the universe that you
were safe. You were being watched and guided the whole
time.

CHAPTER 37

MAY 2023

A WEEK AGO, I GOT a call from a solicitor's office. They told me I must go to their office urgently.

When I got there, I was met by an old guy called Stephen at the door, who was very sober and serious with bushy eyebrows and a funny looking suit. He told me he was Tara's personal solicitor. I was brought to his office which was a higgledy-piggledy room with nooks and crannies. I wasn't surprised Tara picked him to be her solicitor.

'You are here because Tara O'Loughlin passed away last night and in her will she requested that I give you a special message,' he said.

'No! The last time I spoke to her she was as fit as a fiddle. She was enjoying her life in Florida. I had plans to go visit her soon.'

'I'm so sorry, Jane. You must have meant a lot to her. She asked me to play this recording to you.'

He pressed play on the remote control and her face filled the screen. She looked tired and old. Not as I imagined her. And then, as Tara began to speak, my face crumbled, my composure went and grief swamped me. I stopped caring that he was there. My heart broke in two, and I thought my life would never feel the same again.

'My dearest Jane. My time on earth is over. I've known this was coming for some time now. I've lived a good life. A long one. A whole one hundred and two years on earth.' She laughs. 'Who would have known I was that old? It was the cards that made me look so young, for I asked them a long time ago to prolong my life. It was you, however, that kept me alive after I passed them on to you. It's my time now to go and I'm ready. I've so much to thank you for.

For helping me with my shop when I felt so ill and for helping me let go of Candice ... so she could move on and finally be with my beloved Harold.'

At that moment I felt grateful that I got to know Tara and be such a big part of her life for a while, and that I got to help her when she needed it. I owed her so much.

'The answer to life is not about reaching the end or getting everything you want, but instead discovering what strength and beauty lie inside. And of course the relationships we have with others. Love is the greatest gift of all.'

She pauses, and tears well up in her eyes.

'I love you, Jane. Always remember that you are very much loved.'

I stare into Tara's beautiful eyes, and a rush of love fills me.

'I've left you money. A lot of money. Where I'm going, I can't bring it with me. Use it wisely, but most of all enjoy it. I leave you now with my final message.'

'Stop. Stop,' I said to Stephen. 'I need a second.' I took a deep breath.

I hated the thought of this being Tara's final message, after a few minutes I nodded my head and indicated to Stephen to continue the video.

'Death is a funny one,' she said. 'When you know it's around the corner it makes you question your life. Your every being. Why am I here? What is my purpose in life? I still don't know, but what I do know though is I was deeply unhappy until magic came into my life. Magic came to me at the right time – when I felt I had nowhere else to turn to those magical cards appeared.'

I glanced over at Stephen; he had his mouth open in shock when she mentioned the cards.

'When you are ready and no longer need them, you must pass them on to someone else, for they are too powerful to just sit on a shelf,' she continued. 'I worry they could end up in the wrong hands. The cards will find their new owner and when they do I want you to hand them over. Teach them all you know and keep them in circulation. Perhaps they may even discover who the group from the photograph are.'

Tara smiled and then I paused the video, to keep her on the screen for a while longer. One thing I knew for sure, as I stared at Tara's shrunken form. She was extraordinary. Spectacular. She was like a mother figure to me, at a time when I needed it, and our relationship was something I could never have with my own mother.

I let the video play and listened to Tara say her final words.

'I've come to the realization that the world is connected by a web of energy. This must be the energy that the cards tap into to make wishes come true. I don't know how it works, but I believe you need to know how you want to feel and choose this feeling as if your desired outcome has come to pass, and it will. Amongst this web of possibilities, the highest good will always shine through. Goodbye, my dear, Jane.'

After watching the video of Tara, I went straight to the bookshop and sat in her favourite red armchair, and just thought about her, and our time together.

I wished she was sitting in her favourite chair – drinking tea and eating chocolate biscuits. I just wanted to listen to her voice and her wisdom, I wanted us to sort and stack books. To serve customers together and to find them the perfect book that could change their life. And if she had gotten too tired, I would have placed a warm blanket around her, and watched her sleep.

But I understood she would never be back. I understood sitting there, that she gave me the shop for something to hold on to, for when she was gone.

To protect me, and keep me safe.

I think back to how we first met – she made an impression on me at first sight. She shimmered and shone – took me under her wing – made everything better, and continued to do so, each time I visited the bookshop.

Before she gave me the cards, I believed if I worked long and hard, I'd get the things I wanted, and be as good as Gillian. The job, the apartment, the life, and find love. That the future was simply a ball of clay waiting to be shaped. I even tried to ignore my feelings for Ben. Even though he loved me all along.

I was walking down the wrong path, and chasing the wrong dreams.

Tara was part of my life I was missing for so long. She helped me learn how I misunderstood my sister – and my life. She put me on the right path.

Tara was one of the most special things in my life, and I loved her too.

I stayed in the bookshop for some time. I'm not sure how much time had passed. Ben came and wrapped his arms around me. I rested my head on his chest, I felt the pressure of his fingertips on my back. I closed my eyes and breathed in his scent. And then I realized, I didn't need to count to calm myself anymore.

As the news spread about Tara's death, customers came in crowds to the shop – all with good words to say about Tara and their time in the shop. Lots of children came. I set up a special children's area, full of bright colourful chairs and tables and artwork. I expanded the children's book section. Inside there were remote control flying airplanes and mini hot-air balloons. I filled the windows with novelties and trinkets. I wanted them to feel welcome, just like when Tara was the owner.

Chloe, Tara's sister, contacted me. 'Tara thought very highly of you, she mentioned you as if you were family,' she said. 'She wrote a piece, that she wanted you to read out at the funeral.'

Four days later. The church overflowed with people. They stood out onto the street. I was asked to sit at the front row, beside Chloe. People thought I was family; they didn't even question it. *I'm so sorry for your loss,* they said, *no one was expecting this. She lived such a full life.*

When it was time I cleared my throat, and begin to read:
The best part of my life was when my family were together,
and when they were gone, I muddled along,
and tried to find my way in the dark.
It wasn't until my customers came, that I found myself,
full of smiles and laughter, comfort and love again.
My books guided me to find their new owners,
who gained an understanding that most don't ever grasp.

In my magical shop we spent endless hours together — you and I.
Sometimes with no words spoken.
Time stood still, as we enjoyed each other's company.
We shared a common bond, and played with the same deck of cards,
dealt with our choices and consequences,
and found our light at the end.
In the blink of an eye, everything can change,
so, remember to make the most with those who mean the most.

Please know, that I am not gone forever,
I am only taking a breath, until we meet again.
and when the wind catches the smell of freshly mowed grass,
or the sea glimmers in the light, look to the sky,
and I will be there.
And your memories of me will help me live on.
Forever and always.
Tara xxx

CHAPTER 38

JUNE 2023

BEN AND I ARE now married. We got married in Toronto with all our friends and family. It seemed only fitting we got married in the city where he proposed to me.

Sorcha was one of my bridesmaids and she brought her husband Matt with her. He's just as nice as she is. Even though she still lives in Australia, our friendship is stronger than ever. Gillian was my other bridesmaid, and she looked positively blooming. Blooming because she was pregnant at the time with Michael's child. She found out she was pregnant not long after they broke up. Michael questioned whether it was his child, and still hasn't accepted it. But Gillian insists it's his. When she came out to the world as being bi-sexual the response was super positive. It took my mam a while, but she has finally come to terms with the fact that Gillian has a girlfriend.

Ben and I live above the bookshop. We converted the empty rooms on the top floor into a fabulous apartment. We've put the days of the bank behind us, and life is much simpler now. Not only do we sell books, we created a retreat centre for people who want to leave their busy lifestyles behind them. Who want to discover what they really want out of life. Our children's section is also very popular. It's a big part of our shop, just like when Tara was alive.

I'm a better person now, compared to before the cards came into my life. I'm happier and full of life. I've faced up to my fears and discovered an inner strength I never knew I had.

CHAPTER 39

AUGUST 2023

I'M SHOCKED WHEN I see the online newspapers this morning. My mind is spinning. I thought the first allegation that came out recently was made-up, but now there's a second one. It can't be true. I shake my head as I read the article.

Second woman comes forward to accuse actress, Gillian O'Hara (25) of assault.

Accusations against Gillian O'Hara first came to light earlier this month, when the Oscar-winning actress was accused of assaulting a woman in the past.

Following the initial claim against Gillian, this week a second woman has now alleged that the actress once 'slammed her against a wall' last year at a private members' club.

The second victim, who wishes to remain anonymous, claims the actress accosted her in a bathroom and then threatened to 'make her life hell' if she spoke out against her.

'I was afraid to say anything for so long because of Gillian's power and her threats to destroy myself and my family's life,' stated the victim. 'She seemed high on drugs at the time, but that doesn't excuse her behaviour. I finally managed to get out away and shouted "Leave me alone" before she let me out. That same night, later on in the club she came up to me and warned me not to tell anyone about what happened or she would make my life hell. I used to be a huge fan of Gillian's, but not anymore. She has serious issues.'

The victim explained that she is speaking out now about her experience to show support for the other woman who has accused Ms. O'Hara of misconduct.

'The more people that come forward to share similar experiences about Gillian, the better. She should be made accountable for her actions,' she added.

In a statement issued to The Hollywood Reporter, *the star said: 'I don't know why these claims are surfacing now, but what I do know is: I did not assault these women.'*

The allegations, which have yet to be proven, have done untold damage to the actress's career, and she's now been dropped by three sponsorships to date. Ms. O'Hara has also been dropped by her talent agency, United Talent, a spokesperson for the agency told the Daily Mail *on Wednesday.*

This comes at a bad time for Gillian, who is currently heavily pregnant with her first child and has split up with her girlfriend, Colleen O'Keefe, this week.

Colleen has released the following statement: I wish Gillian all the best. We are just in different places in our lives right now and want different things.

The father of Gillian's unborn child is thought to be her ex-fiancé, famous actor Michael Boudet, who has a successful production company with his girlfriend, up-and-coming actress Jasmine Wentworth. Michael has refused to comment.

Pictures from months ago stare back at me from the *Daily Mail* newspaper of Gillian. She's shopping for baby stuff at a fancy London shop and holding hands with Colleen over the table during dinner. I can't believe this is happening to her now.

Later, a text comes through from Emma.

Jane. You and your sister better watch out.

The allegations must be Emma's doing.
I think I have an idea where the cards could go next.

The End.

ACKNOWLEDGMENTS

A MASSIVE THANK YOU to the following people:

To my parents, Tom and Susan, for their unwavering support and encouragement, and igniting a love of reading at a young age. To my siblings, Jonathan, Lisa and Louise and sisters-in-law, Susan and Wendy Curran, for their interest and support.

To the members of the Pencil Pack Writers Group for giving feedback at the earliest stages of this work. To the Boyne Valley Writers Group for your positivity and feedback – Jess, Louise, Morgan, Noel, Ollie, Paula and Peter. Every word of encouragement was appreciated. As a group we lift and inspire one another, and I'm very grateful to be part of such a wonderful group.

To my lovely old friends, Avril, Deirdre and Amanda, for their thoughtful feedback, when all my words began to blur into one.

To An Táin Arts Centre and Nicola Cassidy, for selecting me as a mentee for their 2022 publishing mentorship programme. Nicola's guidance and practical advice was greatly appreciated.

To my daughter, Isabella, for bringing my opening chapters to life by acting out the scenes with great enthusiasm at home. Lastly, to my husband, Mark, for his unending belief and love. For giving me the time and space to write all the way to the end.

NOTE FROM THE AUTHOR

IF YOU ENJOYED READING my novel, please take a few minutes to leave a review on amazon. I really appreciate your support! Thank you for taking a chance on this book. If you wish to contact me you can find me on my social media accounts below:

Facebook Joanne Ryan Curran Author
X @JRCurran4